I need to convince myself that you're not an unspeakable horror using a woman's skin as a disguise while it sates its hellish appetites.

"I wish it hadn't come to this." Jonathan withdrew his hand from his coat, bringing the pistol into the open, and aimed it at Fran's chest. "I need you to answer my questions, miss. I won't say the fate of the world depends on it, but your continued survival certainly does."

The knife sliced through the air next to his head and embedded itself in the wall of the trailer before Jonathan even saw her move. He froze, gun still aimed at Fran, who was now holding a throwing knife in either hand.

"The way I see it, you might be able to shoot me before I put a pair of these in your throat; then again, you might not," she said amiably. "Do you really want to go down this road?"

For a moment, Jonathan couldn't think of a single thing to say. He was saved from needing to by the small white mouse that popped out of his pocket, ran up his arm to his shoulder, and gleefully declared, "Hail, Priestess of Unexpected Violence!"

Fran dropped her knives.

—from "The Flower of Arizona" by Seanan McGuire

Also Available from DAW Books:

Human for a Day, edited by Martin H. Greenberg and Jennifer Brozek

Here are sixteen original tales, by authors such as Seanan McGuire, Fiona Patton, Tanith Lee, Jim Hines, and Kristine Kathryn Rusch, that examine what it means to be human in all its positive and negative aspects. If you were an intelligent robot would the opportunity to become human for just one day be worth the risks? And what would the consequences be at the end of that day? If a magic spell switched a vampire and a teenage girl into one another's bodies would both savor the experience or search for a way to undo the enchantment? And what if only one of them wished to switch back? What tests would an angel face if transformed into a mortal for a day? Can a statue brought to life protect its turf? Will becoming a man for just one day put an end to a pet's happy home life? These are just a few of the inventive stories—some humorous, some sad, many thought provoking, and all unique—to be found in this thought-provoking anthology.

Courts of the Fey, edited by Martin H. Greenberg and Russell Davis

In the world of Faerie, there are two courts—the Seelie and the Unseelie. According to legend, the Seelie Court, also called The Blessed Ones, are those faeries representing light and goodness. They are the heroes, the judges, and they serve the Queen of Air and Light. The Unseelie Court is the opposite: dark, malevolent, and often dedicated to evil. They are the riders in the dark clouds of a storm, travelers on the night winds. From Lilith Saintcrow's magical tale of a half fey ready to take on the entire Unseelie court to rescue the one he loves . . . to Rob Thurman's twisting account of mortals, Seelie, and Unseelie caught up in a Hunt at the end of the worlds . . . to Amber Benson's compelling story of a girl's desperate bargain to escape her evil stepmother . . . to Michelle Sagara's poignant exploration of what it means to be a fey among mortals—here are visions bright or dark, terrifying or seductive, fascinating glimpses of both the highest royals and the lowest rogues as they vie with one another or league together against those of the mortal realms.

After Hours: Tales from the Ur-Bar, edited by Joshua Palmatier and Patricia Bray

The first bar, created by the Sumerians after they were given the gift of beer by the gods, was known as the Ur-Bar. Although it has since been destroyed, its spirit lives on. In each age there is one bar that captures the essence of the original Ur-Bar, where drinks are mixed with magic and served with a side of destiny and intrigue. Now some of today's most inventive scriveners, such as Benjamin Tate, Kari Sperring, Anton Strout, and Avery Shade, among others, have decided to belly up to the Ur-Bar and tell their own tall tales—from an alewife's attempt to transfer the gods' curse to Gilgamesh, to Odin's decision to introduce Vikings to the Ur-Bar . . . from the Holy Roman Emperor's barroom bargain, to a demon hunter who may just have met his match in the ultimate magic bar, to a bouncer who discovers you should never let anyone in after hours in a world terrorized by zombies. . . .

WESTWARD WEIRD

Edited by
Martin H. Greenberg
and Kerrie Hughes

DAW BOOKS, INC.

DONALD A. WOLLHEIM, FOUNDER

375 Hudson Street, New York, NY 10014

ELIZABETH R. WOLLHEIM
SHEILA E. GILBERT
PUBLISHERS

www.dawbooks.com

First Printing, February 2012
1 2 3 4 5 6 7 8 9

DAW TRADEMARK REGISTERED
U.S. PAT. AND TM. OFF. AND FOREIGN COUNTRIES
—MARCA REGISTRADA
HECHO EN U.S.A.

PRINTED IN THE U.S.A.

Acknowledgments

Introduction copyright © 2012 by Kerrie Hughes

"The Temptation of Eustace Prudence McAllen," copyright © 2012 by Joseph E. Lake, Jr.

"The Last Master of Aeronautical Winters," copyright © 2012 by Larry D. Sweazy

"Lowstone," copyright © 2012 by Anton Strout

"The Flower of Arizona," copyright © 2012 by Seanan McGuire

"The Ghost in the Doctor," copyright © 2012 by Brenda Cooper

"Surveyor of Mars," copyright © 2012 by Christopher McKitterick

"Coyote, Spider, Bat," copyright © 2012 by Steven Saus

"Maybe Another Time," copyright © 2012 by Dean Wesley Smith

"Renn and the Little Men," copyright © 2012 by Kristine Kathryn Rusch

"Showdown at High Moon," copyright © 2012 by Jennifer Brozek

"The Clockwork Cowboy," copyright © 2012 by J. Steven York

"Black Train," copyright © 2012 by Jeff Mariotte

"Lone Wolf," copyright © 2012 by Jody Lynn Nye

Table of Contents

INTRODUCTION

Kerrie Hughes

Science fiction meets the Old West is clearly not a new idea, as evidenced in shows like *The Wild Wild West* (1965–1969), *The Adventures of Brisco County Jr.* (1993–1994), and *Firefly* (2002). These shows were pure Hollywood because they had clear heroes and enemies, used liberal amounts of fantasy, and could only exist on the movie lot.

The truth of the Wild West lies somewhere in between those celluloid fantasies and the harsh, often brutal reality. The mass migration westward was devastating for those who had been living there for centuries, but allowed thousands to begin new lives, to remake themselves in the tough crucible of the last true frontier settlement of history. Cities were founded, fortunes were made and lost, tales were told, and lawmen, criminals, inventors, and crackpots all lived there, sometimes all in the same dusty town.

The West also gave rise to its own style of storytelling—incorporating the tropes of classical myth and legend, but with its own spin featuring larger than life characters that could only have sprung from the imagination of those who had seen and lived in this new frontier.

THE TEMPTATION OF EUSTACE PRUDENCE MCALLEN

Jay Lake

You know that place out west of Casper? Wild badlands like you've never seen, all rocks and salt and twisty dead end ravines that'd swallow up a man and his horse both like they was watermelon seeds. Hell's Half Acre is its name these days, but folks used to call that the Devil's Kitchen.

What do you think, biscuit-head? On account of him cooking up sin there. What else'd the devil his own self set to boiling over a fire?

Now this fellow, name of Eustace Prudence McAllen, rode for Hotchkiss Williamson what had the Broken Bow Ranch out that way. Williamson held a good spread, with two different springs and a box canyon full of cottonwoods running down through his grasslands. Drought didn't bother him nearly so much as it troubled his neighbors, though he did have a problem with range fires there through the summers of 1864 and 1865.

McAllen, he might've been a Southern man, ain't no telling now. But he'd showed up the autumn of 1863 and signed on. Working over the winters on the range here always has called for a special kind of cuss, so Williamson and his brother ranchers didn't ask a lot of questions of a man what rode strong and didn't backtalk and kept the cattle out of trouble. Anyone who came west in those war years was avoiding something, somewhere. So long as they didn't bring their troubles in their saddlebags, that was generally good enough.

No, I can't rightly say exactly what he looked like. You talk to people who rode for Williamson in them years, you get different tellings. Time plays tricks on memory, don't you know. There was a lot of panics, from Indian attacks and the range fires and what all. Can't even say if'n he was a colored fellow, some kind of quadroon, or just white, like a black Irishman. Taller than most, maybe. Carried an ivory-handled double-barreled LeMat revolver what had been engraved real tiny, some folks said it was the Book of Jeremiah writ real small, always close to his hand.

Why anyone would carry that particular book of the Holy Bible so I can't rightly say.

So here's McAllen working the cattle for Williamson and minding his own business. Don't drink too much, don't fight hardly none at all, don't cuss in front of Williamson's wife and daughters, lends a hand even when he ain't been asked. Everything's fine until the second summer of range fires and somehow word gets around that McAllen has been setting 'em.

Firestarting is worse than rustling, in its way. You don't just lose the cattle, you lose the land. And fighting a range fire is somewhere between suicide and hopeless. Best you can do is get livestock and people out of harm's way and pray the wind don't shift wrong.

Mostly you know what done it. Dry thunderstorm, often as not. But sometimes they got a pattern. Summer of 1864, and again 1865, it was like that. Visitations, almost.

And people was talking. Cooks and runners and the feedlot boys and the fancy women and whatnot. McAllen's name was on a lot of lips. For a fellow ain't made no enemies, he sure didn't have a lot of friends. It was all around peculiar.

So Williamson, he got the wind put up his own self and went and had a quiet talk with McAllen. I can't reckon the old man had pegged his hand for a firebug. More like he wanted McAllen gone a bit, out of the way to let rumor run its course. So he sent the poor bastard out riding trail west of Fort Caspar, what the city was called back then afore it was really a city. Said McAllen was checking springs and shelter in case they needed to drive the herds through the Powder River country.

Which was so much horse puck and everybody knew it, but it did serve to calm the hard words down some.

McAllen, he got himself out toward the Devil's Kitchen. That's a wild, wild land, looks like God

dropped some old mountains into a thresher the size
of Kansas, then let Leviathan vomit all over what fell
out the ass end. All gray and brown and furze, covered with sand and ash and alkali and salt, nothing
a fellow with any sense would ride into.

But he saw smoke, you understand. And fire was on
his mind more than anyone's. Range fires could take
his life in a hanging, if those hard words stuck around
and took root in people's thoughts. So McAllen probably figured on picking his way on in there and finding
some camp of layabouts or Indians or deserters, or
something he could lay them fires at the feet of.

Off he went, leading his horse down a slope of
scree and into one of them little, twisted canyons,
following the smoke and his own sense of what was
right and what was not.

Now the Devil, he's one crafty son of a bitch.

Yeah, I said that. You just mind your piehole or I'll
mind it for you, and you won't like that one tiny bit.

Crafty on account of that's how the Creator made
him. Lucifer, he's practically the first of God's children. Old Adam, more or less an afterthought he was.
A gardener, really, set to watch the fruit trees and keep
the snakes off the lawn. No, all the pride and power
and glory went into the Prince of Light. When he fell
from Heaven, he took a piece of the Old Man's heart
with him. The meek might could inherit the Earth, but
it was the prideful for whom the beauty of the day
was first forged.

After the Fall, though, the Devil he had to slink

around in the dark patches and hide in the shadows and walk with the rotten side of a man's soul in his hand. That's why he hangs around even to this day in places like Hell's Half Acre, what was the Devil's Kitchen back then. Ain't no place for him among the shaded cottonwoods or along a quiet bend in the river with a fishing pole.

Still, a fellow's got to eat. That's part of our earthly estate, don't you know? And the Devil likes him some barbacoa as much as the next man.

Yeah, what they call barbecue now days.

A good loin of pork or brisket of beef, dry rubbed with salt and some spices, then cooked long and slow over a bed of coals afore you slather on a compounded ferment of vinegar and tomato sauce—that's a ticket to heaven through the gates of the mouth. Food as righteous as any toe-curling sin.

So here's the Devil got him a roasting spit down in a dry ravine in the Devil's Kitchen, and he's got a dozen lesser dark angels to tend the fire and turn the spit, and a whole heifer off of Mr. Williamson's land stuck up there roasting to feed his own hungers and keep his myrmidons at their labors. It was a good place for Lucifer, on account of no one ever goes there, and he could rest in peace until time called for more of his mischief to be spread upon this earth or down in the dominions of Hell.

Yeah, like that, kid. And you wouldn't be the first one ready to sell their granny down to darkness for a mouthful of that hot, sweet meat fresh off the fire. No, sir.

Devil was resting his spurred heels on a shattered knob of gray-white rock, a jug of white lightning in one clawed hand, a corncob pipe in the other, when Eustace Prudence McAllen led his old bay mare into the mouth of the ravine.

Them demons, they giggled and cackled and sizzled as demons is wont to do. Old Scratch looked up to see what the fuss was and saw a beanpole of a man with week's beard looking back at him. Dark fellow, for a white man, in a pale canvas duster and a busted down slouch hat pulled low over his eyes.

"Boys," the Devil announced in a voice like a flash flood down a canyon, "We got us a visitor."

You got to understand the Devil speaks all languages and none. Adamic, what everyone talked before the Tower of Babel, that's the tongue of Heaven. Any man born of woman will understand it, on account of it's the language God made us all to know and be known by.

So while his vowels sizzled with lightning and bedded coals, and his consonants were the fall of hammers and the snap of bones, the cowboy McAllen heard this in English as plain as any what got spoke in the bunkhouse back at the Broken Bow Ranch, and in an accent as melodious as General Nathan Bedford Forrest himself.

Which is to say, McAllen, he wasn't fooled one tiny bit. The Devil can make himself fine and fair as any Philadelphia dandy, or he can be small and slick and mean as a scorched badger, or anything in between. But this day Old Scratch was taking a rest, so his tattered wings spread black and lonely behind him while the horns on his head showed their chips and cracks and stains.

The only characteristic that marked him out from the chiefest among his lesser demons was the blue of his eyes, which were as deep and quiet as the lakes of Heaven. No creature born of Hell could ever have possessed such a gaze, and it was them orbs of light that marked the Devil still as being directly the work of God's hand.

McAllen saw the wings and the flickering, scaled tale and the great clawed feet and corncob pipe and the jug of shine, but most of all he saw those blue eyes, and he knew his time had come, and probably already gone past.

He also knew from the barbacoa spit who'd been setting those range fires.

"How do, neighbor?" he asked pleasantly, careful not to let his hand stray to the gun butt at his right hip. McAllen knew perfectly well that the six or seven wiry, bright red bastards tending that cow a-roasting could take him down before his second shot got off, and he knew perfectly well his first round wouldn't do no more than irritate Old Scratch.

"Smartly enough, I reckon." The Devil sat up straight and set down his jug. "Strange place you picked to be riding fences, son of Adam."

McAllen touched the brim of his slouch hat. He dropped the bay mare's reins, on account of she'd been pulling hard. "It's rightly son of Allen, your worship," he said, calm as a millpond. Behind him, the horse bolted with a scream of fear to melt a man's heart.

Go, he thought, *and carry the news of my death if not the tale of the manner of my passing.* For it is given to some of us to know the manner and hour of our passing.

Well, yes, you're right. Even a deaf-mute idiot Frenchman would have known this was the manner and hour of his passing. And Eustace Prudence McAllen was none of those things.

The Devil smiled, which was not a sight for the faint of heart. "Still no fences down in these lands, son of Allen."

"Just a fire down below." McAllen summoned the courage that had stood him up against Yankee bullets and Oglala Sioux arrows and Wyoming winter blizzards and Texas summer droughts—that courage was needful now for him to walk slowly toward the Devil, measuring his steps with every care a man could bring.

"My cooking could bring a circuit preacher to his knees," the Devil said proudly. Pride was, after all, his overweening sin and greatest accomplishment.

McAllen touched the brim of his hat again. "But your worship, the sparks from your fire keep setting the grasslands east of here to flame."

With a shrug, the Devil smiled again. "Fire is my servant and my only friend. What does it matter to me that the prairie burns?"

Here is where Eustace Prudence McAllen showed what a clever man he was. He smiled back at the Devil, though his guts liked to turn to water, and said, "Except folk are setting the blame on me for them range fires. You ain't getting the credit you rightly deserve."

At those words the Devil's teasing of McAllen vanished in an eruption of wounded vanity. He stomped one great clawed foot, what shook the ground so hard they felt the tent poles rattle over in Laramie. "By all that's unholy, I shan't be having you take the credit for my deeds, son of Allen!" His shout smoked the air blue and called dark clouds into swirling overhead. Flames snapped at the broken tips of his horns, and his wings spread wide with a creak like a barn in a tornado.

No, no, they ain't had no real buildings in Laramie 'til after the war was done and the railroad come to town. Of course it ain't a camp *now*.

Anyway, I got a story to tell, if you don't keep aggravating me like that. Who taught you manners, anyhow?

"That's why I come to you, your worship." McAllen somehow kept his voice steady, though he nearly voided himself in his drawers from sheer, raw terror. "It ain't right, and I reckon to set the record straight."

"I'll straighten the record," roared the Devil. "I'll show them who's Prince of Flame and Darkness around these parts."

At this point, McAllen realized he might've overshot his mark just a little bit. He hadn't aimed to set Old Scratch on the folks of Fort Caspar and the Broken Bow Ranch. He hadn't aimed for much at all, except to live a minute or two longer in the face of such wrath.

He had his second fit of brilliance. "Before you go

wreaking havoc across the land, your worship, maybe you ought to partake of your dinner."

Well, those words brought the smell of barbacoa back to the Devil's nostrils, along with a strong whiff of the sulfur that has been his natural estate since he first fell from grace. Like I said, there ain't many that can resist the crackling lure of the slow-cooked meat.

"Be damned if I won't," the Devil replied, then began to laugh at his own joke.

McAllen, he laughed along with the Devil, because what else is a man to do in such a moment? The two of them stood there, cackling and howling like two lunatics, even the lesser demons capering and giggling through their needle-toothed mouths.

Old Scratch strode with a purpose to the roasting cow and tore off a long, lean, juicy strip of meat, all crisped dark on the outer edge and dripping fat within. The smell that came off the carcass like to set McAllen's brain on fire, reaching right through his nose and his tongue and lighting up the sin of gluttony as nothing else in the world could have done.

"You want some?" the Devil asked, drippings running down his face from both sides of his mouth, his rotten fangs chewing the soft, sweet meat like it was manna fallen from God's hand.

The scent nearly undid McAllen. He was tempted, knowing he'd taste of the finest meal ever to be eaten by himself or any other man. Knowing likewise if he took food from the Devil's hand, he'd be a servant of darkness for the rest of his days here on earth and damned for eternity beyond.

He never was a churchgoing man, McAllen, but anyone who's stood when the bullets fly or watched over the herds when the wolf packs are hunting down the moon knows better than to disbelieve. Life is too short and hard and strange not to blame God for what He done made of the world.

Yes, even now. And I know none of you knot-heads ever dodged a bullet in your young years.

No, acorns out of a slingshot do not count.

McAllen looked at that most perfect barbacoa steaming in the Devil's grip, and reckoned if he didn't take it from Old Scratch's hand, he'd be next up on the spit. But like I said, he reckoned if he *did* take it, he'd be bound then and forever more in ser-vice, like that Faust fellow out of the old days in the Germanies.

Death or barbacoa?

That right there was the temptation of Eustace Prudence McAllen.

What would you have done? This here's the point of the story, ain't it?

What would you have done?

Really and truly, on your best swear, what would you have chose?

They heard the shot at the Broken Bow Ranch, clear as if someone had loosed a round off the porch of the bunkhouse.

Folks heard it in Fort Caspar, too.

Later on some claimed they heard it in Laramie, reckoned the noise for a boiler explosion or some such, but the railroad ain't reached Laramie yet that year, so you can figure on them being liars or at the best misguided in wanting to be part of history their own selves.

But the howl that followed, everyone heard that clear on to Fort Benton in one direction and Omaha in the other. Like a storm off the plains grabbing up sod houses and snapping telegraph poles it was. Anger and pain and rage and loss that caused drunks to stop beating their wives for a day or two, and sent even the randiest cowpokes scurrying into the revival tents for a good dose of prayer and preaching.

You see, Eustace Prudence McAllen shot the barbacoa spit right off the posts and dumped the Devil's dinner into the ashes and sand of the firepit below. He resisted temptation and bought himself a ticket straight to Heaven on account of nixing Lucifer's vittles and vexing the ambitions of evil that day, in that place. Hell didn't let out for dinner, see, on account of what he done.

The earth split open so that the Devil and his minions could chase themselves straight down to Hell, taking that ruined carcass with them.

When Williamson and a posse of his hands came the next morning on the bay mare's backtrail looking for McAllen, they found him lying flat on the ground deader than a churchyard dance party. His clothes were nearly burnt off his body, his hair turned white as the Teton glaciers.

One last piece of crispy barbacoa was stuck between his teeth, and Eustace Prudence McAllen had the expression of a man who'd died with his hands on the gates of Heaven.

They buried him where he fell, on account of none of the horses would sit still for the body to be slung across. Williamson kept the LeMat revolver, which the metal of them double barrels looked to have been frosted but never did thaw, and dropped that piece of barbacoa into a leather pouch to take home and study, for even then he knew it for what it was.

There weren't no more range fires for a long time after that. Some folks took that to mean McAllen had been the torch man, but Williamson and his hands knew better. They kept their dead compadre's name clear, and they kept the herds well away from the edges of the badlands.

Even now, if you ride out west of Casper toward Hell's Half Acre—for the Devil don't cook there no more, so it ain't his kitchen now—if'n you ask around and folk like the set of your shoulders and the light in your eyes, there's a barbacoa pit run by some of Williamson's daughters and granddaughters. McAllen's Barbecue, they call it. Place ain't on no signpost or writ down in no tax rolls, but it's there.

Head for the badlands and follow the scent. Just mind who's eating on the porch when you get there, because even the Devil himself can be tempted back to this corner of Wyoming when the wind is right and the cuts of meat are just good enough.

THE LAST MASTER
OF AERONAUTICAL WINTERS

Larry D. Sweazy

The platform was rickety, leaning deeply to the left, each post bound with an unknown variety of a prickly vine that had climbed up about six feet, promptly froze, and died—just like everything else within sight.

I found the air to be pungent, more of an assault on the nose than the frigid cold. The smell of rotten eggs was so prevalent that I thought I might not be able to breathe again until we had fully arrived at our final destination, some three hundred feet in the air above us.

Steam escaped from a nearby fumarole, and not far from us, an unused geyser boiled, ready to blow upward. The Yellowstone River was frozen over; there was at least a foot of crusty snow covering the ground for as far as the eye could see. The wind tapped at my face, and the thought of climbing even higher into the sky seemed like one of the more foolish things I had ever done.

"The contraption ain't been used in several years, Mr. Lockwood," the guide said. He was a wisp of a man named Harry Norman, gaunt in the eyes and uncertain in every move he made. If the man had ever eaten a meal in his life that he'd found to be enjoyable, I would have been surprised. A shame, really, to think of such a thing, no pleasure in food, or anything else, by the look of the poor old sod.

It wasn't the bad smell of eggs that provoked my thought of a fine meal, just a desire to be somewhere else; in the warm restaurant of a fine hotel or an even not so fine hotel . . . but as far away from the stench and cold I'd found myself in as possible. As with most of the predicaments I encounter, it was much too late to back out now.

"I can see that, Mr. Norman. Are you sure it still works?" I asked, rubbing my hands together, still cold even in the thick fur mittens I was wearing.

Harry Norman looked up to the sky at our destination, cupped his eyes against the bright midday sun, made even brighter by the reflection off the snow, then eyed me with a look that held more than a tinge of fear. I was certain his breath would freeze right in front of my very eyes and break into a million little pieces.

"You'd be best off if it didn't work at all, I'll tell you. That place is infested with evil, and I swore I'd never lead another soul to the top of it, and I ain't

real happy about standing here again, mind you."
He wore a pair of pearl-handled Colt .45s, both exposed on his hips, and within easy reach of his gnarled, bare fingers. They weren't red or bothered from the cold. It might as well have been summer for all Harry Norman was concerned. I accounted the oddity to assimilation, to the years he'd spent surviving the Wyoming winters. Word was, the man had been in the valley long before the contraption, as he called it, had been built.

I nodded, believing every word Harry Norman said. He didn't look happy about our presence. He didn't look happy about anything, really.

I glanced quickly over my shoulder. Raul was staring at me. He was as tall as a mountain, well over six feet, his shadow reaching out past the platform nearly twice that far. He was so ever-present in my life that I sometimes could not remember when he had not been standing behind me, or next to me, on one adventure or another.

As it was, he was buttoned up in a buffalo coat, not a speck of snow, ice, or moisture of any kind to be seen on his person. A leather case sat at his feet, not a scratch on it, either. I have never seen Raul without the trusted case within his reach.

I am as accustomed to Raul's fastidiousness as I am to a bad turn when it shows itself, at the least welcome time. His weapons are concealed. But I would never bet against Raul Scarlato because of that.

"I have paid you good money, sir," I said to Harry

Norman. "I shall expect nothing but what has been promised to me."

Truth be told, it had taken nearly every cent I could access to convince Harry Norman to allow us upward.

The invention was a one of a kind, an anomaly, but also a testament to the reach for greatness and the workmanship that it took to build such an amazing thing. Or something more sinister, if one was to believe the tales and the fear that was frozen permanently on the old man's face.

"Money and evil is regular bedfellows, Mr. Lockwood, but a man's got to eat, and buy himself entertainment once in a blue spell, or at least when the opportunity such as yours presents itself. But I am only intent on honoring your purchase because of the letter sent up by Buffalo Bill Cody himself, I'll tell you that."

The letter I carried from Bill, the same Buffalo Bill of legend, proprietor of the famous Wild West Show, was stuffed inside Harry Norman's coat, along with what was my money—not Bill's.

Luckily, the letter was of true origin, and our mission direct and straightforward for the most part. There was one certain requirement left out of the directive. Bill and I knew no man would allow us within a hundred miles of the place if our escapade was fully revealed. We would have been killed on the spot, along with our quarry, if success came to us as we hoped.

"Opportunities or foolishness?" Raul's words

were thick with his Italian accent. Even I had to strain, at times, to figure out what it was he had to say. Other times, I ignored his words even when they were clear. His stoic face never showed an ounce of pleasure from being right, but I could see victory in his eyes dancing like a twelve-year-old boy scoring a run in cricket.

As a former member of the *Corazzieri*, the protectors of royalty and kings in his home country of Italy, Raul has taken every assignment from me with the oath of honor and a promise of not quitting until a satisfactory outcome has been achieved . . . or death, whichever one comes first.

"What'd he say?" Harry Norman asked.

I shrugged. "Pay him no mind; he is only my manservant, and has no currency in matters of consequence such as this. We need to go up."

I heard a slight, indistinguishable, exhale behind me, but did not look over my shoulder this time to give Raul the pleasure of knowing I had heard him. Still, he stood at attention, another common pose, waiting for whatever was next.

Manservant, of course, might have been too strong a word since I am neither a royal nor a king. I am only the bastard son of a generous man, who *is* a king. Luckily for me, I have not led the life of a pauper, nor was I cast out into the street, left to beg for my supper. A taste of gruel would leave me looking much like Harry Norman, as I think of it, and that would have been a sad turn of events for my palate and my joy of humanly comforts.

I know the value of my own good fortune, leading an exciting and privileged life as I do and have. But my lack of station has not been without consequence. There is not a bottomless pit of money available to me for my every whim and favor. I still have to earn a living, even though I do receive a small allowance, bestowed on me annually through a tangled network of banking drafts, so that it may not, of course, be traced back to the king. As long as I keep the secret of my lineage, I will be rewarded with an annuity and the freedom to pursue my curiosities and desires—and the constant presence of Raul is mine to keep and rely on.

It is a fair deal, and without question, I will continue to honor the arrangement for as long as I shall live.

My mother was just a young scullery maid who caught a traveling prince's eye. There was never a question that the future king owned the loss of her virginity. It would have been understandable for the prince to consider my mother nothing more than a conquest, and move on down the road, but that is not what happened. Somehow, moral responsibility came in to play with the man, and my mother and I were hurried out to the country and tucked away in the sweetest cottage one can imagine. It was an idyllic life, at least until my mother died, and I was forced off to a horrible boarding school that only got better once Raul showed up. Sad thing is, the king went on to marry another royal, and the queen, a beautiful woman in her own right, who knows nothing of me, has not been able to produce a son for the king. There are six daughters lined up for the throne.

My only interest is in the present. I know nothing of the interior of castles and the requirements of more stringent manners than what is currently expected of me. America has not yet aged enough to demand all of the suffocating rules of everyday life that the Europeans have to navigate just to survive.

Now, being at the end of my fiscal year, and down to the last few coins in my purse, I have found myself in the midst of a frozen adventure, and most certainly, I am not lost to the question of how I got into this mess in the first place.

There was a lovely, curvaceous, Scandinavian blonde in Minneapolis who whispered my first name, Ethan, in my ear more than once, and made it sound like she was saying, "Even." There is no way that was true, however, because I will always be in her debt for the memories on a string of *almost* unbearably cold nights. But that is another story. I got involved in this adventure because I needed the money, plain and simple. That and an adventure at the behest of Buffalo Bill Cody was an offer I could hardly refuse.

"You'll be takin' your life into your own hands if'n you go up, Mr. Lockwood, but I won't be responsible for the outcome," Harry Norman said, trying to warn us off one last time.

"I have not asked for a warranty, Mr. Norman. Just a ride. Besides, I have protection."

Harry Norman looked Raul up and down with an

unbelieving smirk on his weathered face. "Suit your-self," he said "But I would be worried about another way down if I was you."

Raul glanced at the case by his feet. "I will see to it that we get back down, whether the elevator fails or not, *signore*. It is my duty to have a backup plan."

The old man let out a definable groan of disbelief, then pushed up to the top of the platform with an arthritic limp.

I followed, holding my breath. Buffalo Bill told me that the ride up would be one of the more har-rowing aspects of my journey. At the moment, I did not disagree with any of his speculations, but as I have said, it was too late to turn back now.

A shadow pushed over my head as Harry Nor-man attempted to spin an iron spoke three times the size of a wagon wheel. Metal on metal argued and complained from the cold and lack of use, but finally broke free with a great heave from the seemingly weak, old man. The effort looked to have drained Harry Norman of all of his energy. His face was ashen gray.

I looked upward, focusing, for the first time, on the elevator that would take us to the contraption, or the skystead as it was more widely known.

I do believe that Elisha Graves Otis himself would have been in awe of the contraption if he were stand-ing before it, and still alive, of course.

Advancements in technology had been rapid since 1853, when Otis first invented the elevator, but it was the skystead that was the greater accomplishment of the two. Greatest failure, as well, hovering over us, like an island in the sky, that would have and should have provoked an unbound amount of wonder and amazement in the capabilities of mankind.

The skystead was nothing less than a town that had hoped at one time to become a city, propelled and held upward, by the power of the earth itself. In this case, the steam that was captured from the entire Yellowstone caldera.

The town, New Ithaca, floated on pillars that looked very much like the smokestacks of London. There was no factory here, just an opportunity and a hopeful amount of construction, given over to greed, miscalculation, and of course, the unforeseen manifestation of evil. That evil was said to have escaped from the bowels of the world . . . or hell, depending on one's beliefs. That bit of information bore me no comfort. Only a bounty, so to speak.

The ground in the skystead of New Ithaca was a light platform constructed of a wood frame fifty acres wide. Hard woven grass and buffalo skins strengthened the foundation, and as I saw it, the construction was a feat worthy of a wonder of the world. The fact that such a thing floated in the air— still, after all that had happened—was a complete success of engineering skill. Even the underbelly of the skystead was an incredible sight to behold.

New Ithaca had been built by a small group of investors, hoping to populate an inhospitable land.

Buffalo Bill Cody was one of the main investors,

who, of course, lost his entire investment once the project . . . failed, as it were. It nearly bankrupted him, and the plan he has shared with me would help avenge that loss. That is, if Raul and I were successful in our quest.

The elevator arrived at the foot of the platform just as a heavy push of wind spun around me.

Flecks of diamond-hard snow crystals stabbed at my face, and somewhere in the distance, I heard a wolf howl. Whether it was a warning or a coincidence, I'll never know, but the howl sent a shiver coursing up and down my back like never before.

Deep in the recesses of my mind, I remembered Raul reciting the motto of the *Corazzieri* upon our first meeting: "*Virtus in periculis firmior*," which means "Courage becomes stronger in danger." I drew no comfort from the motto, and I doubted it to be true at the moment.

"You know what to do if we don't come back?" I said to Harry Norman.

He nodded his head, and broke my gaze. "It'll be about time, that's all I have to say about that. About damn time."

The elevator jerked upward, and I watched Harry Norman become a smaller man, the change of perspective not lost on me. I have never been one to consider myself fearful of heights, but my knees trembled as we inched slowly toward the gates of New Ithaca.

Raul, as always, stood stiffly, unaffected, holding

the leather case now, instead of leaving it to sit casually at his feet.

Interestingly, the air grew still the higher we climbed, and the stink and sourness of the sulfur, so prevalent in the Yellowstone air, began to dissipate. It was not that I had become accustomed to the smell; it was actually vaporizing, disappearing. I could still feel the cold attacking every bit of exposed skin that it could find.

I was quite perplexed at the thought of a town being built at such extremes, height and location, as it were, but people have lived in far more remote places in the world. I could see how a man with the imagination of Buffalo Bill Cody could dream up such a thing, though.

Halfway up, Raul reached inside his buffalo fur long coat with his free hand, and pulled out a gold-plated revolver that he called "The Cannon."

Instead of one grip, there were two, one in the normal place at the rear of the weapon and the other being in front of the double-trigger. A small cylinder sat atop the two barrels, holding a chemical mixture that upped the propulsion of the bullets, if they could be called that, since the cannon balls were four times the size of a normal .45 caliber cartridge. Exactly what the chemicals were, I could not say. Nor could I say what the add-on chamber was on the side of the weapon. Raul was the scientist and munitions expert, not me. My talents lay elsewhere, or so I have been told, and I trust Raul's skill with weapons implicitly.

The Cannon was not Raul's everyday weapon.

But then again, this was no everyday job. I had no idea what he'd packed in the simple case he carried, but if I knew anything about Raul, it was that he was always prepared. If that were not true, I would have been a dead man ten times over.

"Expecting more trouble than usual?" I asked.

"There will be no welcoming committee."

"If the stories are true."

"You doubt that, *signore*?"

I nodded. "I have seen some strange things in this life, Raul, but surely in broad daylight there will be no threat."

"Evil does not require darkness to breathe—or breed—you should know that by now. This is like no place we have ever been before. I will lead."

"Of course," I said, just in case I was wrong. It had happened before.

Some of the flooring of the elevator had rotted away, allowing for a stomach-tumbling look down . . . if one dared. Thankfully, a thick cloud of geyser mist had obscured a clear view of the ground. There was no sign of Harry Norman. It was as if he had vanished into thin air.

My knees continued to tremble as we lurched upward into the sky.

From what I could tell, we were nearly two-thirds of the way to our destination, the only sounds now the strain of the ropes that pulled the elevator to the gate, the whoosh of air caused by our movement, and the weights on the opposite pulley traveling downward.

There were no other live creatures to be seen in the landscape. Not a crow, vulture, or an eagle. Neither scavenger nor hunter had the lack of sense to be out in the weather we faced, or were stupid enough, like Raul and I were, to ride high into the sky on a rotting contraption, our next stop a man-made island in the sky.

Raul reached down and opened the case again. He handed me a weapon, smaller than the Cannon, with one trigger, but the same propulsion chamber and a smaller barrel.

"Silver bullets, just in case," he said. "Do you have your other armaments?"

"Of course," I answered, taking a deep breath. The elevator carriage was slowing down, and the shadow cast down from the skystead was growing darker. Oddly, it looked like we were journeying down instead of up. The light was growing dimmer, grayer, and then nothing but the blackness reached out to us as we approached the raftered underside of the island itself.

"Are you sure?" Raul insisted. His experience with me in critical situations was showing, as I had been less prepared in earlier adventures that had nearly caused our early demise.

"Would you like an inventory?"

"*Sì*, I would."

I nodded. There was no time to argue or to be glib. I knew the risks we were facing, as it were. "Three vials of holy water, blessed by the Pope himself. One wood stake for piercing hearts, if the need and night comes. The small knife that saved our lives previously in that hideous town in Pennsylvania. Two Colt Single Action Army pistols, and two belts full of cartridges. My inate talents—and this contraption you have just handed me. What do you call this one?" I tumbled the weapon over in my hand, having never seen it before. It fit my hand comfortably, like it belonged there.

"*La mia ultima occasione di vedere domani*. My last chance to see tomorrow."

"Very funny."

The rope groaned, and from somewhere beneath us, Harry Norman applied a brake to the elevator, slowing it to a crawl and a shuddering stop. I could hear nothing but the quickening beats of my own heart. Perspiration began to show itself—and freeze almost as immediately—on my forehead and under my nose.

If I hadn't known I was standing on a steam-raised platform three hundred feet in the air, I would have sworn I was standing solidly on the earth.

New Ithaca looked like any other small town in the Yellowstone Valley, or west of the Mississippi River, for that matter.

There was a three-story hotel, a bank, two saloons, one at each end of town, a livery establishment, and of course, a single-level whorehouse. The front door to the whorehouse banged open and closed in the wind, and the sign, LADY ANNE'S HOUSE OF PLEASURES, was faded but still readable. It didn't look like there had been one second of pleasure to be had in New Ithaca in a very long time.

I found the idea of a livery company interesting, since it sat on the very south edge of the skystead, acting as a port for the flying ferries, steam-powered airships that of course never arrived. There would have been a need for horses and carriages, if the western expansion had been needed, had the population grown as hoped, instead of dwindling to nothing—all in the matter of an hour.

There was no church in sight, which may have, at least, kept some of the evil at bay—or housed it. I have seen it both ways in my adventures.

A solid layer of snow that felt more like hard-as-stone ice covered the entire town, and there was not a creature to be seen. No birds, no ghosts, nothing to suggest any evil there at all. The place was vacant, desolate, crumbling under the weight of winter, neglect, and the erosion of time.

The door to the elevator car clanked behind us. Allowing Raul to lead, as he had demanded. I left the door unlocked, fearing it would freeze shut, barring a quick escape—if it came to that.

I took a deep breath, and stood behind Raul, just off to his right. All the better as far as I was concerned.

There were no noticeable smells, which was another good sign. There always seemed to be something rotting, traces of evil, announcements to the presence of any kind of vile creature from the dark, but there seemed to be none here. Maybe Buffalo Bill had been wrong. Maybe the stories of the horrors were untrue, concocted to steal him of his investment and good name. Or maybe, the evil had vacated, gone back to where it came from in the first place. I doubted that, though. We would have heard the tales by now.

The sun glanced out from behind a cloud, then hurried in retreat to hide itself, casting deeper gray shadows over all of New Ithaca than existed before.

Raul took a confident step forward, the Cannon securely in one hand, the munitions case in the other, and headed straight for the hotel.

I hesitated. Surely the creatures knew we were here by now, had a sentry system of some kind to alert them of interlopers and trespassers. The prospect of lunch, human flesh that constituted a collection of the finest food available in the west, must have had a delectable smell all of its own. Thinking of one's self as lunch is not a habit of mine, nor was it a lack of belief in my skills or Raul's. It was fear, pure and simple. I was scared.

But then again, I had been scared before, and here I stood, facing another adventure.

I gripped my weapon, sucked it up with a deep breath, and followed after Raul like a secondhand partner ready to shoot himself in the foot.

The inside of the hotel was darker than it was outside, and for the first time, my nose detected something foreign, not of this world—the smell stung my eyes, too, like ammonia, and quickly coated my tongue. The whole inside of my mouth tasted like I'd taken a lick of chalk. I coughed, holding it in my chest as deeply as I could, so not to make any loud noise, so I wouldn't set off an alarm. Honestly, I wanted to go back to Minneapolis where this whole thing had started and forget about the whole adventure. Raul and I could have made it through the winter, surely not in high comfort, but comfortable enough to feed ourselves—and not have to worry about being food ourselves. Courage grows in danger, my foot.

Raul scowled over his shoulder. I pointed to my mouth, feigned a gag, to see if he'd experienced the same thing, but all he did was roll his eyes like I was being childish and moved slowly ahead.

The hotel had been a grand vision. Opulence without consideration for expense was the obvious goal. What had been fine red velvet draperies hung at the windows, shredded now, presumably by the weather and time. The glass had long since been shattered from the panes. A patchwork of crusted snow and ice was scattered across the floor, as well as on just about everything within reach of the windows and front door.

The finish work, moldings and trim, were all hand-carved mahogany, still straining to hold to a shine and a sense of glamour and arrogance at three hundred feet in the air. Most all of the furniture was toppled over, legs broken off chairs, upholstery ripped out, perhaps for nesting material for all I knew.

The foyer looked like it had been the scene of a

momentous fistfight, something memorable for certain. And the carpet was lush when it could be seen under the snow, Turkish in design but faded and covered with red splotches that I could only assume were dried blood.

A portrait of Buffalo Bill hung over the fireplace, long hair flowing behind him, dressed in his buckskins, pale blue sky the only background, and a smile of success plastered on his legendary face. I looked away from the picture. For some reason, the man's eyes gave me the shivers. It was like they were real, burrowing into my own eyes with anger and resentment or maybe doubt of my fortitude. Perhaps I was being a bit touchy, but it was Bill's island, and I was nothing more than a hired hand with a killer for backup. I had a right to feel uneasy about those eyes, I tell you.

Raul stopped at the foot of the stairs, and cocked his head sideways . . . listening for something above.

For a moment, all I could hear was the beating of my own heart, reminding me of my current state of fear.

But then I heard it.

Faint scratches against the wood floor above us; tenuous and cautious steps, like a cat with overlong nails sneaking up on its prey, or a single fingernail dragging slowly across a hard, but penetrable surface. Scrape. Stop. Scrape. Stop. Scrape . . .

Raul took a step up, completely focused on the landing at the top of the stairs. I wanted to shout at him to stop. *Are you crazy!* But I couldn't bring myself to. Besides, I knew the answer to my question was yes, he *was* crazy, to a certain degree. Our life together was a testament to that.

We had come to New Ithaca for this moment, and I knew what we would face. I had just hoped that the creatures were gone, were truly a thing of myth and campfire tales, but that is not the world we live in.

Scrape. Stop. Scrape. Stop. Nearer. Closer. Right over my head.

The smell of death in a nonexistent hot sun surrounded me, encased me so immediately I could hardly breathe.

I expected an acid goo to seep through the cracks in the floor at any second, scald my hands, and send me writhing back from where I came in pain that could not be diminished or ever healed. Once touched by the poisonous blood of this kind of evil, there is no serum to heal the wounds. At least that I knew of.

I was two steps behind Raul. My fingers were sweaty, and the cold and stench could not stop me. My awareness of any physical reality was quickly vanishing. Running was not a choice. I could have been standing on the moon, for all I knew.

Raul stopped. So, too, did the scraping.

A hard, cold wind pushed in through the open doorway, hitting me square between the shoulder blades, like a boulder had been thrown at me from some unseen creature. I glanced backward, and nothing was there. Nothing but roiling clouds, twisting from sinister gray to outraged black. Ice began to fall; pellets bounced off the ground and roof of the hotel with the force of bullets shot from a million warring rifles.

Somehow I could still hear breathing. My own, Raul's, and the creature's. It was just beyond the landing. I could see its shadow looming, waiting for us to move on it. My guess was that there were more of them on the upper floors. This one was a mere scout to judge our capabilities or the tenderness of our flesh.

A slight red glow began to emanate from the shadow on the second floor, demon eyes burning downward. I was sure of it. I had not been warned of Medusa eyes, but I would take heed anyway. I would avoid looking into the creature's eyes at all costs. Hell burned in those soulless eyes. A hell beyond this world that I had no knowledge of nor desire to learn.

It's not like we were the first ones to ever venture upward to the skystead with a mission to terminate the existence of the creatures. Each human attack had failed miserably, leaving the creatures to thrive and grow confident in their surroundings. At some point, arrogance and the need to colonize would force them to venture away from the island in the sky. Buffalo Bill had no plan for that occurrence—not that I knew of, anyway.

Every human that had stepped on the skystead took it upon themselves as an act of war, and we all knew it. But Raul and I were not a brigade and destroying the nest was not our cause. Perhaps that would trip them up. They would automatically assume we would want them dead, that our goal was the same as theirs—survival at any cost. But that was hardly the truth. We were after money, not blood.

Before Raul could ease his finger around the Cannon's trigger, we felt an unexpected rumble under our feet.

At first I thought it was snow thunder. A clash of energy above or below us, a natural reaction of the altitude in a winter storm. But the rumble was not thunder or a reaction of nature. The next quake of the ground proved that. We were nearly thrown off our feet, and there was a great creaking below us. The floor began to shudder and tilt downward, then back up.

A geyser of unrestrained steam blew up in the middle of the street, just beyond the door of the hotel. One of the foundation stacks had blown open—or had been opened by some unseen force. Perhaps I had underestimated the creatures.

Raul and I both managed to keep our balance, but the creature stumbled forward, completely exposing itself.

It was like no other demon I had ever seen.

At about four feet tall, its body was composed of nothing but muscles, rippled across the blackest skin one could imagine. Coal. A lake on a moonless night. The coat of a stallion not marked by any white. Nothing compared to the demon's naked, shiny skin. At best, it probably weighed fifty pounds.

Its five fingers on each hand were tipped with

nails that looked like the blades of the sharpest knives known to mankind. Not silver, but black, of course. The only other color apparent on the creature were its burning red eyes, now frozen in fear, realizing it was at risk of being killed.

The smell of death grew exponentially around us, tipping both Raul and me back on our heels. The demon had remained standing only by the balance of its tail, a hooked triangle on the end, stabbed in between the floor boards.

There was no humility to the thing. Its male genitalia dangled casually, and I thought of it immediately as a secondary target—if I got the chance to take a shot at the demon.

Raul drew in a deep breath, and countered what he thought, correctly, was the next rumble of the faux ground beneath us. The floor of the hotel groaned and tilted in the opposite direction, the foundation of the building rising upward and breaking apart on impact.

There was much more at risk here than a normal earthquake. If the island broke apart, as it seemed intent on doing, the fall would be fatal for any living creature who did not have the luxury of wings—which meant all of us, human and demon.

I did not have the foresight that Raul had had and fell to the side, tumbling over the banister, and sprawling to the floor.

I wasn't hurt. I hadn't fallen that far, but I was vulnerable—the gun had spun out of my hand and stopped ten feet from me.

Outside the hotel, I heard a chorus of demon screams, high-pitched squeals that were the most unearthly thing I had ever heard. More scraping and screaming came from above us—panic reigned on the top floor as the hotel threatened to collapse. And just as suddenly as I had smelled the foulness of the demon, I now smelled smoke. Something was on fire.

"Get up!" Raul screamed. "This is our only chance to get it, and then we have to go!"

I shouldn't have been surprised that he was still set on completing our mission. I was just trying to figure out how to get back to the ground . . . alive.

Raul focused on the demon, who seemed dazed and unsure what to do—attack or flee.

Just as I stood up, I saw Raul pull the trigger of the Cannon, and to his surprise, and to my amazement, nothing happened. The giant gun had jammed.

The demon seemed to understand that it had a chance. A smile grew on its face, exposing a mouth full of black, slobbery, picket fence teeth. It jumped at Raul.

I had a second to react. The gun was too far and my other weapons seemed to be inadequate. Raul was pulling the trigger repeatedly, trying to fire the gun.

I ran and jumped upward, one foot out in front of me, the other spinning in a circle. It was a move I'd learned a long time ago from a Chinaman before I met Raul, who had taught me some of the secret Oriental fighting arts that he had brought from his homeland.

The heel of my foot landed just below the demon's sternum, so I knocked the wind out of the thing. It screamed like it had been stabbed instead of kicked.

I landed on a step just above Raul. I ran through my inventory of weapons. I doubted the holy water or a stake would waylay the demon. Before I could reach for a six-shooter on my hip, Raul stepped up beside me, nodded, which was as much of a thank you I could expect for saving him from an attack, and pulled the Cannon's double-trigger one last time.

This time the gun fired. But instead of a bullet coming out of the barrel, a net made of pure silver exploded from the side chamber, flying through the air, landing directly over the demon, pinning it down in another fury of screams.

"We need to get out of here," Raul said. He rushed to the captured demon and picked up the silver cage like it was a feather.

The next part of our mission was to get the demon to Buffalo Bill's Wild West Show, in exchange for our payment. The demon would then go on display, its presence a guarantee to increase ticket sales, and restore the fortune lost on the skystead. We would be justly rewarded.

I rushed out of the hotel with Raul on my heels. LADY ANNE'S HOUSE OF PLEASURES was on fire, as were all of the other buildings. The smoke had devastated the demons, rendered them incapable of thinking, planning, moving—or jumping off the island to an obvious death.

I was shocked when we reached the elevator. It was not there.

I looked over the side of the skystead. The entire shaft had fallen over, most likely taken out by the first rumble.

I turned to Raul, who had set the demon to the ground and was digging in the munitions bag. The silver kept the thing from moving. "Here," he commanded, tossing me what looked like a large sheet with armholes in each side. "Put it on and jump. Don't hesitate. Jump." He looked over his shoulder, and I saw the same thing he did: a crowd of demons rushing toward us, trying to outrun the fire and smoke.

"This is your backup plan for getting down? A sheet with holes in it?"

"Put it on and jump." It was an order not a request.

I did as I was told, and jumped. I held my breath, closed my eyes, and put my faith in Raul's invention.

Miraculously, the wind caught the material, and I floated down to the ground safely. Only to find myself face to face with Harry Norman and a Winchester '73 aimed straight at my head.

"You best get up from there before that thing falls on you," he said.

I stood up, untangled myself, and looked to the skystead just in time to see Raul jump over the side with the captured demon in tow.

"You set this in motion, didn't you?" I said. "You're destroying it."

"I am," the old man said.

"Why, when we've done what Bill asked? We just have to make the delivery."

"Ain't gonna be no delivery. The king is dead."

"What did you say?"

"The king is dead. There's more money to be had with your head than that demon's face behind zoo bars in Bill's Wild West Show."

"There's a bounty on my head?"

"There is now. The Queen is set on eliminatin' any claim you might have on the throne, Mr. Lockwood."

"How'd you know that?"

"What, you think I'm just a stupid caretaker for Buffalo Bill Cody? I'm a business partner. Always have been. I need my money back from this tragedy just like he does. He told me in his letter. We get the demon and you. I'll be sailing the South Seas before spring comes to the Territory, you can count on that."

"That's what I get for being noble and not reading the damn thing. Bill's no killer, though. I can't believe he's a part of this."

"I got my own values and debts to see to." Harry Norman nodded, then glanced upward, eyeing Raul as he floated down. I realized at that moment that Raul was a target. I wondered who Harry would try to take out first.

Pieces of the skystead started to break away and fall to the earth. Steam from the other stacks started to blow out the side, and black smoke and demon screams filled the air.

I spun upward again, knocking the Winchester

from Harry's gnarled fingers. The old man stumbled backward and fell straight on his back. He yelled out in fear as soon as he hit the ground, as a huge piece of the flaming skystead fell on top of him, crushing and burying him in a giant thud.

"So you are the king now?" Raul asked.

I shook my head no. "I serve my country at the pleasure of the Queen."

"But she seeks your death."

"She does. But I understand why. We'll just have to keep our eyes open—and make sure our weapons work when they're supposed to."

Raul nodded sheepishly and flipped the reins of the draft horse, driving the wagon over the snowy ridge.

The skystead was gone. Only a stream of black smoke survived behind us. The demon hissed from its cage, and both Raul and I ignored it.

"We've got some business to see to with Buffalo Bill," Raul said.

"And money to collect," I said. "Since I'll no longer have an annuity to rely on."

"We will survive, *signore*."

I smiled and nodded as we made our way west. "We always do. Somehow, we always do."

LOWSTONE

Anton Strout

The gunslinger looked worn; at least so it seemed to Alice Hartwell, watching from her stool at the saloon's bar. Then again, the mother of one *was* wearing a fine silk jacket, lace collar, waistcoat and heavily ruched skirt, her boy standing at her feet dressed down drinking a tall mug of the fizzy caramel water that the bar's new gearmachine produced. The figure wasn't the usual sort of gunslinger she or her son saw stumbling in through the saloon doors of Babbage's after dark. Not here in Lowstone, South Dakota, anyway.

The long denim duster, the low cowboy hat, and worn leather bags hanging off the gunslinger's figure wasn't what caught Alice or her boy's eye. It was that they were being worn by *a woman*, and by the mixed reactions of silence, laughter, and occasional male catcalls, the rest of the saloon's patrons had never seen a woman dressed that way either.

The gunslinger had taken to a table by herself, and ordered a hot meal of barbeque biscuit pie, scalloped corn, and fried tomatoes. The woman's eyes were mere slits. She half fell asleep while waiting for the meal to come but also while eating it. Some travelers looked tired when they came into town, most looking for work in the skymines along the drop off at the far end of Lowstone, but this woman looked the very definition of hard-ridden and road-weary, dust smudged thick on her face, hiding what little femininity she had. Nonetheless, the lady gunslinger set to the food on her tin plate while the bartender placed a steam compressor under a mug on her table, which heated the coffee to drinkable in mere seconds.

One of the men sitting at a table with several other miners off to the left stood up, a hint of menace in his dark, tiny eyes. Alice didn't recognize him from her husband's crew of aeroship drivers, gear grinders, or piston drill operators, but that didn't mean much. Plenty of people came to the burgeoning town now that mining gold and other precious metals was starting to prove profitable. This man, however, had a face harder than the stone they drilled. Alice reckoned he had come to Lowstone with not only greed on his mind, but with much of what hard men wanted, no doubt.

The gathered crowd fell silent as he crossed the room to the lady gunslinger's table while she helped herself to the coffee once it was ready.

"Now this here's a woman after my own heart,"

he growled out with a lascivious laugh, loud enough that it could be heard halfway across town. "Weathered duster, range ridin' hat . . . no bonnets for *this* one!"

He leaned forward on the gunslinger's table, but she paid him no mind.

"Mind your manners, mister," she said, not even looking up from her tin plate. "I may not dress in frills, lace and bows, but that don't mean I ain't a woman, worthy of respect nonetheless. All I want is to finish my meal and hopefully get me a little time to rest. Now, are you going to keep interrupting a lady while she's eating?"

He laughed at that, then looked around the main room of the saloon, catching Alice's eye for a moment. She tightened her grip on her son's shoulders, but let go once the man's eyes moved on.

He leaned back over the gunslinger's table, planting his hands hard on it, the mug of coffee rattling on its heating plate. "Dressed like that, though, I bet you're looking for a lady yourself, ain't ya? Bet you're looking for something else to be chowing on instead of just this grub, too."

The woman laid down her fork, taking her time, and looked up at him. "No need to be vulgar . . . *friend*. World's got enough troubles without you adding to them."

"I ain't your friend," he said, lunging for her across the table.

"Good," the woman said, standing up quick as lightning and stepping back from the table as her chair slid off across the floor, toppling over. "Because I don't like shooting friends, unless'n I have to."

The gunslinger made no move to back away and the man took advantage of the moment, grabbing her by her wrists, staring into her face with his wild, angry eyes. She met them, unmoving. A grim smile crossed her lips.

"What the hell are you smiling at, girl?" the man asked, his voice suddenly wavering, unsure.

"Works every time," she said, then pulled her left wrist back, hard.

The man held his grip, but a sharp metallic *click* rose up from within the gunslinger's sleeve, the cloth pulling back from it. The man looked down in time to catch a gleam of metal where the woman's forearm should be. A sharp *crack* sounded out, a flash of a muzzle, and the man pulled his hand away, clutching what remained of two of his fingers, the rest of his hand a mess of bloody flesh and powder burns. He cried out, stumbling back.

"Jesus Christ!" he shouted. "My hand!"

"I'm not the worst thing that's going to happen to you today, mister," the woman said. "Believe me. Now let me finish my meal in peace. I'm so damned tired, and there's so much I need to do. Now go on, get! I suggest you have that looked at right quick instead of standing here blubbering at me like a little child who done soiled himself."

All wildness had left the man's eyes, replaced by a dull obedient shock. Without another word, he backed towards the doors and stumbled down the steps. By the time he hit the mud of the darkened streets, he was loping off at a steady gait, presumably towards the town's resident saw-doctor.

The gunslinger looked around the silent room, meeting the eyes of everyone who was staring, including Alice, until they turned away. Conversation resumed throughout the saloon. Alice busied herself with anything but looking at the gunslinger, adjusting the lace of her collar and straightening her waistcoat. When she could make no more pretense of fixing her clothes, she chanced another look back at the gunslinger, her eyes widening in rising horror. While the rest of the saloon had decided to leave the gunslinger be, one of them was set on approaching her. *Her own son.* He was at the gunslinger's side now, his arm raised out to her, reaching for the exposed metal of the arm that stuck out from beneath the cloth of the gunslinger's sleeve.

"Michael!" the woman called out, hopping off her stool and running over to him. "Do not touch that . . . *thing.*" Alice realized she didn't know exactly what to call it.

The boy stopped his hand mid-reach and the gunslinger shifted her eyes to the boy's mother, but made no effort to move her arm away. After a moment, the gunslinger looked back down at the boy and offered her arm to him, pulling the sleeve of her coat back even further.

While the gunslinger flexed the joints of her metal hand, the pistons, gears, and cylinders spun, whirled, and slid in near constant motion. The boy's eyes went wide as his fingers lit gently on the frame of the metal housing.

"Is that your arm?" he asked.

Alice stepped over to her son, pulling him away so hard his mug of fizzy water fell from his other hand. "I am so sorry, ma'am," she said. Her face reddened as she looked her child over, her eyes darting back to the machinations of the woman's arm. "He didn't mean no harm."

"It's fine," the gunslinger said. "No harm done. It's good for a child to not shy away from the modern wonders of our world." The gun hand was still smoking with tiny tendrils of gray rising up from it. Her thumb rose to meet her middle finger, and she snapped them against each other. A shower of sparks flew from her hand, causing the boy to laugh. "Ain't that right, Michael?"

Alice's face relaxed a little, but still kept itself serious. "I do apologize. I didn't mean to call your . . . *arm* a thing," she said. "Are you here looking for work in the skymines?"

The gunslinger held up her gun hand. "Now, do I look like I'm looking for work?" She grasped hold of the hand, pressing in on a hidden release mechanism, pulling it free. She laid it on the table and slid her good hand into the leather bag strapped to the side of her thigh, pulling out another and snapping it into place at the end of the replacement limb. "Name's Sadie."

"I'm Alice," the woman said, shaking the mechanical wonder. The grip was strong, but unnatural, and she fought the urge to flinch. She let go and rested her hand on her son's shoulder. "You've already met Michael."

The gunslinger tipped her hat to the boy and he smiled, nodding back.

"I'm sorry," Alice said. "I thought you might have been a miner, what with . . ." She stopped herself short of pointing at the hand again. "Do you miss it?"

"My real arm?" The gunslinger said. She rolled it back and forth, looking it over before pulling the sleeve of her jacket back down over it. "I don't miss what would have become of it, no. However, I am not a miner. My calamity did not come from hard labor, Alice. I have no love for mining or working in the deep roads of the world. Strange things . . . *lurk* in that darkness, as my husband would attest to if he could, the Lord rest his soul."

"I'm sorry," Alice said, uncomfortable still. The boy was still staring at the gun hand lying on the table.

"Don't be," the gunslinger said. "It is I who should be sorry."

Alice gave a nervous laugh, grabbing the shoulders of her son, squeezing them. "You? For what?"

"For what I may have brought to this town," she said, her eyes narrow but filled with sadness. "I am hopeful, though. This place isn't like Guyet, Marshall, or Parkington—all mining towns where the streets were already silent and stained red with soaked up blood. All those towns were so quick to tear the earth open looking for more material to make gears, pistons, compressors, never thinking about the consequences of what they might unearth." She tapped at the metal of her gun arm. "Not that I'm not thankful for all some of those discoveries, all things considered. I just thank the Lord I'm not too late this time." Her eyes fluttered with exhaustion. "I just need to rest a spell . . ."

Alice's voice dropped to a whisper, timid. "Sadie, what happened to those towns?" she asked.

"Something from the darkness," the gunslinger said. "Something not quite alive yet not quite dead, either. Something took my Ward's life. Something that is heading for this town."

Alice's throat went dry. "What is it?"

The gunslinger looked down at the table and shook her head. "I do not right know, but I aim to stop it."

A scream rose up off in the darkened streets— human, scared, pained. Alice and little Michael both flinched.

"What was that?" Alice asked. "Sadie . . . ?"

The rest of Babbage's came alive. The crowd moved to the doors of the saloon but none were willing to step outside. The gunslinger stood, and as she came forward with calm, cool strides, the sea of people parted. Sadie sighed. "More time," she said. "I just need to rest." The crowd stared at her. Her face looked tired. "I had hoped to have more time. There's never enough."

"What *is* it?" the woman asked.

"Listen up," the gunslinger said, taking off her

hat, revealing a dark blue bandana covering her dirty blonde hair. "Do *not* stay here. All of you get yourself home, get to your families, and then get the hell out of Lowstone. Take to the skies if you can."

"Abandon town?" asked one of the men. "Why the hell would we do that? What's out there?"

The gunslinger looked around the crowd, dead serious. "I can't rightly tell you what is out there, only that they came to my town, too. Those that should be dead, ain't. They rise . . . and they hunger. They took my husband, then my town, then every mining town I've come across since, and they meant to lay waste to this town, too. If you do not leave now, you *will* die."

"We'll fight!" someone called out.

"And you will die, just like my town did," she said. "Now get!"

The crowd shifted uncomfortably, but made very little effort to leave.

The gunslinger let out a weary sigh. "I know; it's dark out there. You men with guns . . . mind those without them and the ladies. Remember, their numbers are few, but they don't die like regular folk. If you see one of them undead bastards, aim for the head if you intend on actually dropping one of them. Remove it if you can, but do not for a second think you can take them. Shooting 'em anywhere except the head just seems to piss them off. Run when you can. It ain't a coward's road to run. I've chased these rotten bastards from town to town and each and every one is now only fit for ghosts."

"You seem to have survived," another man near the doors called out.

The gunslinger pulled off the left side of her duster and rolled up the sleeve of her shirt, revealing more of the mechanisms and the stump of her upper arm where it meshed with the gears, levers and piston rods of the replacement limb. "Not without paying a hefty price, I'd argue."

Part of the crowd marveled at the technological wonder of it, while others turned from it with pained expressions on their faces. Those were the first to shuffle out into the night. The rest followed shortly after, the quiet of the bar falling over the gunslinger as she watched them go.

"What about us?"

She spun around to discover Alice and little Michael still standing there. "Shit," she said. "Didn't I tell them others to watch after the women? Where's the boy's father?"

"My husband Harrison works as the night watchman cliff side at the skymines, along the drop off. We had no one to run off with."

The gunslinger let out a long, slow hiss. "Let's get you to the mines, then, and get all three of you skybound in one of those mining rigs I saw riding into town." She grabbed up the hand she had left on the table, stowed it in her bag and cocked the mechanism in her arm to reload the chamber. "Stay close and stay quiet."

The gunslinger crossed the floor to the swinging doors leading out into Lowstone. The streets bustled with families on the run, chaos in motion, but the gunslinger ignored the throng and pressed through them, heading off towards the far side of town.

Alice ran hard to keep pace, practically dragging Michael along behind her as she fought to keep up. Fancy shoes and muddy streets were not well matched and before too long Michael led his mother, pulling her along in pursuit of the gunslinger.

"What's out there?" the boy called out, nervous and uncertain.

"Something I should have stopped before it started," the gunslinger said, continuing her way through the crowd. A few of them took hits from her gun arm as she shoved them out of her path, a dull metallic clang ringing out each time. "Something I should have stopped before it took my own damned fool arm, at the very least. I know that now, in hindsight."

"Yes," said Alice, "but what did that?"

The gunslinger stopped and looked down at a lone boot lying in the street. It belonged to the man she had shot earlier. Part of the leg was sticking out of it still, and she pushed the boy quickly past it before he could notice it, but Alice saw it.

"Sadie, *what did that*?"

The gunslinger looked up at her for a moment and shook her head before continuing on. "I don't rightly know, but whatever it was I think my husband and his miners unearthed it. It killed him and it would have killed me too . . . if I hadn't taken matters into my own hands, that is."

The woman stopped. Her boy, still holding her hand, jerked to a halt as he came to the end of her arm. "You did this to yourself?"

"Had to," the gunslinger said, waving them on with her good arm. "Keep moving, now." She didn't wait to see if they followed, but the sound of their footsteps right behind her was indicator enough. "I was nursing my husband when he came home with the sickness. He and his men drilled far too deep into the earth, releasing . . . I don't rightly know . . . something. I tried to save him but he was feverish, incoherent, and then . . . he bit me. He died, and rather than wait to see if I would suffer the same fate, I cut it off when I started to feel a bit of that fever coming on. There weren't no one left to help me by then. Most of the town was dead."

Alice fell silent after that, words eluding her, and she and her son continued along dutifully behind the gunslinger. The docks along the drop off came into view a few minutes later, the too-few gas lamps showing most people had either fled on foot already or had taken off in their aeroships and zeppelins. Large mechanical drills hung off the underside of dozens of sky ships, most rising up in the air, but some still docked there. The woman and her son moved along the cliffside, searching, but when the first of the shots rang out off in the distance, Alice stopped and hugged her son close to her waist.

"Keep moving," the gunslinger said, urging them on. Several other shots rang out, each of them sounding a little closer, a bit more panicked, but the gunslinger kept the other two in motion.

"Harrison!" the woman called out a short while later, breaking into a full-on run past the gunslinger. A man with goggles resting atop his cowboy hat spun around near one of the ships, his face filling with relief.

"What in hellfire is going on, Alice?" he asked, hugging her tight as she threw herself into his arms. Little Michael joined them seconds later, wrapping himself around both their legs. "The whole town has gone wild . . ."

"We have to go," Alice said. "Now. Something terrible is coming."

The man glanced up in the sky at all the departing aeroships. "This is madness!"

The gunslinger stepped towards them. "That it is, mister," she said, "but that don't mean it's not time to get. Is there a ship here you can use?"

He nodded, but spoke with hesitance. "This one here is the private ship of the master foreman, but Mister Halsey will have my hide if I ruin it."

The gunslinger grabbed him with her good hand, pulling him free from the woman and his son. Her eyes met his and she stared hard, unwavering. "You keep delaying and you can be sure to lose not only your hide, but that of your wife and child . . . as their flesh is torn from their bones. If there's a ship, you take it. Understand?"

Even with the sparse lighting, the gunslinger watched the color drain from his face as he nodded, wide eyed. Shots rang out closer this time, along with frantic sounds of people retreating from town in the darkness.

"Sure, lady," he said, turning to the short gangplank to the hanging basket of the underside of the aeroship's balloon. The man ran out onto it and threw himself up over the edge of the basket, scrambling in, going head first. He righted himself, stood, then held his arms out to the edge of the cliff.

The gunslinger looked at Alice. "You next," she said. "I'll hand the boy over last. I know that you won't drop him. Your husband . . . well, I'm not too sure about. Looks a little too scared to be trusted with that right now."

"Thank you," Alice said, grabbing the gunslinger by both her arms.

Sadie gave a dark smile. "Don't thank me until you're all up in the air."

The woman nodded, let go of the gunslinger's arms, and teetered out onto the plank, grabbing for her husband. He caught her arms, pulling her up as she flailed into the basket beside him.

Little Michael stared wildly into the open space on either side of the thin wooden gangplank. The gunslinger knelt down before the boy.

"It's your turn, little man," she said. He shook his head so violently she thought it might twist off. She put her good hand on his shoulder, giving it a gentle squeeze. "Don't worry. I won't let you fall. You need to go with your mother, son. Do you understand? Can you be brave for me?"

He paused while he thought about it, then Michael gave a reluctant nod.

"Good," the gunslinger said, standing and grabbing him under the arms, lifting. Watching her footing, she stepped out onto the gangplank towards the boy's mother and her open arms. The sudden sound of low moans caught her ear, but before she could react, she felt something hit her back hard, driving her off to her side as she let go of the boy. She landed on the ground, rolling along the edge of the cliff as the boy flew through the air towards his mother.

Alice caught one of her son's hands in hers for a second, before the grip broke and he fell back onto the plank below. The wood of it cracked like thunder, the boy scrambling for the safety of solid ground behind him. The plank snapped in two and fell into the open air of the drop off as he hit the ground hard, safe for the moment.

The gunslinger rolled to her feet as a dozen or so slow shadows shambled around the boy, disjointed bodies that moved like marionettes on strings that were being jerked violently around.

"Michael!" the mother cried out. "Run!"

The gunslinger wondered just where the hell the boy was supposed to run, surrounded like that.

Michael's eyes darted around the crowd, as a low whimper rose up in his throat.

"For God's sake," Alice cried out. "Save him!"

There was little time for the gunslinger to act. Certainly there was not enough time to kill them all before they tore the boy apart. Sadie couldn't—

wouldn't—let that happen. Town after town she had come to find desertion and death, but that ended tonight. This boy would not die, even if it meant she did.

The gunslinger tore off her hat as well as the cloth bandana she wore wrapped around her head. Her long blond hair fluttered down off from the right half of her skull, but the left side was covered by a half dome of riveted steel plating. She reached up, felt for the release mechanism along its back and triggered it. Gears whirred and the steel plate lifted; the gunslinger was sure she could feel the cool western air blowing across the open hole in her skull. Another present from the night everything in her town had gone crazy.

The heads of all the shadowy figures raised, catching the scent on the air. They turned together as a group, unable to resist what she knew they wanted. One of the shadows she knew in an instant, as it sported a sharp, pronounced beard she was all too familiar with.

"Hello, Ward," the gunslinger said, sadness thick in a word as simple as his name.

"Your husband?!" Alice called out from the basket of the ship. "I thought you said he was dead!"

"He don't look all that alive to me," the gunslinger shouted back, then beckoned the mass of shamblers towards her with her good hand. "Come here, you undead bastards. Come and get that singular food you rotting sons of bitches seem to crave."

First she had to control the rest of the group, the

bulk of which was closing in on her, their putrid stink filling her nostrils. She reached down into the bag across her shoulder and pulled out two lengths of tubing roughly the size of her forearm, each with metal tabs jutting out underneath them. She slotted them into fixed points on her mechanical forearm, locking them in place before cocking the switch on the outside one. The gears and pistons in her arm built up pressure within seconds before she triggered the device.

With a *whoomph*, a wire mesh net flew free of the tube, spreading out as the weights at its corners flew out in four different directions. The main pack of walking dead were caught in the expanse of it, the net wrapping all around them, their flailing only furthering the tangle. The gunslinger struck the activator of the second device, letting pressure build up in it. She snapped her fingers, sparking them the same way she had for Michael back at the saloon. A spray of fluid shot forth out of a tiny nozzle in the tube directly above them, the sparks igniting it. Flames shot forward across the gap between her and the mass of undead, a widening cone of fire engulfing them. Sadie prayed that the wire mesh of netting would keep them bound in place. She had made the mistake before of setting one of them on fire, uncontained, which had only left her to struggle with the flaming undead until the fire eventually consumed it, but this time she was leaving nothing to chance.

The heat coming off them was intense, the odor of burnt rotten flesh foul, and she turned away from it, securing the steel cap to her head before setting her hat back over it. The gunslinger turned her attention to the lone figure still free—her husband. She raised her arm in his direction. The creature stood stock still, head cocked at her, giving her pause.

"*Ward* . . . ?" Sadie held her fire. Was that recognition that she saw?

She looked away, closing her eyes for a minute, shaking her foolish wish away. No, that thing was no longer her husband, the twinge where her arm used to be reminded her. She raised her gun arm, leveling it at his head as tears ran down her face, leaving tiny trails in the dust covering it.

"I'm sorry it's come to this, my darling," she said. "I'm sorry this happened to you and that I didn't stop it when I could." She tapped at the metal of her arm, a lonely hollow sound in the now quiet town. "But my chase ends here." In the end, she wasn't sure she could shoot, even after all the ruined towns she had been through. She couldn't do it.

Whether the creature understood her or not, the gunslinger didn't know, but it spun away from her, instead lunging for the boy who was still frozen in place with fear. Without thinking, she shot at the creature who used to be Ward, a chunk of his head evaporating into the dark night air. The lifeless figure toppled over the edge of the cliff, which, all things considered, was probably best. She wasn't sure she could have examined the body if it was lying there next to the boy.

The gunslinger walked over as the sound of distant

gunfire faded and scooped up the boy, who was trembling. "I'm sorry you had to see that," she whispered into his ear before handing him up to his mother.

His parents scooped him into the basket of the aeroship and hugged him hard, calming as the moments passed. They barely noticed when the gunslinger extended a blade from her mechanized arm to cut the ship's mooring line, sending the aeroship sailing up into the night sky. Alice caught one last look at the gunslinger as the ship rose, her good hand deep in one of the leather bags around her shoulder, pulling out a chain gun attachment, slotting it into place on top of her mechanical arm. She grabbed one uncoiled end of an ammunition belt from the bag on her other side.

"I tended my own, may the Lord forgive me," the gunslinger said, slotting the first of the bullets into the chain gun. She cocked back the mechanism. "Now to tend the rest." She took off through the town, walking off into the darkness, dropping the walking dead as she went. The chain gun made enough noise that it drew every last one of the bastards to her, a half dozen or so closing in on her once she hit the end of the town's main street. She dropped all but one of them when the last bullet fired, leaving the whir of the chain gun the only sound, except for a low moan to her right.

Teeth dug into her shoulder, and without hesitation, she popped the blade in her mechanical arm and jammed it into the face of the monster. The brain would die, she knew, bullet or no. The bite on her shoulder, however, well . . . it was a shame she had just run out of bullets. In the chain gun, at least . . .

Alice and her family sailed up through the clouds. The night sky was filled with dozens of other aeroships, silently floating over a sea of cotton white. All of them remained aloft for several days, until food and water began to run short and the first of them descended back to the town in the light of day. Alice and her family returned with them, fearful of what they might find.

Those who had fled on foot had come back to Lowstone, the hard work of removing their dead friends and their dead enemies already under way. Alice searched the town, following the trails of chain gun fire that the locals were already patching up. She found the gunslinger at the far end of the town's main street, lifeless, surrounded by a thick circle of the dead. Alice thought she looked at peace.

As a reminder to all the citizens of Lowstone, they buried the gunslinger in a place of honor along the top of the cliff top—but not too deep. And the workers returned to the Lowstone sky mines, all of them passing by her grave each day on their way to board their aeroships as they headed back to their task of drilling—also not too deep.

THE FLOWER OF ARIZONA

Seanan McGuire

Tempe, Arizona, 1928

Jonathan Healy stepped from the relatively cool confines of the train coach and onto the station platform. A rolling wall of heat promptly struck him across the face, bringing him to a sudden stop. He'd been warned that the Southwest was nothing like his native Michigan. He hadn't been warned about the fact that it was apparently one of the higher circles of Hades.

"Sir? You'll need to move. The train is about to depart."

Desperate for a reprieve, Jonathan turned to the conductor. "Are you certain this is Tempe?"

"I've been riding this route for years, sir. This is Tempe." The conductor's smile was strained. He'd seen this reaction before, usually from city boys who'd assumed that the civilization of the West included somehow turning down the heat. "It's a good town. You're going to have yourself some fine times here."

I genuinely doubt that, thought Jonathan. His business in the west involved a lot of things, but wasn't likely to be heavy on the "fine times." Aloud, he said, "I see. Well, thank you for the confirmation."

"It's no trouble at all." The conductor picked up Jonathan's bag, intending to nudge him out of the way just that little bit faster. Then he paused, an odd look crossing his face. "This bag seems remarkably heavy for its size. What did you say you were going to be doing here in Tempe?"

"I'm conducting a geological survey. You're holding my samples," said Jonathan, hastily reclaiming his bag. He didn't seem to have any trouble handling it. "Thank you again for your help."

The conductor managed a strained smile. "The heat must be getting to the both of us. I could have sworn that something in there just cheered."

Jonathan's own smile froze. "Yes. It would be best to get out of the heat, wouldn't it?" Then he turned and hurried off the platform, vanishing into the crowd of travelers.

The conductor watched the skinny city boy vanish, musing for a moment about the deceptive nature of appearances. Who would have thought a man with arms like that would own a bag full of rocks, much less be able to lift it unassisted? "The world is full of mysteries," he said, mostly to himself.

Then the train whistle blew, summoning him back to work, and the strange man from Michigan was forgotten. Lots of strange men rode the rails to Arizona. They always seemed to sort themselves out, and if they couldn't, the state was happy to do it for them. No matter how tame people might think the west was in this new, modern world, it would always have surprises left for the unwary.

"All aboard! All aboard for Buckeye!"

Engine laboring like a dragon caught in chains, the train pulled away, and Tempe was left behind.

The hotel was nice enough to have a fan in every room, although those fans did little more than move heat from one place to another. By the time Jonathan made it up the stairs, he'd been encouraged to have a lovely time in Tempe by the woman at the desk, the bellhop, the waiter in the hotel restaurant, and a man who'd been on his way down to the lobby. Closing the door of his temporary lodgings between himself and all their good cheer felt like a victory.

"I swear, the heat must be broiling the locals' brains," he said, engaging the deadbolt. He locked the chain for good measure, before putting his bowl of ice water on the nightstand and setting his bag down on the bed. "All right. The coast is clear; you can come out now."

The top of the bag sprung open, revealing a gun case, a hatchet, several large books, and half a dozen mice wearing brightly colored bandanas.

"HAIL!" greeted the mice, exuberantly.

"Yes, yes, hail," said Jonathan. "You shouldn't have made noise before. You could have spoiled everything." The mice looked chastised, their cheers dying as they bowed their heads in shame. Jonathan sighed. "There's a bowl of ice water on the nightstand for you. Get out of there and cool yourselves down."

"HAIL!" shouted the mice again, their sorrow forgotten as they scurried out of the bag and over to the water. Jonathan watched with mild amusement as all of them reached the bowl and began composing hymns about how lovely and cool its contents were.

With the Aeslin mice safely out of the way, he turned his attention to unpacking his things and preparing himself for the night ahead. The conductor had been puzzled by the weight of Jonathan's bag. Had he seen its contents, he might have amended that impression to "alarmed."

Jonathan removed the large gun case first, opening it to check his pistols. Both seemed to have made the trip unharmed. Under the case were several boxes of specially tailored ammunition, chosen to give him the best chance of hurting whatever might be trying to kill him. He and his parents had spent days choosing the right bullets. Even so, he'd be in trouble if they'd been wrong about the local ecosystem. If there was something in these deserts that could only be killed with holly wood or solid gold . . .

The life of a cryptozoologist was never destined to be safe or easy, but it would have been nice if it hadn't included quite so much mortal danger. Jonathan sighed, setting the bullets aside and removing the next item: a rolled poster for the Campbell Family Circus, which boasted, in large letters, the presence of Fabulous Fran, the Flower of Arizona. The drawing showed a blonde woman on a spotted horse, twirling a lasso overhead.

"Claptrap and rubbish," he said, scanning the print at the bottom until he found the line he needed, the one stating that the next show would begin at seven. Every place the Campbell Family Circus had performed in the last six months had been the site of multiple gruesome deaths . . . and they always happened right after the show was finished.

With a few hours left to prepare, Jonathan set the poster aside and picked up the first of the field guides he'd brought with him from Michigan. He had time for one more review of what he might be up against.

On the nightstand, the mice rejoiced.

The Campbell Family Circus was set up on a patch of land just outside the city limits. Jonathan called for a taxicab, not wanting to walk in the heat while wearing a jacket. It would have been better to leave it behind, but that wasn't an option; not with a more than strictly civilized number of weapons to conceal and not with one of the Aeslin mice coming along. They'd chosen the lucky acolyte through a complex series of divinations that Jonathan didn't even pretend to understand.

The driver urged him to have a fantastic time as he was paying his fare. Jonathan smiled tightly, and didn't tip.

The show seemed to skirt the line between traveling carnival and proper circus. There were multiple tents, sideshow wagons, and a small, tidy midway. Strings of lights were everywhere, fighting to supplement the rapidly fading daylight. The woman selling tickets was bright-eyed and chipper, smiling at everyone like she was afraid of being graded. Jonathan handed over his two quarters, receiving a piece of stiff red cardboard in exchange.

"Have a wonderful night at the circus!" she chirped.

"I'll try," he said, and walked on before anyone else could encourage him to have a good time in this blasted hellhole of a climate. *It's not enough that they choose to live here*, he thought darkly. *They have to make the rest of us believe it's a paradise.*

He was so sunk in his thoughts that he didn't see the diminutive blonde coming toward him until he walked right into her, bringing them both crashing to a halt. His jacket squeaked indignantly. Jonathan clapped a hand over his pocket, signaling the mouse inside to stay quiet. "I'm so sorry, miss, I didn't—"

"Watch where you were going? I picked up on that. Observant fella, aren't you?" The blonde stepped back as she recovered her balance, glowering at him. "Try looking at what's around you, why don't you?"

"I will." Jonathan found himself smiling. It was actually refreshing to have someone who sounded like a local being short with him. "Can you point me to the main show tent, please?"

"It's that way." She pointed back the way she'd come. She'd been paralleling the largest of the tents, he realized, making her way from one end to the other. "Better hurry. They're going to be starting soon." That seemed to be her idea of a dismissal; she turned on her heel and resumed her rapid walk toward the back of the tent.

Jonathan watched her for a moment, and then turned to walk the way she'd indicated. The killings never began while the show was going on. That meant that whoever was causing them was somehow occupied until it ended. Maybe, if he was lucky, they'd be careless enough to show their hand, and he could go home before he actually melted.

"My money's on that Fran girl," he informed his pocket, and stepped into the tent.

The seating inside the tent was bleacher-style, arranged around roughly two thirds of a large central ring. Jonathan took a seat about halfway up, adjusting his jacket in an effort to keep from roasting to death. It was a futile endeavor.

The first act involved a group of clowns, some supposedly comic mishaps, and the obligatory cream pie. Everyone applauded.

The second act involved tumblers—quite good— and a fire-eater who Jonathan strongly suspected of being an Oread passing for human. Everyone applauded again.

The beginning of the third act was signaled by the ringmaster, who approached the front of the stage to announce, in a booming voice, "Ladies and Gentlemen! Children of all ages! The Campbell Family Circus is proud to present our star attraction, the flower of Arizona, the star of New Mexico, the lovely, the fabulous *Fran!*"

He dove for the side of the ring as soon as he finished speaking. The echoes of his introduction were still bouncing off the back wall of the canvas tent when an Appaloosa stallion burst in through the rear flap, running hell-bent toward the bleachers. People gasped. One woman screamed.

None of them paid much attention to the blonde who was chasing after the horse—not until she grabbed hold of his bridle and somehow used his own momentum to give herself a boost up to the saddle. The horse kept running, unhindered by the sudden addition of a hundred and forty pounds of blonde woman in sequined leotard and knee-length tulle skirt.

The horse had almost reached the first of the paying customers when the woman hauled back hard on the reins. The horse came to a stop, rearing back on his hind legs and kicking madly at the air.

The audience applauded, interspersing their delight with nervous laughter and exclamations of relief. If the rider—Fran, it had to be—noticed, she didn't give any sign. She just turned her horse, easy as you please, and started him cantering around the ring. His head was up, eyes bright with the sheer delight of the performance. That was one thing he and his rider had very much in common.

"It's her," Jonathan breathed, sitting up a little straighter. She'd curled her hair, and traded her blue jeans for that ridiculous sequined thing, but the woman on the horse—the woman on the poster— was definitely the woman he'd collided with outside the main tent.

"Her who?" asked the small white mouse sitting on his shoulder.

Jonathan clapped a hand over it, scooping it up and sliding it back into his pocket. "I told you to stay out of sight," he whispered.

"I was well-concealed," squeaked the mouse. Its tiny eyes widened, and it began to applaud. "Truly, she is Blessed by the Gods!"

"What?" Jonathan's head snapped up, attention returning to Fran.

She had the horse moving at a full gallop now, and was standing on its back as calm as you please, like this was the sort of thing a person did every day. For all Jonathan knew, this *was* the sort of thing she did every day.

Impressive as it was, her position wasn't the main attraction. That honor had to be given to the throwing knives she was somehow producing from inside her skimpy costume. After holding them up for the audience to see, she smiled brightly, and began flinging them in a seemingly endless stream at the targets studded around the central ring.

Some of the targets were obvious—bullseyes and

plywood cutouts of coyotes, steer, and other local icons. Others were less so, like the hidden flags she whisked expertly from the tent's support posts. Not a single knife came anywhere near the audience. Finally, inevitably, she bowed, dropped into a proper seated position, and rode her still-galloping horse out of the tent, buoyed on a tide of cheers and applause.

The man next to Jonathan leaned over to shout to his wife, "She's amazing!"

"She's dangerous," murmured Jonathan.

Wisely, the mouse said nothing at all.

Paul Campbell was a man with a circus to run, and when well-dressed young men from the Midwest offered him the princely sum of ten dollars just for the opportunity to meet his star attraction, he wasn't going to turn it down. "Right this way, Mr. Healy," he said, leading his guest across the dusty ground behind the main tent. "I'm sure Frannie will be delighted to meet you."

"As you say," Jonathan replied, neutrally.

"Have you been enjoying Tempe so far?"

"Everyone's been telling me I am."

"Oh, good for you!" Paul stopped next to a small, white-painted trailer. "Here we are. Give me a second to let Frannie know she's got a visitor."

"Thank you, that's much appreciated." Jonathan had no particular interest in startling a woman capable of that much accuracy in her knife-throwing—

not unless he was startling her with a bullet, something he was prepared to do if necessary.

Paul opened the trailer door, sticking his head inside. "Fran? Fran, you've got company. A nice young man who's come a long way to meet you—"

Fran's response was inaudible. Jonathan slipped a hand into his coat pocket and through the hole cut in the lining to his pistol.

"Now, Frannie. He's come a *very* long way."

This time, Fran's response was audible, if not comprehensible, and didn't sound happy. Paul stepped rapidly back from the door, turning a sickly smile on Jonathan.

"Why don't you go on in?" he said. "I'm sure she's thrilled."

"Thank you for your kindness," Jonathan replied, and moved cautiously toward the open door. He kept his hand on the pistol. There was no sense in tempting fate.

Fran was sitting with her back to the door. It wasn't as poor a tactical position as it could have been, since the mirror attached to her vanity gave her a perfect view of what was happening behind her. She looked up as Jonathan entered.

"Now, why did I expect it would be you?" she asked. She returned her attention to the mirror, resuming the arduous task of plucking pins from her hair. She was still wearing her sequined thing, although she had thankfully added a bathrobe to her ensemble, making her slightly less naked. "How much did you have to pay the old coot to show you where to find me?"

"Ten dollars," said Jonathan, and closed the trailer door. Fran tensed slightly, but didn't move from her vanity. "Have you been with the circus long?"

"All my life," she replied. She pulled the last of the pins free and shook out her hair. It was longer than he'd assumed at first; she must have already had it up when they'd met outside the tent. Fran dropped the pin with the others and twisted around to face him. "I was left outside the main tent one morning when I was about a week old. They named me after the snake-handler's favorite python. Is that enough of a family history for you? Are you satisfied with the savage circus girl of Arizona? Because I have things I ought to be doing about now, and you're not one of them."

"Not quite," said Jonathan. "Have you noticed anything . . . unusual . . . about the circus lately? Anything that made you feel uncomfortable?"

Fran sighed deeply, somehow managing to roll her eyes and glare at the very same time. "You're a reporter, aren't you? Here to ask me about the murders, maybe get yourself a nice little quote for your paper? Here's a quote for you: get out."

"I'm not a reporter."

"Oh, you're the kind of freak who gets his jollies from hearing about dead people? That's *much* better. Do I need to repeat my quote for you?"

Jonathan scowled. "This would be much easier if you would just cooperate. I need to ask you some questions." *I need to convince myself that you're not an*

*unspeakable horror using a woman's skin as a disguise
while it sates its hellish appetites.*

"Ask away. I don't need to answer them." Fran
folded her arms, continuing to glare at him.

"I wish it hadn't come to this." Jonathan withdrew his hand from his coat, bringing the pistol into
the open, and aimed it at Fran's chest. "I need you to
answer my questions, miss. I won't say the fate of
the world depends on it, but your continued survival certainly does."

The knife sliced through the air next to his head
and embedded itself in the wall of the trailer before
Jonathan even saw her move. He froze, gun still
aimed at Fran, who was now holding a throwing
knife in either hand.

"The way I see it, you might be able to shoot me
before I put a pair of these in your throat; then again,
you might not," she said amiably. "Do you really
want to go down this road?"

For a moment, Jonathan couldn't think of a single
thing to say. He was saved from needing to by the
small white mouse that popped out of his pocket,
ran up his arm to his shoulder, and gleefully declared, "Hail, Priestess of Unexpected Violence!"

Fran dropped her knives.

Ten minutes later, Jonathan was sitting on Fran's
bed, Fran—now wearing jeans and a proper shirt—
was sitting at her vanity, and the mouse was sitting
on Fran's hand. Of the three of them, only the mouse
appeared to be pleased with the situation.

"You're a mouse," Fran said.

"Yes, Priestess!"

"And you talk," Fran said.

"That is so, Priestess!" The mouse showed no sign of tiring of this exchange, even though they'd had it six times already, word for word.

Jonathan, on the other hand, was rapidly losing patience. "He's an Aeslin mouse," he said sharply. "They all talk, and they never forget anything. That's why they travel with me. They're more accurate than a diary and much harder to lose. And you: she's not a Priestess. She's a woman who happens to have been at the site of more than fifty truly disturbing killings."

"So you brought your talking mouse to make me admit to mass murder?" Fran finally looked away from the mouse, turning a frankly bemused stare on Jonathan. "That was your plan? Trick me with confusing rodents?"

"Actually, my plan involved getting you to admit that you're an inhuman creature, using the guise of a trick rider to bring you closer to your prey." Jonathan sighed, pushing his glasses up his nose. "The first of the deaths corresponded with the poster that I used to track your show to Tempe."

"Aw, hell. I told Paul that thing was a bad idea. Mr. Mouse, do you mind if I put you down?"

"No, Priestess," replied the mouse, worshipfully.

Fran gave it a quizzical look, but said only, "All right, then," before setting it down atop her vanity. She stood then, crossing to the free-standing wardrobe that served her tiny trailer as a closet. "See, the show, it runs on a narrow margin in the best of years, and we've lost some acts lately, so Paul thought he'd try to make me out to be a bigger draw than I am."

"A bigger draw?" Jonathan raised his eyebrows. "You seemed like a lovely draw to me."

"Thank you kindly, but I can't do anything a half-trained rodeo rider can't do, and I won't wear less than a leotard. About the only thing that's impressive is the knife-throwing, and that's a dangerous party game. One slip and, well. Dead rubes don't do a circus too much good." Fran rummaged around the top shelf of the wardrobe until she found a shoebox and pulled it down. "Here it is."

"Here what is?"

"My clippings." She walked to the bed this time, not the vanity, and sat next to Jonathan before opening the box. "I used to figure my mama would come looking for me one day, and that she'd want to know what I'd been doing to keep busy. It turned into habit, so I kept going after I knew she wasn't coming."

"That's very sweet," said Jonathan uncomfortably. He wasn't sure what one was supposed to say to beautiful, heavily armed women who'd given up on waiting for their parents to come for them. The only time his parents had been more than a few miles away was when he went to college, and he'd returned home as soon as he graduated.

"It was damned stupid of me," Fran replied. She flipped quickly through the pile of clippings, tugging one loose. "Here. This was the first one."

Jonathan took the piece of newsprint, frowning as he saw the headline. "This isn't in our files."

"Of course not. It wasn't a townie." Fran scowled. "Bull was a good strongman. He loved this show. We found him in pieces behind the trailer where we keep the horses. I couldn't ride Rabbit for a week after the scare that gave him."

"Your horse is named 'Rabbit'?" asked Jonathan.

"Your mouse talks," countered Fran. "I don't think you get to say a word."

"Fair enough," Jonathan said. "Please continue."

"The first dead townies were found the next night—*after* we lost one of our own. I don't care what you think I am—and if you didn't have a talking mouse, I'd think you were crazy, just in case you wondered—but there's no way I'd ever hurt one of our own."

Jonathan nodded. "I believe you. I'm sorry to have troubled you. And now, if you don't mind, I'm going to be going." He stood, extending a hand toward the vanity to let the mouse climb back up his arm.

"Really?" Fran set her shoebox aside. "Where're you headed?"

"There's something out there that needs to be put down before it slaughters anybody else."

Again, he didn't even see her move. The knife was simply in her hand, appearing as if by magic. "Sounds like fun," she said. "Let's go."

"This is not a good idea," said Jonathan.

"This is a fantastic idea," countered Fran, tightening the straps on Rabbit's saddle. "We already know he doesn't like the smell of the whatzit. So if he starts panicking, we know that we should consider running away. Or killing something. I'm not feeling picky right about now."

"This is a terrible, horrible, incredibly foolish idea," said Jonathan.

"Oh, it's probably all of those, too," said Fran amiably. Grabbing hold of the pommel, she hoisted herself onto the back of the Appaloosa. "You can ride behind me, city boy."

"This idea somehow mysteriously manages to get worse by the moment," muttered Jonathan, struggling to climb up into the saddle. It didn't help that Rabbit kept shifting his weight, apparently unhappy about having two riders at the same time. "And I have a name, you know."

"No, I don't know. You never told me what it was."

"I . . . ah." Jonathan grimaced. "My apologies. My name is Jonathan. Jonathan Healy."

"Pleasure to meet you, Mister Jonathan Healy. I'm Frances Brown. You're a monster-hunter?" She tugged lightly on Rabbit's mane. He started forward at a slow trot.

"I prefer the term cryptozoologist."

"What's that when it's at home with its boots off?"

Jonathan sighed. "Monster-hunter."

"That's what I thought. Hold on tight, monster-hunter." Fran leaned forward. That was all the warning Jonathan had before Rabbit broke into a canter, forcing him to grab Fran by the waist if he didn't want to go sprawling.

"How in the name of all that is good and holy in this world did I wind up in this position?" he demanded, raising his voice to be heard above the sound of hooves.

Fran laughed. "Good luck and clean living!"

Not to be left out, the mouse in Jonathan's pocket cheered.

"I'm going to die out here," Jonathan muttered, tightening his hold on Fran's waist.

Rabbit maintained his canter until some signal from Fran told him to slow down to a walk. "This is about the distance we normally find the bodies," Fran said, looking over her shoulder at Jonathan. "Never closer to the tents, not since that first night. Never much farther away. I figure the whatzit follows the light, but doesn't want to be seen."

"That, or the whatzit is starting out at the circus, and prefers to take its kills a certain distance away when possible," said Jonathan.

Fran sighed. "I was hoping you wouldn't start thinking in that direction."

Jonathan stiffened. "Miss Brown, I truly do hope you haven't led me out here to dispose of my body."

"Nah. If I wanted you dead, I'd have slit your throat while you were in my trailer, and then said you'd been trying to take advantage of me."

"That's . . . quite clever, actually."

"We raise 'em smart out here in Arizona." Fran

grinned before her attention snapped abruptly back to her horse. "Rabbit? What's wrong, sweetie?"

Jonathan tried to peer past her. "How can you tell that something's wrong?"

"You work with a horse long enough, you learn the signs. You might want to hop down now. He's getting pretty worked up."

Not wanting to be on the back of an animal that was getting "pretty worked up," Jonathan scrambled hastily down, somehow managing not to lose his footing on the rocky ground. Once he was a few steps back, it was easy to see that Rabbit wasn't happy. He was pawing at the ground, his ears flicking rapidly back and forth, like he couldn't decide which way to turn.

"This is definitely not a good idea," said Jonathan, drawing his pistols and holding them low in front of him. The landscape was easier to see now that it wasn't moving, even if the quality of light in the desert was strange to his eyes. It was brighter than the forests outside Buckley, while still being dark enough to make navigation difficult.

"You've got that right," Fran agreed, sliding down from Rabbit's back. Her hands were empty, but given that he'd failed to see her draw her knives before, that didn't seem like a concern. "City boy like you shouldn't be out in the desert after dark. You're likely to get yourself killed. Good thing I volunteered to come along."

"You call that volunteering?"

"I didn't stick a knife in you." She smiled winsomely, and Jonathan was forced to admit—if only to himself—that she looked lovely in the moonlight.

Something howled in the distance. He tensed, and Fran chuckled, patting the side of Rabbit's neck. The big horse snorted.

"Calm down. It's just a coyote."

"Charming."

Something snarled, much closer than the howl had been. This time, Fran tensed. "*That* wasn't a coyote."

"Then what—" He didn't have time to finish the sentence. With a loud, whinnying shriek, Rabbit took off running, heading back toward the circus as fast as four legs could carry him. Fran swore, chasing after her horse.

"Pursue!" shouted the mouse, right into Jonathan's ear.

He jumped. "I told you to stay in my pocket!"

"You must pursue! The Priestess is running into danger!" The mouse gave his earlobe a sharp tug to illustrate the point.

"She's not a Priestess!" Jonathan snapped, shoving his pistols back into their holsters, and ran after Fran. She was making decent time across the rocky soil, but was no match for Rabbit, who was easily fifteen yards ahead of her. He seemed to be making straight for the lights in the distance. Jonathan was about to shout at her to stop when he heard a sharp rattling sound coming from the shadows to the right.

Anyone who'd ever heard about the American

West knew what that sound meant. Jonathan found a burst of speed he hadn't been aware of hiding, hollering, *"Fran!"* as he ran after her. The rattling got louder. Not allowing himself to think about what he was doing, he grabbed her arm and yanked her back, just before something the size and shape of a small lion leapt from the shadows and landed where she'd been standing.

It had the body of a cougar and the head of an impossibly large viper; when it hissed, it displayed a chilling mix of leonine and serpentine teeth. The rattling grew even louder as the creature lashed its tail from side to side—a tail tipped with a rattle-snake's noisemaker the length of a man's foot.

"What is that?" asked Fran, eyes going wide.

"I think that's what frightened your horse." Jonathan began to walk backward, pulling Fran with him. "Move slowly. Maybe it's frightened. Maybe it will go away."

"Do you see the teeth on that thing?" Fran demanded.

"Optimism is a virtue," said Jonathan.

The cougar-snake-thing made a sound that was somewhere between a hiss and a snarl, and began stalking forward.

"So is speed," said Fran. "Run!"

They ran. And as is so often the case, the monster pursued.

"What the hell is that?" Fran demanded, between gasps for air.

"I think it's a Questing Beast!" Jonathan twisted enough to fire at the creature that pursued them. The bullets had no visible effect, and he mentally crossed "silver" off the list of things that might save his life tonight. "It must be a North American breed! This is something entirely new!"

Fran grabbed his collar, dragging him behind a large rock. A gun had somehow appeared in her free hand. That was an interesting change from the knives. "You're not going to get to brag to the other monster-hunters if it eats us! Now what the blazes is a Questing Beast, and how do we kill it?"

"It's—ah, it's a large predator, generally faithful to a single master, capable of wreaking untold carnage," Jonathan said rapidly. "It's considered a chimera of the viper and panther families. No one knows how that could be biologically possible. We haven't had the opportunity to study one in generations."

"Well, here's your chance to study one from the inside!" Fran peered around the edge of the rock. "It's about ten yards off, looking at the ground. Think we can make a run for it?"

"No. If it's looking at the ground, not following our voices, that's because it hears like a snake instead of like a cat. If we run, it will sense the vibrations and be on us like a shot." Jonathan drew his second pistol, taking a deep breath. "To answer your other question, I have no real clue how we kill it, and was planning to shoot it until either it ate me or was made so thoroughly of holes that it no longer had any interest in swallowing me whole."

Fran grinned, the moonlight glinting off her teeth. "Sounds like my kind of a party."

The Questing Beast was still studying the ground when they stepped out from around either side of the rock and started firing. The bullets just seemed to aggravate it; it made that horrible shrieking, hissing sound again and charged toward them, gathering speed.

"We should run!" said Jonathan.

"I have a better idea!" Fran dropped her gun, and both her hands were suddenly filled with knives. "Keep it coming!"

"Oh, dear Lord," muttered Jonathan, and kept firing at the Questing Beast. Enraged, it tensed, and leapt, mouth open and fangs glistening with venom—

—only to find Fran's throwing knives embedding themselves in the back of its throat, thrown with her usual unerring precision at the one spot on its body guaranteed not to be armored. Jonathan kept firing as he dove to the side, but it wasn't necessary; the Questing Beast went limp mid-leap and hit the ground in a graceless, crumpled heap.

Jonathan and Fran lowered their weapons, staring at the fallen creature. And the mouse, standing on Jonathan's shoulder, cheered.

"What are you planning to do with this thing?" Fran asked peevishly. They'd been dragging the body of the Questing Beast across the desert for almost an hour, and she was clearly getting tired.

"Dissect it, prepare it for taxidermical preservation, and ship it to Michigan for further study," Jonathan replied. "A new species of Questing Beast doesn't come along every day!"

"And thank God for that," said Fran. "Who do I bill for my throwing knives?"

Jonathan looked startled. "We can recover them easily. The Beast didn't have time to swallow."

"No," said Fran firmly. "We can't. Because that's disgusting."

Jonathan looked at her expression, and decided not to argue. "Very well," he said. "Someone must have raised this thing. We should find out who it was, and tell them not to do it again."

"What? You're going to shake a finger and say 'shame, shame, don't make monsters'? I don't think that's going to be too effective."

"No, I'm going to point out that my family possesses a great many guns, and doesn't appreciate it when people get torn apart for no good reason. This Questing Beast would have been perfectly happy living in the desert, never bothering anyone, but it got brought into contact with man, and this was the result." Jonathan sighed. "People just don't think things through the way they should."

Fran echoed his sigh. "No, I guess they don't. Especially not when they think their livelihood's at risk."

"What do you mean?"

"I mean I think I know who's responsible for your monster." Fran shook her head, tugging a little harder on the leg she was using to drag the Questing

Beast. "Revenue's been down lately; Paul says the age of the traveling circus is ending. That people aren't going to want our kind of show too much longer. So you need gimmicks if you want the crowds to keep coming. Things that no one else has."

"Things like fabulous monsters," said Jonathan grimly.

"Things just like that." She gave him a sidelong look. "He's not a bad man. He was only looking out for his own."

"Tell that to the families of the people the Questing Beast killed," Jonathan suggested.

Fran didn't have an answer for that.

It took them another hour to get the Questing Beast back to Fran's trailer, where they covered it with a tarp to keep it out of sight. Fran went to the stable, looking for Rabbit, while Jonathan went looking for Paul.

He found the circus manager standing next to an empty cage near the far edge of the circus, looking anxiously out on the desert. "Waiting for something?" Jonathan asked, stepping up behind him.

Paul jumped. "Mr. Healy! You shouldn't sneak up on a man like that. I don't know how it is where you're from, but out here, some folks are likely to shoot first and ask questions later."

"Sounds like a quiet dinner at home." Jonathan folded his hands behind his back. "I repeat: waiting for something?"

"I don't know what you're—"

"Because your Questing Beast won't be coming home. I'm afraid we had a little disagreement over whether it was allowed to eat me, and I won." He hadn't consciously decided to leave Fran's involvement out of things until that moment, but it felt like the right thing to do. "What did you hope to achieve? Did you think it could be *tamed*?"

Feigned innocence gave way to real shock, followed by fear, as the circus manager gaped at them. "You—you killed my—but how—?"

"Given the people that it killed, I think I was justified."

Paul's face darkened. "It was going to save my show. I was going to charge the rubes five dollars a head for just a *glimpse*. That would have given us the margin we needed to keep going, to find another way."

"It didn't trouble you that it kept escaping?"

"I was going to get it under control."

"It was going to kill you all."

"You Easterners, you're all the same." The gun appeared in Paul's hand almost as fast as the knives had appeared in Fran's. "The laws are different out here. You had no business coming and poking at things that didn't concern you."

"The exploitation of cryptids always concerns me," Jonathan said, as calmly as he could. He took a slow step backward, followed by another. "As does the panic which ensues whenever a monster is seen by the public at large. It was too great a risk. There's more at stake than just your circus."

"Not more that matters!" snapped Paul, and cocked back the hammer. Jonathan saw the motion and dove to the right. The bullet caught him in the left shoulder, spinning him halfway around and knocking him back a few feet. He drew his own pistol, but before he could fire, Paul made a choking sound and fell, hitting the ground like a sack of wet hay.

The knife protruding from Paul's throat somehow failed to be a surprise. "You're a bastard, Paul, and I quit," said Fran, stepping up behind Jonathan. "Ever been shot before, city boy?"

"More times than I care to count," he said, wincing. "That doesn't make it hurt any less."

"I guess it wouldn't." Fran looked at the body of the man who'd been her employer, sorrow painting her face. "What now?"

In that moment, Jonathan didn't have an answer.

"All aboard for Phoenix, Prescott, Ash Fork, and all points east!" The conductor did a double-take at the young man walking toward him, one arm up in a sling. "Well, sir, it looks like Tempe's been an adventure."

"I suppose one could say that," said Jonathan, putting down his bag in order to extract his ticket from his jacket pocket. "It's definitely been educational."

The conductor punched his ticket and smiled at the pretty blonde next to him, her hair pinned up in curls. "Will this be your first time in Ann Arbor, miss?"

"It will," Fran said, smiling broadly. "I'm looking forward to the snow."

"It's not *all* snow," protested Jonathan.

"And Arizona's not all desert and snakes, but that's about what you saw, isn't it?" Laughing, Fran took his good arm in hers. "Let's find our seats so I can go check on Rabbit in the livestock car."

The conductor waved before turning back to the oncoming passengers, chuckling to himself. It was pleasing to see a couple who looked so well-suited to each other. Why, they'd been so clearly infatuated that he'd almost fancied he could hear the sound of a distant crowd, cheering them on.

THE GHOST IN THE DOCTOR

Brenda Cooper

The ghost had clearly never taken the Hippocratic Oath. Julian Welles Orson shook his head as the light in the teenaged boy's eyes died on the table in front of him. He cursed, a long expletive that pissed off the ghost, but at that moment he just didn't care. Surely this young man hadn't deserved death.

Of course, he probably had. Every time Julian had looked into the past of a person who died on his operating table or under his care, the death had been deserved. At least, that was true since the ghost. Boy probably raped his sister or something. No matter what he found out, it never made him feel better. He was a physician, dammit, not a judge. His eyes felt salty again, and he bit back a powerful thirst for whiskey. He could have some later. He had the mother to deal with first.

He pulled the stained coverlet that the boy's mom

had brought him up over the boy's slender shoulders, closed his eyes, and then covered him completely. The corpse looked even smaller and younger covered, as if he had just killed a child. That wasn't correct: had just failed to save a child. At least he hadn't known Tom well, had only seen him once before when he came in with an ankle the size of a baseball.

Still, Julian pounded a fist into the sturdy doorframe hard enough that it hurt his knuckles.

The ghost faded within Julian until it was no bigger than a breath, sitting inside his chest on top of his lungs, waiting for the next time someone noticed his doctor's valise and asked for help.

Julian opened the door and went out to where the mother and her sister waited, faces as grey as their clothes. He looked the mother in her face and shook his head; no comforting words snuck around his anger at the ghost. The two women collapsed into each other's arms, shivering and crying.

Since they didn't look at him, he continued out to the street and shut the big wooden door softly behind him. He didn't want to leave this town. But people eventually noticed that the times he snatched someone from death's door came no more often than the times people he should have been able to heal slipped away from him. Last week it had been old Jed Scott, who had a heart attack while Julian was setting a broken leg. The boy—Tom—had been delirious with fever, but should have been strong enough to pull through. He was—had been—young and strong, and probably the only help his mother got on the family farm. No man had shown up to check on the boy in the day and half he'd been in Julian's care.

As soon as he finished notifying Sam, the undertaker, Julian took his ghost to the Swinging Gate and ordered a whiskey and water. He finished the water and pushed the empty toward Rachel for more before he started in on the whiskey. He'd miss Rachel—he always missed at least some of the people he had to leave behind. He'd been in Grover's Gulch a year and half, longer than most stops. The whiskey disappeared as fast as the first glass of water. By the time the second glass of water had thinned the vile sourness of the liquor churning in his stomach he felt slightly better, if a little sick. He forced himself to run through the good litany, the one that named the people he'd saved is if by miracle. Karen the nurse whose neck had broken in a fall from a horse, Matt the sheriff who'd been gut-shot, Joe the horse-boy who'd been gut-kicked, and ten more. Lives that went on because he'd accepted the old medicine man's ghost on accident. Iron Hawk had quietly asked if he wanted the same powers the old man had enjoyed and he had unwittingly said yes. He hadn't known what the stiff Sioux was asking when he said yes. Worst choice he'd ever made, and he'd made pretty bad ones a few times.

He shook his head and signaled Rachel to bring him another one. She smiled at him, soft and sweet and a little sad. If she weren't a barmaid, he was pretty sure she'd be telling him to watch his drink. And if he didn't have the ghost curled warm and slightly drunk in his chest, he might ask her to walk with him and count the stars overhead and smell the plains all around them and the first blooming flowers of spring.

Maybe he would ask her anyway. Maybe he could stay, after all. He knew it was the whiskey making him think this way, but it was a nice dream. Rachel's skin looked soft and her laugh was infectious and low. She was strong and quiet. Just the way he liked his women.

The next morning, he woke from a poor sleep, bones cracking as he pushed up from the mean pallet in the back of the small office. His mouth tasted like ash from too much drink and his forehead felt two sizes too small for his brain. This was no way to be a doctor. He kept seeing the boy's fever spiking and spiking on the bed in his office, his limbs thrashing before he finally stilled and then slipped away.

The man he used to be could have saved Tom.

Rachel could have loved the man he used to be.

For a moment Julian thought about the gun in his saddlebags by the door, but he wasn't far enough gone for that. At least not until he got some coffee. He was just stirring up the ashes from the stove to heat water when the undertaker came in and stood in his doorway. Sam's head nearly touched the top of the doorframe and his shoulders nearly met the sides. A big man for a tough job. His eyes spoke accusation but his words were soft. "What happened to Tommy? I thought he had the same fever his sister had."

Julian couldn't look directly at him. "I thought he'd be okay."

"I think he should have been. I've known that boy since he came into the world. He was a good one."

"I know," Julian mumbled, sure the guilt sitting like lead shot in his bones was visible to the other man.

"I've had a lot of business lately."

Julian forced his gaze to meet Sam's and said, "I think so, too. I've done my best." That was true. He knew it was true.

"All right, then," Sam said, looking finished with the conversation. Maybe not happy with Julian's answer, but he'd said his piece. "Good morning to you, then. I hope it's a good day."

After he left Julian stood looking after him, feeling small. The ghost inside him was invisible when there was no one that needed help, except sometimes when he drank. Damned thing liked liquor. Maybe it was as unhappy as he was.

He'd never had that thought before, and it startled him a bit.

After he finished making and drinking his coffee, he washed his instruments in the leftover hot water even though they were all basically clean. He wrapped them in a torn but clean shirt and tucked them into his valise, which he then tucked into the empty side of his saddlebags. The other side held emergency jerky, a bottle of whiskey, a flask of water, and in the bottom, his Colt 45.

He wrote a note, ripping it up twice and starting over. The final version that he stuck to his locked door with a nail was, "The doctor is out for at least a few days."

He was on his way before noon, head still pounding so hard it was tough to enjoy the early spring warmth against his skin. When he left other places, he'd always gone out for a new town. As in those other times, he hadn't left anything behind, but the note was new. It sent a message that he might be back.

He didn't think too hard about where he was going since he didn't want the ghost to hear his thoughts. Not that he was sure it would even disagree. He couldn't imagine living like smoke and air in someone else's body any more than he could really imagine the ghost living inside his body even after five years.

Instead, he thought about the pines and occasional oaks he saw and the taste of the salty jerky on his tongue and the clop and roll of Red's hooves underneath of him. He thought about the mountains he was heading into and the sky above him and the way the early spring grass smelled like babies and the scent of a woman in the morning. He thought about Rachel.

It was three days' ride west to the place where he'd picked up the ghost. Of course, the tribe wasn't there now. But traces remained. Here and there the imprint of a hoof had survived the tracks of other animals and the fall and melt of snow. He spotted

the worn marks of travois heading south and followed them, letting his horse pick its way slowly
while he worried about what he'd say when he
found Iron Hawk.

His ghost woke in his chest by the evening of the
first day he followed the Sioux band and gave him
restless dreams all night. Now he thought only of the
tribe and the ghost and tried not to think about being
free of the ghost or about how the tribe might kill
him when he showed up. Riding up on them this
way felt a little like thinking about the revolver and
how its cold steel would feel against his forehead.
Images of Rachel and young Tom drove him forward
anyway, desire and grief both working his chest.
He'd only been riding a couple of hours on the second day when he spotted a telltale smudge of smoke
rising from trees above him and started looking for
scouts.

Even though he knew the scouts were there, they
didn't stop him or show themselves.

Red's hooves fell nearly silently on the soft, damp
carpet of needles that filled the path, making Julian
feel almost like a ghost himself as he kept going, the
encampment further away than it had looked.

When he got there, he found Black Shawl Woman
waiting for him. She acted as if he had been gone just
a day or two, inclining her head, and saying "Hello,
Julian. Good to see you," in slow but nearly perfect
English.

"And you, grandmother," Julian replied. He dismounted and tied Red's reins to a log that served as

a bench for those too old or too tired to dance at night. "Are you well?"

"None of us is well."

So she was as cheerful as usual. "Is Iron Hawk here?"

"They are fighting. Perhaps that is why you came to us."

"Are they fighting Pawnee?" Please let it be Pawnee. It needed to be Pawnee.

"White soldiers."

His heart sank. The ghost would judge whites. He wasn't sure if it would judge Indians, since none had come to him for healing. But he had been with the tribe for six months a long time ago. Long enough to learn that the value of small talk was nothing. He settled in beside the old woman. "I will wait with you."

Her answer was to make room for him on the log. There were women and children left in the encampment, and they began to move about and make noise after he sat. He thought there should be more of them, but perhaps there were and they just stayed hidden. After watching an hour, he became convinced that there were fewer women and fewer teepees than before.

He heard a high screech that almost sounded like a real hawk. A scout.

Moments later, he heard hoofbeats, and then a group of ten or so riders poured up the path, calling out in Sioux to another. Two of the men pulled extra horses with white captives tied bleeding onto the bare backs, maybe alive, maybe not.

The ghost filled Julian's chest, straining toward the men, although it didn't make its preferences clear about whether it wanted the Sioux or the captives or both. It pulled so hard Julian had to lean back and plant his feet in order to remain respectfully seated until Iron Hawk acknowledged him.

Black Shawl Woman stood and Iron Hawk came to her. Blood stained his elkhide shirt but he slid easily off of his pony and stood in front of her, loose and easy.

Black Shawl Woman's looked full of fear, the first emotion she'd shown. "So few?"

Her husband nodded. "We left some of them dead."

She spat on the ground and looked at Julian.

Julian had been holding his breath. He let it out slowly, careful not to move too fast. The ghost went as silent as he felt, as if a veil of quiet had fallen over the four of them, the two Indians, Julian, and his Indian ghost. No matter that just beyond the small circle, other men talked to other women, ponies stamped and blew, and one of the captives whimpered. Between the three of them, it was all quiet and assessment.

Iron Hawk's face was stony and his eyes dark and still full of the fury of the fight and the race back home. After a long time he spoke slowly, in English, almost as if he talked to a child. "You are still a doctor. Please take care of mine first."

Of the Indians. Julian's hands shook as he dug his instruments out of his bag. He spoke to Black Shawl

Woman. "Please bring water and ask someone to heat more water."

She nodded. They had done this before, he and Black Shawl Woman. Before the ghost. The ghost had come from here, from this tribe. It had happened after a different fight. Indians to Indians. A fight that rushed into the circle of teepees and resulted in the death of the old medicine man, Speaks to Trees. He never called the ghost that anymore, couldn't bear to call it anything. To think he had once thought that the essence of the medicine man would make him a better healer. He had come here to study with him. He shook his head, letting old disappointments go for now.

Julian recognized the first brave that came to him. Running Bear. His hand flopped at the end of an arm so shattered that white bone showed near the wrist. Worse than a splint could heal. He asked for three sticks anyway, and sinew. While he waited he ignored the wrist and looked at the rest of Running Bear, careful not to touch him. It was always all right to look. The ghost seemed to need touch to choose the fate of a man.

Not much else looked wrong. A scrape on the other arm, and a few old scars, one of them from a time Julian had sewn him up in the past. Everything about the man was muscle and ligament, no fat at all. Running Bear's back was so thin it looked like it sagged off of his shoulders. Julian remembered him being almost fat, for a Sioux.

A small boy raced up with the sticks and sinew,

his eyes shy as he handed them up. Julian gave Running Bear one of the sticks to bite on and pulled on his arm, snapping it as close to correct as possible given the shattered bone. The brave grunted once and blinked, looking up at the blue sky above him. Strong. They were all strong, these Indians. Even the ghost inside of him.

Julian wrapped the break in the other sticks and some clean rags from his bag, then tied it with the sinew. The ghost began to rise in him, nearly gagging him as it filled his chest. Sweat poured down the back of his neck. He should never have left Rachel. He should have just stayed in Grover's Gulch and taken his chances.

His hands encircled the wrapped wrist and stayed there, heat flowing up through the soles of his shoes and straightening his spine, catching in his heart so he took a deep breath to encourage its passing up to the small dimple by his clavicle. From there, it flowed down his arms and into his hands. It took a few breaths. It was never instant, him standing there and the ghost doing its work for good or ill. He let go when he felt the heat slowing inside him.

The man's face had lost its thick pain lines.

At least this warrior was a good man.

The next task was almost the same, only a nasty cut that looked better before he even finished washing it in the water that Black Shawl Woman had brought him and salving it with supplies from his valise.

The ghost backed off for the next two patients,

who presented simpler problems: a jammed finger he splinted like he had the arm and a set of nasty-looking but shallow gashes. At least when there was no possible way to explain a death the ghost didn't create one.

Maybe he would survive this day and be able to ask Iron Hawk how to give the ghost back. He stopped and drank from his flask of water, words running through his being. *Thank you for the gift. It has two faces and I don't want it. Can you help me kill your old magic man? Can you make me just another white man again?*

His mouth tasted like dust and death and the ghost.

The two white captives had been taken from the mounts and put on the ground, their legs tied and children set to watch them. An insult, or maybe just acknowledgment of to how beaten they looked.

Black Shawl Woman had stepped away somewhere, perhaps to get more water, but Iron Hawk stood watching him, his face inscrutable. If he had something better to do after just returning from a devastating fight, he didn't show it.

The first man was young, maybe just a few years older than young Tom back in Grover's Gulch. His beard was fuzz at best. He had been the one whimpering, but now he was silent and wide-eyed, almost accusatory. As if Julian was a traitor for being here. Julian didn't bother to introduce himself. No reason for rumors of him with the Indians getting out. People got killed for less in some towns, especially after a long night of drink.

An arrow had gone through the thick of his thigh. The shaft was close enough to veins that Julian was afraid to draw it out lest he miss the exact path it went in. He snapped off the head and the fletch and stared at it for a moment, checking the shaft for barbs or splinters. It was well-made. "Grit your teeth," he said, and then he pulled slowly and steadily, still not touching the captive.

The boy cried out, his eyes wide, sweat beading his white brow where a hat he no longer seemed to have had shaded it from the sun.

Julian kept going, feeling the ghost in him, not sure which way it was going to choose.

He handed the broken arrow to a child and said, "Put that in the fire" in a mix of English and bad Sioux. The boy seemed to understand him. He ran off.

Julian took a deep breath and clamped his hands over the bleeding holes on either side.

Cold seeped through his fingers. He knew— because it was still running through his fingers— that the blood was hot and alive, but all he *felt* was cold.

The cold seeped all the way to his own heart. Fear.

When he felt this he fought. He always fought. It happened inside him, something no one could see. His stomach soured with it. He could just let go of the patient and tell someone else what to do if he could make them understand him, but Iron Hawk stood watching, eyes narrow.

He held on, his lips thinned against his teeth, his

hands shaking, the blood that should have stopped by now pouring out from between his fingers like a cold river.

The young man's heart sped up and he cried out more softly, struggling and falling all at once. His face whitened.

Julian forced his eyes to stay with the young man.

It took a very long time, the blood running through his fingers and the stoic Indian standing above him watching and the ghost working against him and against the life that still throbbed under his hands.

Eventually, as always when the ghost decided, the young man stopped bleeding.

Two men came and carried the body off silently. Someone would end up with the scalp but at least they didn't take it in front of him.

Iron Hawk nodded at the other captive. Maybe if Julian rushed Iron Hawk the old man would kill him, run him through with a spear or a shoot him. The tribe had a few guns.

Julian stood up. The world swung around him, tilting.

Black Shawl Woman plunged his hands in a dented metal bucket of tepid water.

He shook himself and nodded thank you at her, scrubbing hard as if he could wash the death off of him.

The other captive was older, maybe even as old as Julian. Blood caked his scalp and the side of his face as if someone had tried to scalp him alive and done a poor job. Pain filled his eyes and thinned his mouth. He sat with his knees drawn together, arms wrapped tightly around them. He had watched in silence while the young man died. Hadn't, in fact, said a word or uttered a whimper on his trip in. Julian circled him, looking for other signs of injury. He didn't see any, but the man was folded tight across his torso.

Iron Hawk watched.

Julian knelt in front of the captive. "Can you stand?"

"No."

"Why?"

"My stomach might," a pause, "fall out of me."

Julian gestured Black Shawl Woman over. "Blanket, please, and hot water."

While she directed a younger woman to do her bidding, Julian arranged his surgical instruments out onto the a square of leather he carried for that purpose, carefully setting each in its place, letting the man see them, and see how carefully he handled them. The ghost stretched inside him, curious.

"You live with the tribe?" the man asked.

"No. I'm just visiting."

"But they let you work on them."

Julian didn't want to explain the details. "I haven't been here for five years."

"Lucky me."

Julian shook his head. Maybe.

Black Shawl Woman brought the blanket. She didn't speak to him, but neither did she watch him as carefully as her husband did. It felt almost comfortable to be around her again, as if he were falling into old habits or she were an old friend. He knew better, knew she allowed him in her camp because of Iron Hawk. But still, they worked together to lay the blanket out and help the old man scoot onto it.

"Why don't they just kill me?" the man asked after he'd gotten squared onto the blanket, still protecting his torso.

"Maybe they will," Julian replied. "Let go of your knees." He hadn't been holding his knees when he came in on horseback. Whatever was there, the man wasn't going to bleed out instantly. But Julian would touch right away, get this done, give in to the ghost. And then he'd ride away and shoot himself.

Julian sat on one side of the man, ready.

Black Shawl Woman sat on the other.

The man rocked until he was on his back, his knees up in front of him. Then he straightened out his legs fast, his hands coming up with a knife between them. He slashed toward Black Shawl Woman, opening her upper arm and digging in with the knife as if it were an awl instead of a blade.

Julian knocked his arm to the side, holding it down, knife blade digging into the blanket.

Black Shawl Woman scrambled away.

Julian leaned on the man. "You shouldn't have done that."

"Kill me."

"No."

The ghost was in him, pressing toward where Julian leaned on the man.

Julian couldn't let go of the knife or risk it himself. He bore down harder, letting the ghost choose.

"That your squaw?"

"No." Julian barked, leaning hard on the man's arm, holding it down with his knee so he could take the weapon.

Warmth spread down his arm, his own heat and the ghost's heat pouring into the man who was now struggling under him like a wounded fish.

Julian threw the knife away from him, heard it skitter against the stony ground and then stop.

The damned ghost was going to heal this one, after taking the other one.

Julian kept his weight on the man, watching in fascination as blood stopped welling up from his scalp and color came back to the cheeks.

Black Shawl Woman had returned with ropes. She and two women bound the captive in place, under Julian, while he lay there, the heat of the ghost running through him like a river or a volcano, feeding the man color and life and breath.

After his blood cooled and he sat up, he stared at Black Shawl Woman. She stared back, and then cracked a small smile that might even be approval. Blood still ran down her arm.

He reached toward her, but she took a step back and gestured for the women to help her move the bound captive. Julian wasn't sure he'd place a penny bet on the man's life, but at least his hands would have no part in his death if it came. He stayed on the blanket, now bunched and dirty from the scuffle, and tried to get his breath.

Iron Hawk still stood watching. He hadn't even moved in to help Black Shawl Woman, but had merely watched. And it was Julian he watched.

Or the damned ghost. Who knew what Indians could see?

"I do not want this inside me any more," Julian said.

Iron Hawk shook his head. "Until you die. It is part of you until you die."

"There is nothing you can do?"

"We will take Speaks to Trees back when you die."

Julian imagined Rachel back at the Swinging Gate, chatting with customers or wiping down the bar and humming. He imagined her exposed to the ghost and what it would be like for the life of someone he loved to ebb away from him. For Rachel to die under his hands.

He pushed himself up, his knees weak and his hands shaking. He walked past Iron Hawk and over to Red, running his hands down the horse's thickly muscled neck, feeling its warmth. He reached into his saddlebag and folded his fist around the grip on his Colt. It felt light as he slid it out of the bag and into the air. In spite of how tired he was, he cocked it and held it to his head, the weight wrong now, pressing down on his wrist. The barrel felt as cold as he expected.

He pulled the trigger.

The gun bucked in his hand, the shot off-center, pain blossoming in the back of his head.

He staggered.

No way he had missed, but he still moved and breathed.

Heat forced him to his knees. The gun fell onto the ground.

Iron Hawk stood above him, chanting in Sioux.

Heat burned through his veins. He fell forward onto his stomach, biting his tongue to keep from crying out.

He rolled over, looking up at Iron Hawk, his visions fuzzy. Iron Hawk's hands and lips moved but Julian heard nothing. The heat stopped, cold. Literally. Every place that had been burning felt like ice, and for a brief moment he felt the ghost had judged him, felt anger rolling into his heart.

He took in a shuddering breath.

The ghost was gone.

He would miss Rachel. The tribe would care for Red. He let go, falling into darkness as his eyes closed.

When he woke, he ran his hand across the back of his head, which should hurt like hell but was only a bit sore, the way it felt after a headache. Dried blood caked his hair but he couldn't feel the place the bullet had seared his skin.

The stained hide of a teepee circled above him, light from a small fire playing across painted images. Night. Stars overhead, just a few winking in the black hole that let the smoke out. Furs under him felt lightly scratchy against the bare skin of his hands. Someone was singing.

Black Shawl Woman. He looked. Her arm had been bandaged. Good. He couldn't bear to touch her and have the ghost judge.

It didn't rise to fill his chest anyway. He closed his eyes, felt inside his body.

No ghost.

Water boiled nearby, and by the time he opened his eyes, Black Shawl Woman was approaching him with a warm wet cloth. She wiped his face and his head, the cloth coming away stained almost black by old blood.

He looked around for Iron Hawk, didn't see him, lay back down and passed out, the soft singing of Black Shawl Woman following him into dreams.

The next time he moved, natural light bathed him through the open teepee door. Black Shawl Woman offered him water and a bit of rabbit soup, both of which tasted so good he might be dead, although by now it was clear he wasn't.

Red was saddled outside. Iron Hawk stood at the horse's head. He nodded, still solemn, but his eyes had lost the cold assessment and instead he— almost—looked friendly.

"What happened to Speaks to Trees?" Julian asked him

"What do you think his job with you was?"

Julian let out a long breath while he checked his

saddlebags to ensure the Colt was there and that he had fresh water. "It acted like a judge."

"In the end, what did the ghost judge the most?"

Julian felt the emptiness where the ghost had been. "Me."

"And through you, others like you."

Julian wasn't sure that was entirely a good thing. The ghost had only healed about half of the patients he's seen in the long five years. He didn't ask what Iron Hawk would do with the information. That was for the old man to decide. At least the ghost had found Julian worth saving.

He reached out and clasped Iron Hawk's hand and clucked at Red to get moving. In three days, he would be able to ask Rachel to walk with him.

SURVEYOR OF MARS

Christopher McKitterick

John didn't need to turn his scope alidade to witness the intruder headed his way. The man had been stirring up dust for nearly an hour during his long walk from Acidalium Town, where most of the pioneers lived. In the low Mars gravity, it was easier to keep one's balance by shuffling along than by taking big steps. The cloud lingered in the summer afternoon's still air, reminding John of the smoke a steam engine would leave back home, weaving through the Montana high desert, millions of miles away. The gigantic bulge of the cargo-ship parked at Lowell Space-Port shone like a steel mountain on the other side of town, where laborers were feeding it tons of native Martian artifacts, Mars-stone, and discouraged or broken homesteaders headed back to Earth. This was the 15th day of Second-July, 1902, two Mars-years (four Earth-years) after men first landed here, a little more than four Earth-years since the failed Martian invasion.

John leaned over his metal stand and jotted down his last notes for the homestead survey. The map for the little offshoot of Acidalia Colles Gully that stretched out below him was filling out nicely, too. It had taken more than a year to get around to properly surveying his land, but there was nothing to be done about that: more than three hundred other homesteaders all needed their land surveyed as well. As they say, a cobbler's child wears worn shoes.

He looked down from the dry hilltop into the Acidalia Colles Gully. A dense carpet of red creeper marked where the channel stayed damp through the Martian spring and was only now drying in the late northern summer. Plump succulents dotted the hillsides like spiky orange pots, and dry red scrub bush clung to the rocky soil above the valley. For the two months of spring flood season, the desert of Mars blossomed like nothing on Earth, a riot of colors unseen when the plants lay dormant during the other twenty-one Mars months. Like other Mars pioneers whose homesteads included areas where water flows, John's homestead claim was a quarter-section, 160 acres; if a claim was completely arid, a half-section, 320 acres. All along the center of the homestead, many-legged native cattle—*More like big-eyed elephant-octopus things*, his brother had once remarked—munched the plants that most folks found distasteful, stripping leaves from stems with their half-dozen snout-tentacles.

Good thing people found the cattle and their little Mars-chicken relatives more to their liking, or the pioneers would have expired from starvation long ago.

John stepped back from his equipment and stood straight. The land was bathed in pink afternoon light shed by a tiny sun set in a sky so blue it was almost purple. Just out of sight, a mile beyond Jacob's Mesa (so named in remembrance of his father), lay the ruins of an abandoned Martian trading-post: *his* town, John's Town, well within the boundaries of his quarter-section claim. Burrowed into the side of the mesa huddled the little Martian cottage John called home during the brutal Martian winter and spring, and where he would remain through the summer and hereafter. He felt like smiling.

Son, said his father, *you've finally found your place. It's good.*

Yes, sir, he replied. *I love this land. Reminds me of home, only more remote from troubles.*

Nothing like home, then, said his father.

I guess not, except for how you can be alone.

"John Mulberry," called the intruder, whose face was still half-covered with the bandana most folks wore to block the dust from nose and mouth, and whose head bore a heavy wool hat. John could tell that it was Lucius McCrady by the heavy denim coveralls the man's wife had mended a dozen times with green thread. Lucius wore a gun-belt. From the shape of the hammer and cylinder, John figured the holster held an old Remington percussion revolver. That was different.

John frowned and crossed his arms. It wasn't like Lucius to bear a weapon, even out here in the wilds where one might encounter a pack of little land-squid. Their sting wasn't much of a threat to a man wearing boots and warm clothing. John wore his father's Indian War guns since last winter, when the Company's enforcers had started getting rough. Each night, he cleaned and oiled the pair of Colt Army Model 1873 .45-caliber revolvers against the omnipresent red and black dusts of Mars.

Lucius was clearly spooked—probably got himself in trouble with the subversive talk he was spreading among the homesteaders, miners, and port-workers. He and Martina were decent people; they had braved the rimey sandstorms of January to bring John warm beans and Mars-chicken after John's brother Billy died. Lucius would never draw arms against another man, or so John would have thought. He decided it was time to have a word with Martina; she was smart and level-headed and would put Lucius off the road to getting himself killed.

Lucius stopped beside him on the hilltop over-looking the gully. He watched the grazing cattle for a moment. John waited patiently. On Mars, where the air was as thin as on an Earthly mountain-top, it was only polite to let a man catch his breath after a long walk.

"You heard the Company's looters annexed the Perry claim?" asked Lucius.

"I did," said John. He had surveyed the Perry homestead during last year's spring, and the Perrys had been overjoyed to learn that their dusty half-section encompassed the ruins of an ancient Martian city. Such a claim could be worth more even than a Mars-stone mine, what with the technology one could sell to enterprising folks back on Earth. Ben Perry had uncovered intact Martian water-pumping equipment in one of the cellars.

Lucius was clearly waiting for more; when he didn't get it, he began to fidget.

Careful, said his father. John sometimes wondered if he was crazy, talking with the dead as he was wont to do out here alone with the beautiful desolation of the wilderness.

"John," said Lucius, pulling down his bandana, "you know what I'm asking."

John remained silent.

"Dammit, John, we need your help. You know we've been organizing for a while now. The port-workers are with us; they took the Company men's spare guns and ammunition last night, and we been sharing those out among the homesteaders and miners. Even a few of the Chinese are with us, with the promise that they won't be treated like slaves anymore."

John squinted into the distance from whence Lucius had come, tracing the snake of dust back to Acidalia Town. He couldn't quite make out the buildings from this distance, but he could see that people were kicking up a lot of dust back there.

"I've heard talk about this," John said. "I expect Boss Cooper has heard, too. I don't imagine those gunfighters in his employ will take kindly to your preaching war against the Company."

"It's ain't war," the other man said. "It's revolution. It's freedom! The Company ain't never done nothing for us but eat our lunch. Imagine what we can do without them. We're running the Company's looters and enforcers out of Acidalium for good. Tonight. We got to hit them before the cargo-ship leaves, before the new Company men get dug in. We're planning to ship all the Company men back to Earth where they belong, at least the rotten ones. But we need more men to make that happen." He looked intently at John.

Keep out of this, John. A little breeze gave John the excuse to look away from the man's piercing green eyes and set his solar compass onto his papers to keep them from blowing away.

"We need men with guns," Lucius said. "I know you're no fan of the Company since what they did to Billy."

John remained quiet. He peered through his scope alidade to pick out the red-iron balls he had discovered atop the mesa. His mouth tasted of rust.

"I respect you wanting your solitude. I've respected how you stay out of things. But you know we need boys like you. Boys who harbor in their hearts hate for the Company. And more than that . . ." He gestured at John's gun-belt. "I heard tell that you know how to use those Peacemakers. I heard—"

John abruptly turned to face the man. He savagely

pulled down his own bandana so he could speak more clearly. His face felt on fire.

"What did you hear, Lucius?"

Lucius was about to speak, then looked down.

"I don't know, John," he finally said, quietly. His face was shadowed beneath his hat. "None of us really know what to do with these." He fondled his pistol's old hardwood grip.

Stolen by Chinamen to start a war, said John's father.

"But those enforcer boys," Lucius said, "they know what to do with theirs."

"That's right, Lucius, they do. You've gotten a bunch of ranchers and miners and Chinese box-haulers all riled up so they're willing to make a stand against the Company's gunfighters. What do you expect will happen? Even if you kill them all, then what? The Company will just send a new crew when the cargo-ship comes back again in a couple of months. Are you going to kill every new enforcer who comes to Mars?"

"There's no other way!" Lucius's eyes were bright with angry tears. "Sure, you know what it's like to lose a father and a brother, but you don't know what it's like to lose your baby girl. Martina and I do! Martina's one dream in life was to raise a family. The Company stole her dream. Ben Perry knows what it's like to possess a whole city and watch it taken away, the only thing of any worth on his homestead, and now he'll watch his pretty wife starve to death and his little boy starve to death unless the rest of us do something about it.

"Well, we're going to do something about it." Lucius's cheeks glowed red.

"I implore you," John said, "don't do this. Shooting someone never solved anything. It festers like a disease that produces more spite that someone else needs to let out by the blood of another. If you know I can shoot these," he patted his Colts "you know that I know they don't solve anything."

"But your brother! He—"

"He stuck his nose in somebody else's business." John felt so angry now he shook. It had been all he could do to heed his father's words and not go looking for the man who had murdered his brother in the cold. He wanted to repeat his father's words: *You can't see a man for what he is when you're pointing a gun at him. But he becomes a man again right quick when you see the pain in his eyes. After he dies, you never stop seeing him that way for the rest of your days.*

But all John could manage was, "Guns didn't do Billy much good."

"Sometimes you got no choice but to fight," Lucius said as he began to turn away. "If you're a man, you'll lend us your guns tonight. Right after sunset, outside the Company office in Acidalium Town."

He walked away, retracing his path in the dust.

You're right to stay out of this, son, said John's father. *It's not your business. Killing someone doesn't make you a man.*

A breeze began to hiss across the brim of John's hat. It was a cold summer.

*   *   *

John did not go to town. He sat atop the butte, near a fire made from bundles of dry stalks. Sunset lasted for an hour or more. Rainless storms coming in from the north cast up dust, pink and luminous in the twilight. When the wind settled down, the stars blazed overhead the way they do in fever-dreams, millions of them like milk spilled across a glass sky, white and blue and red like Mars in the daylight. Somewhere up there, one of those blue stars was Earth, source of all that ailed them, where the body of his father lay dead and rotting in the ground, and no amount of killing could ever bring the man back to life.

Daddy, what am I supposed to do? He got no answer.

Later, when his fire had died to cinders and the bitter cold began to claw at his toes and fingers, John heard the unmistakable thunder of a gunfight in the distance. He wondered if it was his imagination getting the better of him, the way he could see Captain Grunwold sitting across the fire, two scabbed-over bullet-holes in his blue Army uniform. The dead man stared at John with unreadable brown eyes, those eyes he could never stop seeing even when he looked away.

John's father joined them, wispy white hair tousled in the breeze, surrender in eyes sunken from seeing the horrors of too many years in the Army during the Indian Wars. He used to talk about the weight he carried on his conscience. The last thing John's father had told him, lying on a cot that stank of dried blood, was *The West is built on taking away from someone else.*

I've surveyed it all, and it's nothing but men here now, men so full of greed they'll climb over anyone who was here first, over women and children even, men so bad their hearts depart their bodies for fear of turning to stone in such hard chests. Ride that Martian ship to the only free place left, where no one has to die or kill to build a home.

Little flashes of light in Acidalium Town told John the thunderstorm existed not just in his mind.

John was glad at that moment for his father's death prior to seeing even this distant land spoiled by the stony hearts of men.

The next morning, John awoke to the sound of hammering at his cottage door.

"John Mulberry!" shouted a man on the other side of the concrete slab. "You come out here!"

John didn't recognize the voice, but he could tell there were two other men outside with him. They spoke to one another in hushed tones. John pulled on his coveralls over the liner-underwear he slept in, stepped into the boots that he kept beside the cot, fitted the knitted-wool cap that he kept on the nightstand, strapped on his gun-belt that hung on an iron hook near the bed, and then fitted his deerskin gloves. The man pounded on the door again.

"We know you're in there. Come out!"

The Martian who'd lived here before John sat pressed into the far corner beneath the one round window, its tentacles quivering, its intelligent black eyes fixed on John's as he crossed the blue-and-green checkerboard floor to the door. When John first found this cottage, he'd discovered the Martian's body, dry skin stretched across the globe of its ribs. It had left the heater on and door open when it perished, dumping warmth into the icy fall air. John had buried it at the base of the mesa. A framed photographic print on the front wall portrayed the creature standing upright with its cluster of tentacles supporting it, and beside the thing stood another Martian, half-turned toward the first who looked out at the viewer. It was taken outdoors on the plains. In the distance, a third Martian squatted among blocks in the sand, looking like a fat octopus rather than jellyfish balanced on spidery limbs. The Martian ghost never spoke, but neither did it seem to disapprove of John sharing its cottage. John had left the photograph where he found it out of respect for the dead.

He swung the door open on creaky hinges. He stood on the stoop and evaluated the three men standing in the pale sunshine. Company enforcers, two newly arrived a week ago that he recognized, and the gunfighter Gerry Ake, former bounty hunter out of Oklahoma.

The bastard who shot me dead, said Billy. John's heart raced.

Their mounts chewed dry creeper leaves down near the Martian's grave; these long-legged variants of Martian cattle refused to climb slopes such as the staircase carved into the stone of Jacob's Mesa, though they seemed not averse to bearing men upon their long, narrow backs. John noticed that there were four mounts, though only three men stood before him. John felt a relief, for if they intended to kill him here, they would not have brought him a mount. He reached for the dial beside the door frame, the one that controlled the Martian heaters that kept the place comfortable through the bitter winters. He turned off the heaters.

"John Mulberry, Martian Public Land Surveyor?" said the young blue-eyed enforcer.

"I'm he."

"You're a known associate of one Lucius McCrady, settler four miles east of town, and his wife Martina McCrady, former sporting woman from the saloon. They are fugitives from justice, having led a gang what murdered four employees of the Cydonia Company and injured six others."

"He's not here, nor is Martina. You're welcome to look around inside."

"We ain't here for them," said Gerry Ake, stepping forward a bit between the two younger men.

At Ake's instigation, the blue-eyed enforcer fumblingly drew a battered .44-40 Winchester pistol from its dry leather holster and pointed it at John.

"Put your hands up and get out here!" the boy shouted.

"You aim to shoot me?" The barrel wobbled just a foot from John's face. "Because it's a hell of a thing to kill a man and have to live for the rest of your life with the emptiness you manufactured in that act."

John, look at his hands shake! said John's brother. *You can take him. He ain't never killed a man.*

That's just it, Billy, John replied. *He ain't never killed a man.*

The enforcer boy glanced down at John's guns, then back into John's eyes. His rapid breathing made clouds of steam that whipped away in the morning breeze. The cold, dry air of Mars was greedy for the moisture harbored in a man's lungs.

"You prepared for that?" John asked.

The boy blinked, his Winchester lowering a bit.

"*I* got no problem killin' outlaws," said Gerry Ake. He smiled, baring tobacco-stained teeth, and rested his gloved left hand on the hilt of his Colt .44-40 Bisley target revolver, pristine with mother-of-pearl grips.

"I know you don't," said John, raising his hands to chest-level. He didn't look at the gunfighter. "I wasn't involved in the shootout you mention."

"Don't care," said Gerry Ake. "Boss wants to talk to you. Now keep your hands away from those Army cannons you like to wear."

The quiet third enforcer unbuckled John's gun belt and slung it over a shoulder. John pulled the door to his cottage closed and led the way down his gritty stone steps to the Martian mounts waiting in the gulley below.

When the blue-eyed enforcer beside him stumbled, John said, "You're new to Mars. It's best to move deliberately until you find your Mars-feet, else you'll spend a lot of time brushing dust from your knees."

They took the long way back to town, riding along the dry gully until it merged with the high country beyond the mesa-land. If a man didn't want to walk, he let his mount pick its own path. They moved more like dogs than horses, round shoulders and hips rising and falling with each loping stride. The early morning's bite faded as the sun rose higher into a turquoise-blue sky.

As they approached the last mesa, they could see the vast hull of a Martian cargo-ship, destroyed in a war that burned out before men arrived. It was split open like a steel watermelon hit by a sledge-hammer, the cables and plating of its innards filling with dust and wind-blown brush. In their exploration of the planet, the Army Cavalry men had discovered that the cargo-ship the people of Mars now used to ferry people and materials back and forth to Earth was the only one of some dozen to have survived the Martian civil war. Three ruined vessels still held ten invasion-cylinders each, like huge rounds in a revolver, ready to fire their War-Tripods at Earth.

As they rounded the mesa, more of John's Town became visible across the plains beyond. Some of the horrible Black Dust that the Martians had used in their invasion of England was still visible in the wind-lee between the buildings, like stubborn shadows. John couldn't shake the memory of the first time he explored the town: desiccated Martians spilled out of buildings, some shuddering in the streets like terrible tumbleweed. He'd found a corral full of heaped bodies of those simple, man-like creatures, surely no smarter than monkeys, that looked to have starved when their masters died. Scientists back home had determined that the Martians kept them for food: They drank their blood—transfused it, actually. John was glad he never met a live Martian.

What the Martians had done to England was nothing compared to what they had done to themselves. The Black Dust had found its way into every crevice all across Mars. They had flooded their world with the stuff. John's Martian room-mate had no answer for why they had done this. John wondered if they'd decided to invade Earth because they'd made Mars uninhabitable to their own people, to escape the war, or out of the same breed of self-hatred that makes men keep killing once they start along that path.

As they drew nearer, John was startled to see activity within John's Town. A dozen or more men were using picks and pry-bars to find their way into the cluster of buildings that weren't smashed like the rest of the town. Four large Martian horseless carriages waited near the edge of town, floating a few feet above the ground with the power of Mars-stone.

Company men, said brother Billy. *Looting your property*.

John watched the men carting off equipment that rightly belonged to him. His cheeks grew hot, even in the icy morning breeze.

"What are Company men doing in my town?" he asked.

"That ain't nobody's town no more," said Gerry Ake, a few steps behind him. "New rule is that all Martian technology belongs to the Company."

"John's Town is on my homestead claim," John said.

"Ha! 'John's Town,' eh? Don't make no difference where it is, that's the new rules. Anyhow, you got no claim while you're in custody of the law."

John felt his heart pound in his throat.

This is what Company men do, said Billy. *They grab until there ain't nothing left, then make new laws so they can grab more. You gonna stand for this, John? Oh, right, you're done with killing.*

How did listening to Lucius and McCrady's ideas work out for you? asked John. *There are other ways to make things right.*

Tell that to Gerry Ake, said Billy. *Tell that to the nine men and three women he murdered in Oklahoma and Kansas. Tell that to the men he murdered here.*

They rode on in silence. A horseless carriage—a big platform with a propeller mounted on the rear—whooshed past them, loaded down with all manner of Martian apparatus looted from his town.

John stared straight ahead for the rest of their journey to Acidalium Town.

"Talk to me about your friends and associates," said Monty Cooper, Company Boss on Mars. He indicated a swivel chair situated in front of the wide oak desk. "And how you're not part of their murderous gang."

John didn't want to sit. He wanted to face his ruin with as much dignity as he could manage. Gerry Ake and the two young enforcers leaned against the

office paneling on the far side of the room, behind
John, near the door to Main Street. All this wood—
everything in the room, desk, chairs, lithographs on
the walls—had been ferried to Mars.

John said nothing. Cooper waited a bit, eyes peering out from his soft face. A breeze rattled the single
window-pane that provided a view across the Chinese and Irish laborer shacks surrounding Lowell
Space-Port. A storm was brewing from the north,
whipping up dust. The laborers pulled their wide-
brimmed hats low over faces obscured with masks
and bandanas against the weather. Finally Cooper
sighed and looked outside.

"Make it easy on yourself, Surveyor," Cooper
said. "We're planning a hanging tomorrow, and it
might as well be McCrady or his whore wife than
you. My boys took care of most of their gang, and
several of my men were killed or wounded. I notice
you bear no injuries. Fancy that."

"I wasn't involved in the gunfight," John said.

"So you say," said Cooper, nodding. He held John
with a piercing stare, then leaned back in an over-
stuffed green leather chair that creaked beneath his
mass. "Can you corroborate that claim?"

Again, John had no answer. He lived alone, as had
always been his wont.

Cooper sighed. "Put him in the cell," he said to
Gerry Ake. "John Mulberry, you had better hope that
Mr. Ake finds that damned Irishman and his murderous Mexican whore before tomorrow noon, else
you'll be dancing above Main Street."

*   *   *

John sat on a cold stone slab in the town's only jail
cell. Steel bars separated the tiny space from a door
that led to Cooper's office. The cell smelled of mold
and piss. Someone had scratched into the stone the
image of a naked lady.

How's pacifism working for you, brother? asked Billy.

Outside, the storm seemed to be growing fierce
until John recognized the sound, not as blowing de-
bris but the steady thumping of a Martian Tripod's
legs against the cobbled street. It grew louder and
then stopped outside the building. Soon after, John
heard the front door open and close, then voices. The
voices grew loud enough for him to hear:

"This ain't none of your business, nigger!" Gerry
Ake's voice.

John could hear Cooper's low rumble, then another man's booming voice: "Yes, it is my business.
The U.S. Army is the law here, and that boy you arrested was not in town last night. I saw who was involved in the shootout, and John Mulberry was not."

Footsteps, followed by the door to the cell opening. Captain George Hughes of the Army company
stationed on Mars stood framed by the doorway, his
dark blue uniform coat trimmed in gold. Slung over
one shoulder was John's gun-belt. The 10th Cavalry
were the first men to Mars, sent back in the giant
Martian ship that had landed near Wolf Point. The
ship had been filled with dead Martians, dead Martian cattle, dead Martian man-like things, dead red
creeper . . . everything homesteaders might need.

Scientists determined that Earthly disease bacteria had destroyed what was meant to be a colonization crew before they had fully disembarked. After engineers deduced how to operate the vessel, the U.S. government shipped the 10th Cavalry back to scout the Martian homeworld, destroy any resistance, and report back on their adventures. Everyone was stunned to learn that all of the tentacled beasts had destroyed one another during their internal war.

In the two Mars years since—four Earth-years— the 10th had explored half of Mars. The Martians had gone extinct without humans needing to fire a single shot.

Captain Hughes stepped into the alcove on the other side of the bars. The young enforcer who had arrested John earlier in the morning followed him in, pulled out a set of keys, and unlocked the cage. John stood.

"Much obliged," John said.

"Don't thank me, Surveyor," said Hughes. "You're in my custody now."

As they walked out through Cooper's office, the Boss worked hard to look busy with papers on his desk. Gerry Ake still leaned against the wood paneling by the open front door and made his left hand look like a pistol, pointing it at John first and then Captain Hughes. He laughed and sauntered outside before them.

Hughes led John across the paved Martian sidewalk onto the cobblestone street where the huge Tripod stood. Articulated steel tentacles swayed around its disc-shaped body. Huge blue lettering on the underside proclaimed, "ARMY 1." A crossed pair of swords in gold scabbards supporting a huge "10" also adorned the machine, as did a pair of bison, which framed the other markings. High above, the Tripod's top lid was hinged open, the leather-capped head of the driver just visible from within.

The driver lowered a rope-ladder, which, upon Hughes's urging, John proceeded to climb. When he and Captain Hughes stood inside the narrow confines of the Tripod, the driver rolled up the ladder and stowed it beneath the steel control console that ringed the compartment. Dials bore alien markings and boxes displayed moving-pictures of squiggly lines; people had affixed paper notes indicating what each device monitored: POWER, PRESSURE, HEAT-RAY, and dozens more. The driver sat upon a wide, flat stool and began manipulating the many levers that surrounded him, clearly designed for the multitudinous limbs of the Martians rather than two human hands.

The machine lurched off, and they proceeded across town in silence except for the clanging of metal feet against stone and the whirr and creak of machinery. They left the lid open, probably because the Tripod's interior stank of hot metal and rot. A little round glass in the front served as the driver's portal to the world, though John could see outside just fine while standing and clinging to hand-holds. This was his first ride in a Martian war-machine, and it made him feel simultaneously giddy and sick to his stomach.

They passed the long row of Martian buildings that comprised the town, ornate stone spaces that had been converted from mysterious purposes into a general store, a trading-post, a combination post office and barber shop, a schoolhouse, both Episcopal and Catholic churches, a bank, Nolan Hersh's mechanic shop where he purported to fix Martian machines, the Dakota Sioux gathering hall, all manner of other little shops run mostly by settlers deterred by the unforgiving nature of trying to homestead on Mars, and of course a saloon. Many of the town's buildings had been converted into homes, but most of the teapot-shaped structures sat empty. Their deceased original inhabitants had been removed nearly two Martian years ago when the first wave of immigrants, the Chinese and Irish laborers and Company looters, arrived, yet explorers still found one of the desiccated bodies every once in a while.

At the edge of town they passed the expanse of Lowell Space-Port, busy with activity and dominated by the massive cargo-ship, their only passage to Earth. A few miles north of Acidalia Town, John could just make out the ruined Martian village that sat on Joe Running Bear's homestead claim, which John had surveyed summer of last year, after the U.S. government had begun shipping the Dakota Sioux to Mars. They seemed polite enough people, kept mostly to themselves—not unlike the other immigrant groups.

At last they passed through the open barbed-wire

gate of the Army camp, situated just on the other side of town from the space-port. The Tripod staggered to a halt outside a long, shabby barracks constructed from sheets of some light, flexible material. Captain Hughes turned to John and handed him his gun belt. John strapped it on.

"Your daddy was a good man. I knew him when I served at Fort Assinniboine out of Havre in Montana, where he was doing surveys for the Land Office in Indian country. I knew Captain Grunwold, too, the son of a bitch what killed him." Hughes turned to face John, his dark features nearly unreadable in the shade of his wide cap. "That one *wasn't* a good man."

John felt his heart race: at last, someone who had witnessed the event. His father had never talked about it before he died of his wound.

"What happened? Why did Grunwold shoot my father?"

"I was a lieutenant then," said Hughes, "and they were both captains. Grunwold, he figured the best way to demoralize the Indians into quitting the war was to just kill everyone, wives and children and braves alike. When your daddy got attached to our unit to survey the lands in Northeast Montana, he got to feeling responsible for how the soldiers behaved, like any good officer should. So when Grunwold sent my platoon to 'pacify' this little Assiniboine village near the Martian cargo-ship, your daddy figured what that meant and joined us.

"Right after sunset we arrived at this little huddle

of tents in the badlands. It was clear there wasn't any Indian braves here, but Grunwold ordered a full assault. Your daddy countermanded the order. The two argued in front of all the men, making Grunwold angrier than I'd ever seen, and he drew his sidearm and shot your daddy in the belly, right there. Army officer shooting Army officer in front of Army soldiers." Hughes whistled.

"The men, they got all heated up—everyone liked your daddy—and it looked like Grunwold was about to face a mutiny. So he ordered the ride back to the Fort. Six of us carried your daddy on account of he couldn't ride with his wound. Interfering with Grunwold's order got him killed. It also stopped a massacre. As I was an officer in charge of one of those platoons, I would have been responsible for what happened. I owe him for that debt."

John felt a rush of mixed pride and anger. Hughes broke his reverie.

"It's not clear in my mind right now what to do about our current troubles. All I know is what I thought was good men and women are shooting each other."

John looked out across the camp with its soldiers formed up in ranks in the dust, twenty-two men drilling before a pair of sergeants. Seeing all those Negro men in uniform didn't feel strange on Mars where everything was different than on Earth. Just past camp rose the steel whale that was the cargoship, swallowing not just piles of Mars-stone dug up by miners working the great Valles Marineris, but irreproducible Martian artifacts that rightly belonged to John's Town and Perry's Town and any number of other towns.

"I didn't ask to be any part of this," John said. He felt as if a cold stone had sunk in his belly.

"Life has a way of throwing things at you that you never asked for," said Hughes. "Sometimes it's good, like when I got promoted to captain so the Army could ship me here to command this little outfit. I bear no illusion that my promotion or these men," he pointed to the soldiers, "getting put in charge of pacifying an entire planet was intended to be an honor." His smile looked more like a grimace. "But once we got here and didn't have to fight, I'd got to thinking that things had worked out for the best . . ." His voice trailed off. He nodded to the driver.

"Follow me, I want you to meet those at the heart of last night's troubles."

The driver unfurled the rope-ladder, and John and Captain Hughes climbed down. Hughes led him to the stone Martian shack that served as Army command headquarters and opened the door. Inside, by the blue light of Martian light-fixtures overhead, John could see two cots along a wall and several busy medical officers attending to their occupants.

"Lucius! Martina!" John said. He felt light-headed when he saw a broad, blood-stained bandage across Lucius's left shoulder, and Martina's black hair half-hidden in white gauze. She was unconscious.

Lucius waved away a medic fiddling with his bandage and sat up on the cot. He regarded John for a moment, then spoke to Captain Hughes. "George, what's this all about? Are we under arrest?"

"Well, you ain't leaving until I decide. You in such a hurry to get shot again?"

"You know what they're doing to us out there, George," said Lucius. "They're taking away everything we own, killing us slowly. Last night they murdered nine good men who wanted nothing more than the freedom to make their own way on this world fair and square! John here might have saved some of them if he'd been with us."

John had to look away. That cold stone was starting to grow hot.

"Seems to me that those 'nine good men' did some killing of their own," said Captain Hughes. "You put me in a tough spot, Lucius. I don't appreciate what the Company's doing any more than you do, breaking U.S. law by claiming what rightly belongs to people. But killing is against the law, too, and if we don't obey law we're no better than them. I won't countenance any massacres, no matter who's behind it."

A commotion outside got everyone's attention. Hughes and John walked to the front door while Lucius swung his feet to the floor and pulled on his boots. Martina began to stir on her cot, her dark eyelids fluttering open. John heard many voices outside, angry shouts.

Hughes opened the door to reveal what appeared

to be all the townspeople of Acidalium plus many of the homesteaders and miners and even a few of the Sioux: dozens of men and women milling about within the wire confines of camp. They carried a variety of guns—mostly stolen, John figured—and many more held dangerous-looking farming or mining tools. The ghosts of those who died last night stood among them. *This would be over if you'd helped us*, one of the dead said to John.

Two squads of soldiers formed a line between the citizens and their captain, holding their rifles and shotguns to make a fence. Hughes strode into the middle of the melee.

"What's the meaning of this?" he demanded. "Y'all're trespassing on Army property. Don't you have anything better to do? I suggest you return to your work, unless you've decided to pursue a life of leisure on this garden planet."

"We hear you're taking the Company's side in what happened last night!" shouted Clinton Perry. "We hear you arrested the McCradys and now John Mulberry, too." The muttering grew louder.

"You heard wrong," said Hughes. "See for yourself." He turned and gestured to John and Lucius, who took the opportunity to step forward and stand beside Hughes.

Just as the mob began to quiet, a large gang of Company men approached the camp's gate, Gerry Ake in the lead. Boss Cooper accompanied them. Seeing this, the citizens grew angrier and louder than when they had first burst into camp.

John heard a noise behind him and turned to see Martina stumble out of the impromptu hospital. She limped as if favoring one leg. A double-barrel, breach-loading Winchester shotgun weighed down her arms.

"Here come the Company's thieves and murderers!" shouted Lucius. "Prepare yourselves!"

Captain Hughes said a few words to his two sergeants, who each led their squads around the mob's flanks toward the gate to bar the way of the approaching enforcers. Across the paved landing-field to the left, the cargo-ship laborers set down their loads and headed toward the camp's fence. Two or three shifted their coats to reveal pistols tucked into their trousers. Out of the corner of his eye, John caught motion—Lucius drawing his old Remington from the pocket of his overalls. Much of the human population on Mars was concentrated into a few hundred square yards, armed to the teeth, and getting themselves riled up to murder one another. No one cast a shadow anywhere on the red soil. The sun shone directly down on them from a dusty turquoise sky but provided no warmth.

Every man's got a time when he's got to decide what's the right thing to do, said John's father, *or events sweep him up regardless of his will. Now's your time.*

John stepped forward through the crowd of citizens until he stood between them and the approaching Company men, directly between the two squads of soldiers. He put up his hands and shouted.

"Stop it, you damn fools!" All eyes turned toward

him. He turned his back to the Company men and faced the pioneers.

"You know what's going to happen if we keep killing each other. The boys working for the Company will kill us for killing them, and then we'll have to kill them for killing more of us, and on and on it'll go, round and round like a revolver barrel, blasting every one of us into oblivion the way the Martians did themselves in.

"Why wasn't a whole civilization of Martians waiting here to pounce on us with their War-Tripods and Heat-Ray guns? You've explored their ruins, full of skeletons. You've had to sweep their once-poisonous Black Dust out of your homes. You've seen those huge unexploded shells buried beside buildings where they once lived and worked and maybe even played. You've seen their big ships, shattered. That's the only one left," he pointed to the cargo-ship sitting across the field, "and we're this close to destroying it, too.

"The Martians didn't put up a fight because there weren't any of them left to fight. It wasn't Earthly disease bacteria that did them in here, it was each other." The people were listening, quiet now.

"Mars is a hard place to stake a life. It's about all we can do just to survive. The soil here won't grow our crops, and the local plants taste like dirt. The only way we survived two Mars winters was together."

John pointed at a few weapons, including Lucius's pistol. "You fire a gun today at another man and you're making yourself like those fool Martians. The only way we win this battle is *not to fight!*"

Lucius stepped forward, hatless, and faced the citizens. "What John says is fine, but consider this: y'all know that the Martians drank the blood of those man-things they kept corralled near their cities. That's what the Company wants of *us*, and they won't stop until they suck us dry!"

Now he faced the Company men, particularly Boss Cooper.

"You don't care what's our property; you keep us corralled here to feed fat shareholders back on Earth. We can't survive if we keep shipping all the working Martian equipment back to Earth without getting fair trade. Hell, we need to keep it for *ourselves*, right here, for the people!"

The citizens were nodding and muttering, even the port-workers and some of the soldiers. John could see Lucius growing brave, working himself up to incite another shootout; he quickly spoke.

"That's right," said John. "We need to get smart. We need to keep our bounty. We need to figure out ways to grow vegetables indoors where they won't freeze. Anything we need, we can trade Mars-stone for it. But none of that will matter if *we keep killing each other.*"

He faced Boss Cooper.

"Here's how it's going to be. We don't need the Company anymore. We're firing you, sir. Homesteading on Mars ain't easy, but we don't need you to survive." A few shouts of approval. Out of the corner of his eye, John caught an odd expression on Lucius's face, almost a smile.

"We're a family here. We leave each to each's business and help each other in need. We won't stand for being taken advantage of anymore. We are our *own* company; we're all shareholders of Mars with our stakes and claims and labor, and we will no longer abide outside forces interfering in our affairs." Men and women began to cheer.

John noticed Gerry Ake tensing, left hand fidgeting.

He's going to draw, said Billy.

John shook his head slowly at the gunfighter. *Don't*. No one among the giddy crowd seemed to notice what was happening except for Captain Hughes off to the right, who watched the Company man and whispered to a sergeant.

Gerry Ake's lips peeled back in an ugly smile. His hand lurched. John drew both his guns as the gunfighter drew. The three pistols thundered together. John felt a blow to his ribs like being kicked by a horse, hot and numb. Gerry Ake tumbled backward, dark holes in his abdomen and the middle of his chest, and fell to the dusty ground.

Not again, his father said. *Son, there should have been another way.*

Sometimes there's not, Billy said.

Another of the Company enforcers drew his pistol. John struggled to respond. The Colt in his left hand felt too heavy to move, and he had trouble aiming the one in his right.

Shots boomed from both Cavalry squads, striking the enforcer from thigh to head. He crumpled like a wet sack. Guns were raised from all quarters.

"Stop, everyone!" shouted Captain Hughes. He stepped forward into the empty space between the two mobs, glancing briefly at John's wound. "Did you hear what this man just said? We need to be done with killing!"

Boss Cooper stepped forward and glanced down at his two dead enforcers before fixing John with furious eyes. "In the next shipment I'll have the Company send an army of peacekeepers to bring law and order to this place. We'll—"

"No," John said. He tossed both of his father's pistols into the dust. He pointed at Captain Hughes. "This man's the law here, and no one rides our cargo-ship unless we invite them."

Lucius stepped forward, putting a hand on John's shoulder, then looked fiercely at Cooper. "We don't need you or the Cydonia Company. Everything on Mars belongs to the people you see around you, not the Company. From now on, *we* determine what we carry to Earth, what we trade for, and what or who we bring to Mars. Every man on this world is a free and equal member of Mars Company."

"And women!" called Martina. She limped forward, her face set. "It's a hard life, but more women will come if they know we'll be free and equal with men."

Lucius nodded. "All men *and women* of Mars will be free and equal," he said.

Martina handed a man her shotgun. She gestured toward the fence where the port-workers stood, then across to the Cavalry. "We'll all be free, Negroes and Sioux and Chinese and Irish—everyone who contributes to the betterment of Mars."

The gathered citizens cheered. John's chest was on fire and his head swirled. The scared and confused faces of the Company men told him that despite the mood of the citizens, they stood at a precipice. He spoke as loud as he could manage:

"Even you Company men who don't have blood on your hands," he said. "If you renounce the Company and stake an honest claim or homestead and put in honest work, you may join our family."

The blue-eyed man who had arrested John that morning dropped his gun and stepped over Gerry Ake's body to the side of the citizens. A few others followed suit, then more, until only a handful stood near Cooper. John nodded to the defectors, then pointed at the Company loyalists.

"The rest of you will go back to Earth where you can't cause us any more suffering." The world began to spin before his eyes. "We hereby declare ourselves independent. Free not only from the Company, but from Earth itself! It's nations that cause war, companies that cause greed, and lack of mutual understanding and respect that causes killing. We hereby declare ourselves free of Earthly ways and name ourselves the Family of Mars!"

John lost consciousness to the sound of cheers. The ghosts of last night's dead began to dissipate.

The last thing John saw before the world went dark was the dead eyes of Gerry Ake.

Ten days later, after unloading most of the Martian artifacts that had been destined for Earth, Montgomery Cooper was escorted back to Earth along with sixteen other Company men, enforcers and looters all. Nine citizens returned with him, disheartened after trying to scratch a living from the hard Mars soil or uneasy with their new freedoms.

Upon hearing the news of the Mars Uprising, the United States declared war on the separatists. As no Earthly military could stand against the might of the Martian war-machines—nor did they possess ships capable of crossing the ocean of space—the Family of Mars politely ignored this declaration and continued trade with Earth as usual.

The engineer who steered the cargo-ship from Mars to Earth and back joined the "Family of Mars." To avoid attack or piracy, he landed the ship only in remote regions of Earth, where the crew traded Mars-stone for needed supplies. He selected a different port of entry each visit.

The U.S. Army discharged Captain George Hughes and revoked his commission. Hughes went on to establish the Mars Defense Corps, eventually comprising infantry, cavalry, and—after Mars scientists deduced the methods of controlling Martian flying craft—air troops. Most served as reservists, working their mines and homesteads for all but twelve days per year, when they trained for emergency.

Over the next few decades, thousands of people emi-

grated from Earth to Mars, at which time it became clear that the planet could not sustain many more immigrants.

John Mulberry served one term as the first President of Mars but refused to accept a second nomination. As this was a part-time job, he continued surveying homesteads until failing health encouraged him to teach others how to survey their own land.

Martina McCrady, who had initiated the Mars Independence movement, served two terms as President after him. Many women did, indeed, emigrate to Mars.

John Mulberry died unmarried and without children at age twenty-seven in Mars-years, long enough to see the Family of Mars become self-sufficient and blossom into a nation rivaling any American state. By all accounts, he lived a contented life. His wound never fully healed.

COYOTE, SPIDER, BAT

Steven Saus

This happened a very long time ago, but not so long as it seems. This country stretches time in strange ways for all people, especially my kind. Europeans scoff at Americans for this. They laugh at my country's history, thinking it only a blip and piddle in the bucket of history. They are often right. But some places, some times persist. They last far longer than they should, ignoring the dictates of the counting of men. Far more people say they were at a place than possible—but they all tell the truth.

And sometimes that stretched-out time echoes back into the measured tread of days and weeks. The relentless passing of seconds and days chops off parts that don't fit, and details are lost. But still they echo outside of themselves, real people becoming myths and myths becoming flesh and blood.

This was one such time.

*   *   *

On this first day—not the first day, though maybe she was there, too—the woman rode across frozen Montana earth toward her home. She rode a nondescript brown horse, but it was a fine animal and well bred for long days on the trail. Her black hair was cut to her shoulders, the fringe not quite touching the white fur lining of her coat. She sat back in the saddle, listening to the crunch of horse hooves on frost-covered grass. A slight smile flickered across her thin face as she thought of home. The early morning light slid across the land, and she knew Robert would be waiting with breakfast.

She came from the hunt, the carcass of an antelope strapped across the back of her horse. Perhaps the metal tang of blood-scent masked the smells of the high cold prairie. The extra weight of the meat, along with thanking the antelope for its sacrifice for her family, must have made riding more difficult. It must have distracted her attention, explains why she did not notice sooner.

When she did notice—when the burning smell reached her sensitive nose, when the crackling sound reached her tuned ears—she did not believe.

And when her cabin came into sight, thought fled.

She leaned forward, the horse already responding. The cold wind bit at her ruddy face, streamed her black hair back from the yellow and grey of her narrowed eyes. She pulled the horse to a stop, sliding from the saddle. She padded the short distance to the body lying in front of the still smoldering ruin of their life together.

His face was untouched, but only his face. The rest of his body was shredded, dressed, cut like she'd planned to do to the antelope that afternoon. Her hands ran across the bloodless cuts and tears in his flesh. Her mouth moved in soft words. Perhaps she spoke to the Great Spirit, though she had yet to meet such a thing. Perhaps she spoke to her dead husband, traveling to the Heaven she'd believed in. We have no way of knowing, and she never said.

We know only this: for the rest of that day, and into the night, Coyote howled in pain, and across the prairie her little brothers howled with her.

That was the end of that first day.

On the afternoon of that second day, as the sun dipped down to kiss the horizon, Lao-shu sat in the back of the saloon. She sat with the black man, the gaze of her dark eyes dancing across the faces of the men. She dealt the man five cards, her caramel voice sliding under the noise of the room. "The girls will be busy tonight, Anthony."

He picked up the cards with delicate fingers and raised an eyebrow. She laughed, matching his eyebrow with her own. "Is that for the cards or the prediction? If you want someone to cheat you at cards, I hear that—"

Anthony shook his thin head, light glistening off his shaved scalp. "No, that's not it, girl." She snorted as he continued. "I'm just waiting for the next thing to happen. Damn near got eyes in the back of my head, and I still don't know what got Coyote riled."

She narrowed her eyes and leaned her head forward so it swept her hair into a tunnel framing her face. "You just stop right there with the naming. It's not—"

"Everyone west of the Mississip knows something happened. That's what got these men all ready to jump into the arms of your girls. They know something—something bad—happened, but don't know what. Just natural for a man to find comfort in something warm, familiar, and female."

He smiled, and after a second, Lao-shu did as well. "Next you'll say it's in their nature, won't you?"

He nodded, and looked at the cards again. "Things act in their nature, but that don't mean they ain't got a choice." He spread the cards in the eight fingers of his hand. "Besides, I know you're cheating."

She laid her cards down, face up. "Four kings, ace high. Why would you say I cheat?"

Anthony put his cards down on hers. Four more kings and an ace looked at them. "'Cause I am, too."

The door to the saloon opened. Coyote stood there, and the humans in the room grew quiet. The humans knew Coyote—though not by that name. They had drank with her, been with her as she married Robert. They'd delivered the letters from his parents in Boston, made peace with the Indians at her urging. They'd laughed as she made a buffoon of the traveling preacher, and hunted buffalo with her. They knew that easy-going person with the coat lined in white fur.

Now something in the back of their minds reminded the humans in the room of another plain, of another time when wild dogs herded—or hunted—humans instead of sheep, and they grew silent.

Anthony waved to Coyote. "Come over. Have a drink."

Coyote's yellow and grey eyes looked at the black man. She slowly walked to the table as Anthony called for beer. Coyote pulled a chair through the sawdust, sat, and began to drink the beer placed before her. Lao-shu looked at Coyote, then to Anthony. Anthony shook his head slightly, and Lao-shu pushed her chair back.

"I go to check on my women," she said. "Sometimes men seek power instead of comfort." Lao-shu kissed Anthony on the cheek before she headed upstairs. Coyote's eyes focused on the kiss, then on Anthony's face. They waited a long while, until Coyote finally spoke.

"Leave her."

Anthony's brow furrowed. "Ain't neither of us offended you, seeing as we're both guests in your land, and—"

Coyote shook her head. "To keep her safe. To keep her from being a target." She took another drink. "Spider, she's not like us."

"Close enough. She ain't human like—"

"She can die."

Anthony shrugged. "It'd only be a dozen years."

"She. Can. Die." The left side of Coyote's mouth

twitched, whites of teeth glinting through thin lips. "Just like Robert."

Anthony felt the goosebumps travel up his back. "Robert?"

Coyote nodded, drained the rest of the beer. A bit of foam rested on her lips. It reminded Anthony of the mouth of a frothing dog. "I'm sorry," Anthony said.

The yellow and grey of Coyote's eyes shimmered in the light from the gas lamp. Coyote's voice came out in a low rumbling growl. "Murdered. By something old. Something that smells dead."

Anthony drained his glass. "No stranger than anything else. So what are we waiting for? Huntin' with the First Anger can't be any worse than riding on a crocodile's snout, right?" He looked to the bartender. "Tell my mouse I'll be back soon 'nuff."

They stepped out of the saloon, mounted their horses, and rode toward the ruins of Coyote's home.

That was not the end of that second day.

It slid from building to building in the darkness. It was of the darkness, yet pale as the sliver of moon high in the clear winter sky. With a soft clattering of fingernails against wood it scaled the general store, then collapsed upon the roof. Its emaciated limbs lay naked against the freezing air, but no involuntary shiver shook its frame.

It stretched under the sky, joints still creaking from the months in the ship's hold. It stretched muscles still weak from the long fast of the ocean voyage, and then the paltry food of bilge rat blood afterward. It had expected to hunt, to feed after the ocean, but had miscalculated.

When it had woken after the weeks at sea, it heard voices from its homeland. Not the smooth voices of the hereditary idiots too smart to listen to the tales of old women, but the coarse peasant voices. The voices of prey that had learned to fight back. It had panicked, not expecting to find the same thing that drove it from Europe in this new land. It had fled, leaving injured dockworkers with a story no educated American would yet believe. And like so many of the prey in this land, it continued traveling west.

The man had been a good start. He had lain with a Name. A Name that had been gone. A Name that was not there with its mate. Even in its weakened state, the man had filled its belly and given it more strength than a thousand prairie dogs, a hundred cattle, or a dozen of the normal prey.

Its nostrils flared. One building still had lamps burning, and the scent came from there. One—no, two Names had been there. Another remained—not a Name, but more than any of the normal prey. And this prey did not know the power of the cross, of garlic, of a Eucharist. Sharp fangs stretched from its mouth in anticipation of warm blood.

It leapt from one roof to the next, an ungainly tangle of pale limbs, leaping toward the saloon.

Lao-shu dipped her brush in the inkwell, then wrote the day's totals on the scroll. The pictograms flowed, a functional form of art. Perhaps Confucius would have approved of that aspect of her work, if not the work itself.

She turned at the knock on her door. "Yes?"

The door creaked open and Sally poked her head in. "Do you have a minute, Miss Mouse?"

Lao-shu smiled at her name, and Sally glowed a little more beautiful under her influence. This was her year; she delighted in giving what favors were hers to grant. "Yes, Sally?"

Sally continued in her Texas drawl. "I was just checking that you got the message about Mister Anthony." The girl wrapped her arms around herself and shivered slightly. "We ain't seen you downstairs since."

Lao-shu nodded and set down her brush. "I did, dear. Would you like an extra blanket?"

"Yes'm. It's a sight colder here than—did you see that?" The girl pointed at Lao-shu's window.

Lao-shu looked. "No, I don't see anything." She handed a blanket to Sally. "Everyone treat you well?"

"Yes'm." A blush colored Sally's cheeks. "Thank you for asking. I ain't never worked for someone who asked before, just so long as they didn't mark . . ." Her lip quivered as she fell silent.

Lao-shu drew the girl into a hug. "Shush. You work for me now. I keep telling you girls that I won't let anything happen to you all."

A gunshot sounded from below, then two more with a chorus of screams, and a final echo of a short, choked shout. Silence settled over the saloon for just a moment before the women upstairs began to scream. Lao-shu pushed Sally down onto the bed, then pulled the cord-wrapped hilt of her dao from underneath. Sally's eyes widened as Lao-shu drew the sword, its curved blade reflecting the firelight.

"Stay here," Lao-shu said, barely able to hear herself over the rapid pounding of her heart. She opened the door, then heard the creak of the mattress ropes. She turned back to Sally. "Stay."

A white hand, streaked with blood, slid around her left shoulder and neck, pulling her off-balance. The other hand—she could see its fingernails, curved and sharper than even her dao—slice across the tendons of her wrist. Hot fetid breath blew across her cheek as Sally started to scream and scream.

As the fangs pierced her neck, her blood spurting into the thing's mouth, Lao-shu remembered that even in its year, a mouse was still a prey animal.

And so ended that second day.

In the first moments of that third day, Anthony noticed the fire before Coyote. Coyote smelt the change in Anthony's scent and looked to his friend. His skin had gone ashen gray, and he did not move in the saddle.

"Town's burning," Anthony said. "Eyes in the back of my head."

Coyote sniffed, then nodded. After a moment, her features softened. "Mouse."

"Yeah, well. Sometimes rat, depends on how you say it. Crazy language."

Coyote guided her horse next to Anthony's. "Will Mouse—"

Anthony shook his head. "No. I can already feel the year going to hell for her people. Probably the whole damn decade at this point. Figure the rest of 'em will probably stay clear for a while, too. Screw all their luck something fierce."

The tear tracks shone in the silver light of the moon. "Anthony . . . I'm . . ."

The black man shook his head. "S'okay. I was thinking 'bout heading back to the ocean myself, being Spider again instead of Anthony. Those folks pay good heed, unlike them that get out here." He wiped the salt water from his cheek, then licked it from his hand. "Good salt water. Tastes like off the coast of Grenada."

Coyote bit her lip, trying to still the roiling in her stomach. "Good speed, then—"

Spider looked at Coyote again with a small smile. "Damn, you stupid or something? I ain't leaving until after we kill that sonofabitch."

The left side of Coyote's mouth curled in a half grin, Spider smiled wide showing all his teeth, and soon their laughter echoed across the prairie.

And all the animals who heard that laughter in the deep dark of the early morning curled in their holes and nests, hoping that mad laughter would pass them by.

It ate flesh and power and blood, changing the townsfolk from people into meat with brutal efficiency. The blood was first, and with blood came power. With power came thought, with thought came planning.

As the sun rose over the bloody charred wreck of the town on that third day, it walked—not scampered, but walked—back to its sheltering hole.

The sun lifted itself into the sky that third day. Antelope and buffalo did not move, grazing nervously in place. Prairie dogs huddled silent in their dens. No hawks screeched across the sky, not a single buzzard drew a lazy circle in the sky.

High noon came and went; there were no men who fought at that bright time.

Different predators would fight on the plains this day.

The sun set on that third day.

Coyote sharpened her long knife while Spider looked out from the cave mouth. "Don't like this place," she said, sliding the blade into its sheath.

Spider did not turn to look at her. "Hush. You wait for it to come to you. Time and place of your choosing."

"That spider nature talking?"

Spider turned that time. "Sun-Tzu. Mouse gave me a copy to read while we were still in San Francisco."

Coyote huffed. "Fair."

Spider turned back to the opening in the rock. "It's coming." When Coyote cocked her head to the side,

Spider opened his side eyes, just above the human ears. "You ain't the only one with little brothers and sisters."

The thing scrambled up the rocky slope toward the two figures hunched around a campfire, pale skin glowing in the nighttime dark. It closed to within fifty feet, then bared its fangs. Both held their breath as its muscles coiled and it leapt—only to twist in midair, landing between the two figures. Each toppled onto its side, stiff and lifeless. The thing turned to face the cave.

"Dammit, that trick fooled me back when," said Spider. "Coyote, why don't you . . ." but Coyote was nowhere to be seen. "Dammit," said Spider. He ran into the cave as the thing loped toward him. He leaned forward, arms and legs splitting to give him sure footing across the pitch-black interior of the cave. He ran on all eight legs, rock sliding under his feet with the sound of the creature gaining on him. A hundred feet to the trap, fifty, twenty-five, then Spider was on the far side of the hole, turning to face the thing that pursued him.

The thing had once been a man, or able to pass as one, staring at him across the pit. Slowly cooling blood circulated through its veins, its eyes glowing like a cat's. It hissed at him.

Spider's webs covered the opening, but the creature did not fall into either his webs or the hole. It bared its fangs, and the part of Spider that thought like a man shook with a deep instinctual fear. Spider showed his own fangs, but it did not comfort him.

The creature's voice rasped, sandpaper across chafed skin. "We are many, old Name."

Spider managed a laugh at that. "An' I have many a name, though there's but the one of me. So that makes us a right fair match, don't it?" Even his sensitive eyes strained to see in the darkness, the hairs on his legs signaling the thing's every small motion. And it wasn't taking the bait.

"This land will be my land," it rasped, a European accent to its words as it shifted forward, inching around the pit. "I can create an army from those I feed from. This will not be your land, it will not be your stories they tell, but mine."

"I like Spider's stories," Coyote said, rushing from the shadows. The creature swung its arm toward Coyote, sharp claw aimed at her heart, but the fur-lined coat turned the blow. Coyote's knife slid through the dark air, a hard chunk as its sharpness slid through the thing's spine. Its head and body fell backward, thrashing the webs into a straitjacket as it fell to the cavern floor far below.

Spider walked around the pit. "Waited long 'nuff, didn'tcha?"

That third day ended quietly, as Coyote and Spider sat at the mouth of the cave under the moonlight, passing a hand-rolled cigarette between them.

Spider looked at Coyote, not commenting on the new silver streaks in Coyote's hair. "Think it was telling the truth?"

Coyote nodded. "There will be more. Just like the white man. It was one of them once, after all."

Spider choked on the cigarette. "S'all we need, innit?"

Coyote looked out into the sky for a long moment. Spider broke the silence. "I'm still headin' back to the islands. You're welcome to travel with."

Coyote shook her head. "There is a river that flows near here. I will flood these caverns, seal them off from humans."

The two did not speak after that, though they held each other's hands warmly before they parted ways under the moon.

All this happened in that three days, that decade, that hundred years. Eventually, the tales of the blood-draining monsters came to be told again and again, but they will not last forever. And in such a wild place, where time flows and ebbs, who can determine the lifespan of a spider or a coyote?

MAYBE ANOTHER TIME

Dean Wesley Smith

The day we dug out the coffins, the miners were fighting again.

The battle had finally stopped outside the two gold mines on the hill above Silver City, Idaho, but underground the sounds of an occasional shot could be heard echoing out of the mines themselves. I couldn't imagine firing a gun inside a shaft of a gold mine, but the men who built the mines didn't seem to have any trouble doing just that.

A dozen men stood guard on the tailings of both mines not more than a hundred paces apart, barricades of upturned wagons and spare mine timbers their only protection.

From across the valley, the heat waves rippling off the sagebrush-covered hills made the crouched men look like they were dancing on very short legs.

Only a couple hundred steps below the mines

was the main downtown area of Silver City. At this moment in time, 1870, the town was one of the great mining towns in the western United States. By the year 2016, the year we left to come back to 1870, Silver City was mostly forgotten even by history because of its remoteness.

I would have never known about the ghost town if my family didn't own an old mine here that hadn't produced anything in almost one-hundred-and-fifty years.

I stood just inside the Last Time Mine, leaning against a rough timber, drinking from a bottle of water I had brought with me from the future, watching the gunfight play out. The Last Time was a thousand feet up the side of Florida Mountain, directly across the valley from War Eagle Mountain and the two warring mines.

The sunny, warm afternoon in September hadn't started out to be a gunfight afternoon, but something inside one of the mines on War Eagle had triggered the battle. Some of those shafts over there crossed from one mine to another and there were always fights over who owned what underground.

And from the historical records, the two mine owners hated each other and eventually, in one fight, one of them got killed. I could never remember which one and actually didn't much care.

The town below showed no movement at all, closer to what I was used to back in 2016, when there were no year-round residents here and only a few buildings left standing.

The 1870 eight-plus-thousand residents of Silver City, Idaho, were more than likely going to stay in their shacks and mines and saloons until it was clear the fighting was finished. When you get the two biggest mining crews in the valley going at each other right up the hill from the town, even though not a miner in the bunch could shoot straight, it got dangerous.

In fact, because they couldn't shoot straight made it even more dangerous for the locals. The bars were going to do a good business today.

I had read in history books about the area, the old ghost town, and how the mining and union battles had happened. I just hadn't expected to be back in time and watching when a fight actually broke out.

The fight wasn't like what you would see in a movie. Mostly just men shooting over protection without standing or even looking where they were shooting.

At this point in history, my family's mine, the Last Time Mine, was played out and abandoned. My great-great-grandfather Clarence Benson had left before last winter and boarded the place up when he left. It had taken me some work from the inside to knock out the boards.

Great-great-grandfather wouldn't be back for at least two more years, if his diary was correct and we hadn't done anything to change this timeline, so we had more than enough time to do the research we were here to do.

Of course, that was before we found the coffins.

Only a few of the locals from the time had noticed me and had come up to ask what I was doing. I had just said I was my great-great-grandfather's son coming to work the mine some more, hoping to find a new vein. That had only gotten laughs and we had been left alone so far by the residents of the valley. They all knew this mine was long past bringing out any ore.

In the next month or so most of the locals would be leaving, heading away from this high mountain valley and the brutal Idaho winters. But we were here until the research was done. We didn't have to try to make it over those rough roads and trails in deep snow. We had a much easier way out. We just stepped back into the future.

"Donnie?"

The voice echoed down the shaft behind me and I turned and shouted back, "At the mouth."

"They still fighting?" Brenda asked a moment later as she came up from behind me and put her arm around my waist, staring down toward the town below.

"I think it's over for now," I said, laughing. "Glad we don't need to go down for supplies."

I was teasing her. We had brought along everything we would ever need and could go back to 2016 and get more supplies much easier than even walking down the hill to town.

I could feel her shudder. "Going into that ghost town with all those ghosts is the last thing I ever want to do."

"They are not ghosts," I said, shaking my head. Since we had gotten here, she had insisted everyone in the town below were ghosts because they were dead in 2016. It was her way of trying to understand and grasp time travel. She could understand the theoretical math of it just fine, but would rather think of the people as just ghosts than think of them as actually being alive and able to hurt us.

I didn't blame her. Being able to travel in time was a very strange thing. And so far, only the two of us had done it to my knowledge.

I turned and gave her a hug. Brenda stood not much over five-foot high and since I was only five-seven, we fit together perfectly. We both had dark brown hair, brown eyes, and the same skin tone. We were often asked if we were brother and sister. I thought that funny, Brenda thought it creepy.

Brenda wore jeans and a thick plaid shirt with the sleeves rolled up. She had on tennis shoes that we had painted an off-gray to hide their modern look in case a local did come by. She always wore a small, black jogging pack around her waist. She called it her purse for the past.

I also wore jeans and a plaid shirt and cowboy boots that were scuffed and in the style of this time period. My hair was cut short and I had a beat-up old hat I wore when outside in the heat for any time at all. Luckily, the mine kept the air inside at a nice comfortable temperature even when it was a hundred outside.

Brenda and I had met at CalTech in graduate

school. She had one of the most brilliant minds in theoretical mathematics the school had ever seen and it fit well with my understanding of theoretical physics. Combining our two areas of focus, both in marriage and in study, had led us to this time in the past.

That and the old family gold mine, of course.

Together, leaving the heat of the afternoon, we walked back down the mine tunnel, hand-in-hand. It was wide enough for both of us to walk side-by-side and tall enough that we didn't have to duck at all. It had been built that way to give enough room for a horse to pull a heavy oar cart.

My distant grandfather had done a good job shoring up the rock walls with thick timbers every four feet, leaving very little rock showing between the huge uprights. Most of these timbers were still strong in 2016, although we had gone in and fixed a few of them before starting too much work.

A narrow gauge railway track ran down the middle of the mine for the small ore cars to be pushed in and then pulled out.

The track ran through the cabin in front of the mine opening, as was normal, and then out to the leading edge of the tailings. In the winter, or when it was raining, my great-great-grandfather had worked the rock from the ore car inside the cabin, making the place dusty and coated in rock dust.

In 2016, the old cabin was long gone, destroyed by the extreme weather.

At first Brenda had wanted to clean the cabin and

set up our camp in there. But after a couple of hours of cleaning, we had given up and pitched our tents and set up camp at a wide area in the shaft about two hundred steps inside. We cooked with an electric stove using batteries we had brought with us; the area around our tent stayed fairly even in temperature because it was so far underground.

We got to our camp and I handed her the bottle of water, grabbing a new one for myself. We were going deeper into the mine, heading for the "crystal room" as I called it, where all our research was going on.

I snapped on the hologram that showed a rockslide blocking the tunnel just in front of our camp to keep any stray locals from wandering in. It only came on when there was movement near the mouth of the tunnel; otherwise it would have taken far too much power to run. As it was, I had to change out the batteries regularly.

Beyond our camp, deeper into the mine, we had strung motion-sensitive lights along the tunnel that came on as we moved deeper into the mountain and then shut off behind us.

The lights actually gave the place a very comfortable feel. I had never thought I would feel comfortable in a mine a thousand feet under a mountain, but here I did.

"Why did you come looking for me?" I asked as we walked.

"I thought I saw something strange behind a set of crystals," Brenda said, "right at the end of the main tunnel."

"Strange in what way?"

"Artificial strange," she said, which made me glance at her.

She was paying attention to where she was stepping along the railway in the tunnel and didn't notice my look.

Beyond the end of the tunnel was nothing but more rock. There would be a tunnel there in the future, an extension, but that tunnel just hadn't been dug yet in 1870 and wouldn't be for another thirty years or more.

At least that was what I had thought. My grandfather had reopened the mine in the late 1920s for a reason he never stated in his diary and I had always assumed he had dug the tunnel. That might be a false assumption.

Maybe Brenda and I dug the tunnel.

Or more accurately, maybe we were about to.

The mineshaft suddenly opened up into a massive natural cave with vaulted high ceilings. The cave had a seemingly-unnatural flat floor and was large enough to hold completely a very large 2016 suburban two-story home without touching any side or the ceiling. The ceiling was almost forty feet above the floor.

Every inch of the entire cave was covered with crystals.

Every inch.

In fact, my great-great-grandfather had to break through the crystals to even get into the huge room and then break through the wall of crystals on the other side to start a new tunnel where he thought gold might be.

The crystals were of all sizes. Just a single light shining in the room seemed to produce a thousand reflections.

Brenda had described it as being inside a giant geode, and I think she was right. The crystals in this room in modern times would be worth far more than the gold taken out of the mine in the first place. My family just never knew what kind of fortune they had found. And therefore had never disturbed any of the crystals, luckily for us.

We had strung very low voltage lights around the crystal room and had set up tables and a ton of machines needed for our work in the middle of the room. It had taken many trips from the future to get it all here and in place. And we were constantly going back for fresh batteries and taking the used batteries to be recharged.

We just didn't dare set up any kind of generator system in the room because of ventilation and not having any idea what higher levels of power put into the crystal room would do.

It seemed, from what we could tell, that every crystal in the room, every one, even crystals not more than a quarter inch long, had the power to shift in time. Working in the middle of a few-hundred-thousand or more time-travel crystals was stressful enough without taking undue chances.

We headed across the big room, following the old rail tracks into the tunnel that had been cut in the far side of the room. Great-great-grandfather had just left the crystals he took off the walls in a pile to one side of the tunnel. I don't think he had even bothered to take a crystal out of the room, which was more than lucky for all of humanity as far as I could figure.

And more than likely he had handled them all with gloves, which had also saved him from ending up in some unknown time or place.

We went into the mine tunnel on the other side and followed the tunnel the twenty steps to where it again ran into a wall full of crystals. It was at that point that great-great-grandfather had decided it wasn't worth working the mine anymore and had shut it down.

Brenda and I had talked a lot about what was on the other side of those crystals, but to be honest, we were both scared to death to even try to dig any deeper. We wanted more information about the nature of how the crystals worked and so far, in three months of research, we had made no progress at all.

How the crystals worked, how they allowed us to just step through time and end up exactly where we wanted to be was beyond us. And that was driving both of us crazy.

As we reached the back wall, Brenda took out of the small pack she carried on a belt what looked like an old spyglass. She handed it to me.

"I've been working on this to help see through the crystals," she said as I looked at the simple, almost childlike telescope. There were lenses screwed in on both ends and one end was slightly larger than the other.

"Nifty," I said. "Magnification?"

"None," she said. "Just looking for a way to first study the insides of the crystals at normal size. I can adjust it later for magnification."

I was impressed. But a lot of things Brenda did impressed me. And I loved that about her.

She pointed to an exposed crystal on the wall on the back of the tunnel. "I thought I might try to see through the crystal to the other side. It's fairly clear here. Take a look."

I glanced at the bottom of the scope. It had a rubber rim, so it would be safe to touch the crystal with. I gently pressed it against the crystal, then put my eye to the scope.

"Adjust the focus with the center tube on the scope."

I used my right hand to do just that, slowly moving the center of the scope first to the left, then easing it back to the right until suddenly the image cleared up.

And I still had no idea what I was looking at.

From what I could tell there was a metal case or something on the other side of the crystal. And it looked very modern and very alien.

I stepped back and handed the scope to Brenda.

"Stunned" wasn't really what I was feeling. "Scared to death" described it a lot better. I wanted to run back to the crystal room and head back to our own time and forget we had even found this room in the old family mine.

"So now what do we do?" Brenda asked as I leaned against a mine timber and tried to think.

When I didn't answer she went and looked through the scope again. "I can't tell what it is," she said after a moment. "But it clearly doesn't belong this deep and this buried in this mountain."

I wouldn't argue with that.

"We need to look at this tunnel from the future," I said. "Before we try anything else. Neither of us have given this tunnel even a slight look before now."

She nodded and started back down the mine tunnel taking very large steps. I knew exactly what she was doing. She was measuring the length of this tunnel and so that in 2016 we would know where the wall had been.

I followed her. Back in the middle of the crystal room I picked up a rubber glove and put it on my left hand, then picked up a crystal from near one wall. It had been a crystal left to the side of the mine when my great-great-grandfather broke into this room for the first time. It had been the only crystal we had used.

Thinking of 2016 I turned to Brenda. "Ready?"

She nodded and at the same time we both touched the crystal with our bare hands.

Traveling through time for those who wanted something special would be a huge disappointment. One instant we were standing in 1870 and the next instant we were standing in 2016, with no sense of movement at all.

We just shifted times.

In 2016 we had filled the crystal cavern with supplies, from food to batteries to everything else we could imagine we might need.

And our camp was in the same place in both times. Only in this time we had a concrete wall in front of the mine with major locks and danger warning signs blocking the tunnel. Too many tourists around the town in the summer to take any chances.

Brenda led the way toward the back tunnel and once there started stepping off with her very long paces until she stopped. "This was where we were standing," she said, looking around at me.

Ahead in the tunnel for another twenty feet was just more mine tunnel through solid rock until it just ended.

There were no sign of crystals on the ground where the crystals had been. Nothing.

"That is so weird," I said. "The crystal wall was right here."

I moved my hand to indicate where the wall had been and banged into something metal that sort of echoed. I yanked my hand back and looked at it. Rust had streaked on my hand.

"That's a hologram," I said as Brenda and I both stepped back.

I instantly started searching for the connection and the projectors and after a moment found them tucked up in a hollow in the ceiling, just as we had placed the ones in 1870 showing a rockslide in front of our camp.

And the power line went to a set of large batteries hidden above a timber. Again, the set-up of the batteries and the wiring was just the same as we had done in 1870.

Exactly.

"Did we do this?" Brenda asked, her voice soft.

I reached above the now very old timber where I would have put the switch and found it and clicked it off.

"I think we did," I said. "I have no idea when we did it, but we will travel back to a time before this and put them in at some point in our future."

When I flipped off the hologram of a mine tunnel that dead-ended, a very large and very old metal door appeared, surrounded by concrete. It looked also very similar and then I realized it was the same kind of door that my father built on the front of the mine in 1990. My guess is that my father had built it the year before I was born.

"This is like the one your father built out in front of the mine," Brenda said, confirming what I thought.

I had no idea how that was possible. None.

No records or conversations I had with Dad had indicated he knew anything about this mine other than he always repeated over and over that it was dangerous. My mother would never talk about the mine, ever.

And my grandfather called the family mine a family curse. And he never once explained that either, other than saying it cost them taxes every year to keep it.

I hadn't told any of my family that Brenda and I were going to the mine for the summer. They thought we were in Europe studying.

"So now what do we do?" Brenda asked.

I pointed at the holographic projector and the batteries. "It seems that whatever we do, we survive to put that in at some point."

"Or at least one of us does," she said.

I ignored that comment and said what I was thinking. "We dig this out in 1870 and find out what's back there behind the door my dad built."

"You are going to need some help," my father said from behind me.

Brenda and I spun around. My dad, my mother, and my grandfather were all standing at the mouth of the tunnel from the crystal room, smiling at us.

Instead of staying inside, my mother insisted we all go back out in front of the mine, to where the old shack used to be and eat lunch and talk. The day was warm, but not hot. And the sun had just dipped behind the ridge to the west.

Two minutes after we had reached the outside and my mother was unloading a meal she had packed for this, a man with a heavy moustache walked out of the mine and joined us, followed a few seconds later by a skinny man in 1880s clothes.

In all my life I never expected to meet both my great-grandfather and my great-great-grandfather.

I just sort of gaped at them, mouth open, as I shook their hands.

And my dad and mom, also shocked, shook their hands as well.

After introductions, Brenda sat on a blanket drinking a bottle of water and giggling every so often.

It seems they already knew me and Brenda very, very well, since after this point the two of us jumped all over in time.

In fact, right before great-great-grandpa Clarence dug to the crystal room in 1868, Brenda and I went back with this entire crew to help him make sure he didn't touch the crystals with his bare hands when he opened up the room.

I have no idea of the timeline implications of all of us doing that at some point in the future, but it seems we had done it and so this chain of events is now the time-loop we are in.

I asked Dad why he built the door in front of the room we were about to open. He said that I told him to in 1990 and helped him build it. But I didn't say why. And he had no idea what was behind that opening in the crystal wall.

But he and Grandpa had trusted me. I had also been the one, a future me, to tell them exactly when to meet Brenda and me.

"You know how damn hard that was to keep secret from you for all the years you were growing up?" my father said.

I laughed. "I can't even imagine."

"I kept the same damned secret," Grandpa said, looking disgusted.

"Not a pleasurable secret to have," Edward said.

"But worth it," Great-great-grandfather Clarence said, "after seeing this family all together now long after my bones have gone to dust."

Suddenly my physics brain kicked in and I realized that the two men had come from the past. From everything I could tell, traveling to an unknown point in the future with a crystal wasn't possible.

Only going to the past was possible, and a past we knew. And if you were in the past, you could only go to a future you knew as well. Every time we had jumped back to the future, we had been gone the same amount of time as we had been in the past.

"How did you know what time to come to?" I asked my great-great-grandfather.

He frowned. "I didn't. A future you, dressed pretty much like you are now, came and brought me forward, told me what to expect out here and then vanished into thin air."

I started to open my mouth and then stopped, stunned.

Brenda giggled again, then said, "You know, this isn't mathematically possible."

Everyone just nodded, even though not a one of us understood what she really meant.

"So does anyone know what is behind that wall or that door?" I asked.

"None of us do yet," my father said. "This is all our present. It hasn't been opened up until we all do it."

I looked at my great-great-grandfather Clarence.

"You worked the mine again a few years after we opened that room, didn't you?"

"I didn't get near this place again," he said, "other than to come back and, with your help, board it up and set up some sort of fancy thing that made it look like there was a cave-in if someone did get in. I just wrote down I had worked the mine again."

It seemed I had a lot of chores in the near future. If I didn't do them, we all wouldn't be sitting here.

"I never went inside the place," my great-grandfather Edward said. "Too damn busy to come all the way up here anyway."

"So it looks like we are all going to find out what's in that room at the same time," Brenda said.

My parents, my grandfather, my great-grandfather, and my great-great-grandfather all nodded.

But none of this was making any sense to my physics training. How in the world did this time-loop get started in the first place? And to keep it going I had to set all this up at some point in the future. Why would I do that? There were so many thousands of possible futures, possible timelines that were not this one, I couldn't even begin to imagine them.

Suddenly I realized what was going on.

"Brenda, the crystal," I said. "We have always used the same crystal, right?"

She nodded. "Every time."

Then her wonderful mind caught up to where I was going and she stood.

"Are you thinking that every crystal in that cave is a different timeline?"

"That's exactly what I am thinking," I said. "If we had used a different crystal, this would have a different outcome. Who knows what?"

Brenda and I stood thinking while my father finished getting out the food and my mom set up some folding chairs and a table. No one said a word until my dad broke the silence of the mountain evening.

"Do either of you know what that room is? Or how it came to be?"

I glanced at Brenda, then at my father. "I have a hunch," I said. "Science believes that time and space are linked, and many are starting to think that matter is linked as well in a way that we just don't understand yet."

"And that from every decision," Brenda said, "two universes are created. Most fold back in together as nothing really changes from the decision. But a major decision with lots of ramifications can have untold numbers of universes created."

All three of my grandfathers just shook their heads in disgust, but my father and mother seemed to be following Brenda.

"You think that room is a natural creation," my mother asked, "from these universes splitting off?"

"Possible," I said. "Again, we are only starting to understand the connections between space and time and matter. But there are not enough crystals in that one cave alone to even begin to account for all possible alternate universes of just this planet's history."

I had a hunch I knew what was on the other side of that crystal now. I didn't really want to see it, but we had to.

"Are you saying there may be more of those crystal rooms?" Clarence asked.

"Maybe thousands if not millions more rooms like it, bigger or smaller depending on the original splitting that started building the room. No way of knowing."

"We need to open that wall to be sure," Brenda said, nodding. "Now this is all starting to make sense mathematically."

All three of my grandfathers just shook their heads and said nothing.

"We eat first," my father said.

"Just like a Benson man," my mother said, smiling at me. "Always thinking of their stomachs first."

"I've noticed that," Brenda said and both women laughed. None of the five Benson men did. We were too busy eating.

One hour later real time, I had everyone transported back to 1870. We all wore long sleeves and rubber gloves to make sure no crystal touched our skin and took us away from this mine and into a different timeline.

Then, carefully stacking the crystals in a certain place in the tunnel near where we took them out, we opened up the wall. After we got the wall opened, we would move the crystals inside the room just in case they needed to be there.

It was clear almost immediately that there was an

even larger crystal room on the other side and that room merged into another and another off into the distance.

More than likely, the crystal room my great-great-grandfather had found would grow at some point to join this larger room. If it was still an active timeline for long enough.

There were millions and millions of crystals in just what we could see, some tiny, some huge, lining every inch of every wall.

And right down the middle there was a very long row of similar-looking coffin-like chambers.

And the coffins stretched off into the distance into the other visible rooms.

I saw the coffins and wanted to stop digging. My mother agreed with me, but Brenda convinced us we had to continue.

As we went back to carefully taking apart the crystal wall, I said, "Simply by wanting to stop, a new timeline started where we did stop and another tiny crystal has now formed in the room behind us."

"Every decision means a new crystal?" great-grandfather Edward asked.

"Every decision starts a new timeline," Brenda said, nodding. "A new one for the choice; the crystal representing the larger main timeline grows a little by absorbing the other half of the choice. So more than likely the crystal we have been using has grown just slightly."

"I took exact measurements of it," I said, "so we will be able to confirm that."

Clarence snorted, then said, "If I wasn't standing here with my son, my grandson, my great-grandson, and my great-great-grandson, I wouldn't believe any of this."

With that none of us could argue.

We finally got the door cleared enough to go through and silently, flashlights on, we walked toward the first coffin. The reflections off the millions of crystals seemed to make the room very bright even with just a few flashlights.

If I weren't so scared, I'd be stunned at the beauty of it all.

The coffins were made out of some kind of metal, with a clear window-like opening over the top half of the casket. Each casket sat on top of a small riser, also made of metal.

There was a slight film of dust on them, but not much. It looked like they had been polished recently, or something was keeping them clean.

As I was afraid I would see, it was an older version of me.

And beside me lay an even older version of Brenda. Looks like I died a decade or two ahead of her.

Either something in the coffin kept our bodies preserved or this had only gotten here recently. But from the look of the line of coffins going off into the distance, that wasn't possible.

"It looks like we had pretty long lives," I said, trying to sound light even though I actually wanted to just be sick.

Seeing your own dead body can do that to a person.

Brenda held my arm with a grip that hurt and I didn't care.

"We clearly come back here after we die at some point in the future," I said.

"And now we're ghosts as well," Brenda said, shaking her head.

I didn't want to argue with her, since basically she was right. We were standing in 1870, over a hundred years before either of us would be born, yet we were staring at our own bodies.

"There's writing on a plate," Grandpa Edward said, bending over. "It reads, *Placed January 1ˢᵗ, 1700 at noon.*"

"How in the world do those bodies look that good?" Brenda asked.

"Something in the future got much better in embalming," I said.

"Or the crystals in this room don't let things deteriorate in here," my father said.

Both Brenda and I looked at him. He had a point.

My mother turned away, but my father kept moving down to the third coffin. "Take a look at this," he said.

I knew what it was and so did Brenda, but we followed anyway and my mother came back, not looking at the first two coffins.

It was another coffin with another me inside, about the same age as the first one. And Brenda was beside me again, again looking much older than when I had died.

The plate on this read, *Placed January 2nd, 1700 at noon*.

"I'm going to have nightmares for the rest of my life," my mother said.

Brenda and I, arm-in-arm, just kept walking along the rows of coffins with our bodies in them, going deeper and deeper into the complex of crystal caves.

Every-so-often one of us would have died young, and every-so-often I lived much, much longer than the first one.

But we were always placed together and each placement followed the other by one day exactly.

After walking past a few hundred coffins, and no sign of the row of coffins ending in the distance, we stopped.

"We are all of them, aren't we?" Brenda asked. "Right now, right here."

"We are," I said. "We decide to be brought back here and buried and all of these coffins are us from this point forward, in all the thousands of alternate universes that allow us to come back."

"So these rooms are where all alternate universes branch," she said. "That's why all of our bodies from all the different universes can be here like this in one place."

I instantly knew she was right.

"Of course," I said, staring off into the dark distance at all my coffins. "This is the gateway to every alternate universe. They all are grounded here. At least all the ones springing from events on this planet. Time and space and matter are all connected."

"And this is the connection point," Brenda said.

"It seems we have some papers to write," I said, smiling.

"You have errands to run first," she said. "You have to bring your family together out of the past, actually the future from here, to first help your grandfather find that first room and second, get them here."

"You are right," I said, slipping my hand into Brenda's hand and turning us back toward the beginning of the row of coffins. "We have to try to keep the start of this timeline together."

In the distance I could see my three grandfathers and my father and my mother standing, talking, waiting for us. About halfway back to them something suddenly struck me as I once again walked past the two of us buried side-by-side.

I froze and stared at the two coffins.

"What's wrong, besides the fact that we are dead?" Brenda asked.

"Both of us are right here, in every universe, side-by-side."

She squeezed my arm and smiled. "I noticed that. It's nice, isn't it?"

It was nice that we stayed together, but there was only one problem.

"Who buried us here?"

Brenda blinked, then frowned.

And behind us an adult voice said, "Hi, Dad. Mom."

We both spun around to see a twenty-year-old

man, short, but solid, who looked a lot like both me and Brenda, smiling at us. He had my father's smile and Brenda's wonderful eyes.

And in the next cavern back were a few hundred more of the same guy, some dressed slightly differently, smiling and waving.

RENN AND THE LITTLE MEN

Kristine Kathryn Rusch

Let me start by telling you this: I'm good with a gun.

In fact, I'm better with a gun than anyone I know, although most people don't believe it. I'm the one who trained my brother Ralphie how to handle his.

Of course, now you know Ralphie as Kid Vicious—at least that's what the dime novels call him. No one else does, or at least, no one else did until he got his own dime novels. Before that he was Ralphie the Kid, which he hated, or Ralph Visch, which is our last name, or plain old RV. Sometimes people called him *That kid, you know the one, not as famous as Billy, but cuter.*

Because Billy was one of the ugliest boys I'd ever met.

But I digress.

I don't have a nickname. Girls don't get good

nicknames. Like Calamity Jane. I mean, really. That's just mean. Little Annie Oakley. Yeah, not for me either.

My parents named me Renn, which they misspelled because they're illiterate. Or really, I think the doc misspelled it because he's barely literate. Or maybe it was the pastor, since I'm actually in the church rolls for my date of birth: Renn Visch, born—

Wait. I'm not telling you how old I am. It's bad enough that I've told you Renn is misspelled. I'm not telling you my real name, the one my parents intended for me.

I learned the treacheries of that path not too long ago.

But I get ahead of myself.

The little men showed up at the farm one Saturday morning, three of them, looking for Ralphie, and I gotta tell you, it's lucky they found me. Ralphie wouldn't've taken them seriously. In fact, Ralphie might've just squashed them with his big old fancy cowboy boots.

Because they were no bigger than my thumb. It took me a while to believe they were real.

At least I had a chance of figuring them out, because I read. Ma says I'm going to lose my eyesight, reading at night by candlelight, but really I think I'm more likely to burn the house down. Twice in the last year, I've put out curtain fires in my bedroom, not that Ma knows that because I stitch up some new ones each time from old cloth. I tell her I like patchwork curtains—the latest are green and pink and some kind of leaky purple (with dye that came off on my fingers as I stitched)—but honestly, I work with what's available. And I hate purple, although not as much as I hate pink.

My room is little more than a box off the kitchen. Ralphie gets the good room, even though he doesn't live at home any more. Ma and Pa, they have the room that should've been the back parlor, but they ran out of building material (and money) before our house got finished, so they improvised. The house is kinda truncated, which means that some parts look big and other parts that you'd expect got lopped off in the back.

For a while, Ralphie brought in real money, taking jobs as a hired gun, but now he mostly drinks the money away and never comes home. In fact, I had no idea where he was that morning that the wee folk showed up.

That's all I could figure they were. In my reading, I'd seen stories about fairies, but not stories about subsets of fairies, like brownies or pixies, and I certainly didn't know how they all worked together, like some little community, which they were. I also expected those communities to be very Old Country, which they aren't, and thought that the stuff in the folklore was true, which it mostly isn't.

Although some of it is, so figuring it all out was tough.

Meandering again. Sorry.

The farm is at the butt-end of nowhere in the middle of the Great State of California. My folks homesteaded, sorta, and thought they were land-rich, which they are, sorta, but they're money-poor, and are destined to remain that way.

Our nearest neighbor is miles away, which is why, when someone whispered, "Hey, girlie," at dawn, I let out one of those screams the dime novels call "bloodcurdling."

"Hey!"

"Shush!"

"Shut up!"

Three different whispers. I sat up and didn't see anything. At that moment, Ma stepped into my room, already dressed with her Saturday apron tied around her waist.

She looked around, saw me, saw that I was by myself, saw that I was white as a ghost, and said, "Another bad dream?"

I was shaking, my feather pillow shoved up between me and the headboard, my favorite quilt pulled up under my chin covering my night rail. The room looked empty to me too.

"I guess so," I said, even though I never had a sound-only dream before.

She nodded like she expected that and to be fair, she was probably right. I had a lot of bad dreams, mostly about being trapped in mud or trapped in amber (from my reading) or being trapped in a mine or being trapped in the storm cellar. I woke up screaming from those too.

She said, "Your pa's out milking the cows—"

Cow, I silently amended.

"—and I need some help with breakfast before you go shooting."

My parents didn't complain about my shooting. They encouraged it. Some weeks, it was the only thing that kept us in food. As I said, I'm good with a gun. Hell, I'm a crack shot if you really want to know, and I can fell a squirrel at 100 paces with one eye closed and the other half-covered with a patch. I'm not too fond of squirrel meat, but I'll eat it when nothing else's in the offing. And Pa, no matter how hard he tries, is probably the worst farmer on the face of the Earth. What he grows, nobody eats.

"All right," I said, but Ma was gone before I could finish. I let go of the quilt and swung my bare feet out of bed. I always hesitate before putting my feet on the cold wood floor, and as I hesitated, I heard squealing.

Then something warm and soft landed on the big toe of my right foot. At almost the same moment, something else landed on the big toe of my left foot. And then something splatted against the floor.

I looked down to see what kind of creature— spider? mouse?—had landed on my foot. Clinging to my big toe was a little man, dressed in green, with a tiny feather jutting out of his tiny cap. He climbed up my toe, got past the nail, and chomped.

"Hey!" I said, shaking my foot.

There was another little man on my left foot. He was climbing the toe and I didn't want to feel tiny needlelike teeth in my tender toe-flesh, so I shook that foot too. That didn't dislodge the little guys (and at that point, I wasn't questioning what I saw, I was just reacting), so I brought my right foot up, grabbed Little Guy #1 with my thumb and forefinger and picked him up by the scruff of his neck.

"Hey!" he said, sounding as upset as I had. Only his voice was little and squeaky and it would have made me giggle if it weren't for the other little man heading toward the sensitive skin on the top of my toe.

I shook that foot so hard the little guy dislodged, did a flip as he went up in the air, two more little flips as he went down, and then he landed on the cold floor with a splat . . .

. . . next to a third little man, who had his feathered cap off, and was rubbing his beaked nose as if it hurt him.

"You bit me!" I said to Little Guy #1.

He grinned, revealing pointy teeth. "Yum," he said. "Toe jam."

Which made my stomach flip.

"Okay, first, toe jam is the stuff between the toes, and you didn't get to that," I said. "Second, that's my toe jam and I didn't give you permission to get near it or my toe."

By this point, I had decided I was having a pretty wicked and realistic dream, and I have learned over the years when you're having a wicked and realistic dream, you just go with it, no matter what.

His grin faded and he started kicking. The kicks gave him some momentum, and he started swinging. The fabric of his tiny shirt collar began slipping through my fingers.

"I'll drop you too," I said.

"Renn!" Ma shouted from the kitchen.

"Coming!" I shouted back. Then frowned. The timing of the dream felt off. Ma would've yelled like that when I was awake, but usually in my dreams, things happen consecutively, not all at the same time.

Little Guy #1 stopped kicking. Either I scared him when I yelled, Ma scared him when she yelled, or he didn't want to get dropped.

I set him on the floor next to his buddies, and expected them to scamper off. Instead, they looked at me, including Little Guy #3 who was still rubbing the tip of his oversized nose.

"We came to talk to you," Little Guy #2 said, as he stepped forward.

I tucked my bare feet under my thighs, then covered everything up with my night rail and the quilt.

"So talk," I said.

"We came to see your brother, but we can't find him. Is he here?"

"No," I said.

"In that barn, then, with the . . ." and here Little Guy #2 shuddered " . . . cow?"

"No," I said. "He hasn't been here in months."

"Do you know where he is?" Little Guy #3 asked.

"No," I said. "Now, if you'll excuse me, I have chores."

I leaned over the side of the bed, found my shoes, and slipped them on my feet. Then I grabbed my unmentionables, my socks, and my housedress and hurried off to the necessary. Even though I believed

I was having a dream, I thought maybe it was one of those dreams where half of it was really happening (like Ma yelling) and half of it was in slumberland.

I figured that with my shoes and my dress on, the slumberland part would disappear.

I managed to get dressed in the necessary without touching any of my clothes to the unsavory parts of the two-seater, then scurried into my brother's room, washed up with the pitcher of water and washbasin Ma always left for him in case he appeared in the middle of night, and then went into the kitchen.

Ma was nearly finished with her famous buttermilk pancakes—which are famous for a really good reason. I managed to get the table set before Pa showed up. He brought in some fresh warm milk. I scooped up a pitcherful, scraped the cream off the top, and we all said grace before tucking in.

I didn't tell them about the little men, and my folks didn't mention anything strange, so I figured I'd finally awakened all the way (and it was good to wake up to buttermilk pancakes).

I pumped and heated water for the dishes, cleaned the kitchen, and still managed to get to my own personal firing range by nine AM.

I practice every day whether I need to or not. Shooting is 90% practice; at least, that's what I told Ralphie when we were training. Used to be, guns scared him. He hated the bang and the boom, he hated the way his gun kicked with each shot, and he hated the way that bullets destroyed whatever they went into.

I don't know what changed his opinion. If his personal dime novelist is to be believed, it was when he saw his best friend all shot up by some sheriff. But I didn't know Ralphie had a friend except me (no one who knows him really likes him much) and I've never been shot; besides, how would that make a man hire out his services as a gunslinger? It just never made sense, and Ralphie wouldn't tell me when I asked.

So I spent my morning shooting tin cans and cow pies, hitting things at impossible angles from incredible distances, squinting and picking off leaves on trees as if they had offended me (both the leaves and the trees). I did all those things that would keep me in squirrel meat, and those things that just might get me a prize at the county fair, if they let me compete again, which they hadn't for the past three years because I so soundly beat all the guys in the previous two years. (They let me back in the second time because they thought I cheated the first time and they planned to catch me. Nope. My shots, while impossible, were clearly legal—and clearly possible, Pa said, since I had done them, even if no one else could. That was when they banned me.)

I had gotten down to my last five bullets and debated whether I'd use them or whether I'd hang onto them, since using them meant spending my afternoon at the smithy begging for some lead. Old Gus had stopped making me bullets. He did, however, teach me how to cast my own.

I had my little case on a gigantic stump that I had

flattened out to work as my shooting table. My hand fluttered over the bullets, indecisive, when someone cleared his little throat.

I froze, flashed on the dream, and thought, *Naaaaw*. I had heard a bird cough, nothing more.

"Missy!" said a squeaky little voice.

I closed my eyes, then opened them again. I was awake. Dammit. Then I looked around to see if anyone had seen me think that unladylike word (most of what I said and did was unladylike, but deep down, it bothered me more than I wanted to admit).

The three little guys were sitting on a tilting post from the collapsed fence that Pa hadn't fixed in two years. He figured Ralphie would do it when Ralphie got home, but Ralphie didn't do manual labor, and of course, didn't bother to tell anyone. That collapsed fence was the reason we had "cow" and not "cows."

"I don't like it when figments of my imagination follow me around," I said.

One of the little guys—I no longer had any idea if he was Little Guy #1 or Little Guy #2—giggled. Wee men shouldn't giggle. It was infectious. Little Guy #3 (I recognized him from his nose) giggled as well, followed by the remaining little guy. And in spite of myself, I giggled too.

That was the moment I lost any control I might have had.

"We're not figments of your imagination," said Little Guy #3. He had a honking big voice, considering how tiny he was. The tip of his nose was red.

Apparently, he had fallen on it when he was jumping for my delectable toes that morning and missed.

"We're in need of help," said Little Guy #2 (or the guy I was designating as Little Guy #2). I squinted at him, hoping to get a better look at him so I could better tell him apart from Little Guy #1—so that I wasn't constantly changing their designation.

"We can't find your brother," said Little Guy #1.

"I don't think anyone can," I said.

They sighed. It sounded like the rattle of an errant summer breeze.

Little Guy #1 sat down and put his face in his hands. Little Guy #2 patted him on his tiny shoulder. Little Guy #3 stood at the very edge of the fence post, and looked like he would tumble off.

I moved closer, just so he didn't have to lean.

"We have approached fifteen gunslingers," Little Guy #3 said. "We are quite disappointed. They are nothing like advertised. Most drink to excess. Many did not believe we existed. Two called us rat babies and tried to stomp us out. Three shot at us *and missed*."

He shook his little head as if he was more offended that they missed than he was that they had fired at the trio.

"None of them would listen to us. Your brother was our last hope."

Then he sat down too and put his head in his hands.

"What do you need a gunslinger for?" I asked.

Little Guy #2 looked at me over Little Guy #1's

feather. "Three days hence, trolls shall invade our village. Their champion will face our champion. If their champion wins, they become our rulers. And if our champion wins, they will not bother us for another five hundred years."

I frowned. "That doesn't sound fair. Why don't you get to rule them?'

"Have you met a troll?" Little Guy #3 put his hand to his exceedingly large nose. "They have terrible habits. They're *huge*, and they all smell like rotted meat. Who would want to rule them?"

"Good point," I said.

"In the past, we have always defeated them. They are not very bright. Our champion could always win, usually by felling the troll, and then biting him until he gave up in anguish."

I could imagine. I didn't like the feel of those razor-sharp teeth on my toes, let alone how it would feel everywhere.

"We have always sacrificed a champion for this, because troll flesh is toxic to us—not intoxicating like your lovely toe flesh." At that moment, he bowed.

I did not thank him, although he clearly expected it.

"We have a champion chosen, but we cannot use him," Little Guy #3 said. "One of our scouts learned that this year, the trolls were determined not to lose, so they hired an advisor. And the advisor told the trolls that we are allergic to metals. He advised the trolls to hire a gunslinger to shoot up our little town—"

(Here I was thinking the gunslinger could stomp

their little town with his silver decorated boots, but I didn't say anything about that.)

"—and not only would our champion be unable to fight, but we would also have to acquiesce to the troll leadership, because only they can remove metals and remain unharmed. Needless to say, we were terrified, until we realized we needed to counter their gunslinger with one of our own. But we cannot hire anyone."

"If you can't handle metals," I said, "what would you hire them with?"

"Their heart's desire," the little guy said, and sat down. He sounded like he was going to sob.

"You would be able to grant them their heart's desire?" I couldn't quite believe what I had heard.

They nodded. In unison. I had never seen anyone do that before.

"If you have the kind of power to grant someone their heart's desire," I asked slowly, "why can't you do that for yourselves?"

"Magic is soooo cruel," said Little Guy #2.

I frowned so hard I could feel the skin on my forehead pulling downward. "You mean you can't?"

They nodded in unison again.

"Well, why not have you—" and I pointed to Little Guy #3 "grant his—" and I pointed at Little Guy #1 "—heart's desire?"

They looked at each other, and for a moment, I wondered if they had never thought of it. Then they shook their little heads.

"Magic is very, very cruel," Little Guy #2 said. "It is not within the rules."

"So break the rules," I said.

"We break the rules and lose our magic," said Little Guy #3.

Wow. That was clearly not a world I could survive in for very long. I would have broken a rule before breakfast.

I was still trying to process all of this. I had accepted that the little men existed. I had accepted that I could see and talk to them. I had also accepted that they were in some kind of crisis. But I was still trying to fathom how they had come upon this solution, and whether or not it was even feasible.

"Let me try to understand this," I said. "You've been going around the West, trying to hire famous gunslingers by offering them their heart's desire."

"Yes," Little Guy #2 said.

I was shaking my head before I even realized I was doing it. "This isn't going to work. Gunslingers are unimaginative men. If they had an imagination —" (and a brain, I mentally added) "—they wouldn't use guns to solve every problem they come across. All they understand is shooting. I'm not even sure they have a heart to desire with."

"It doesn't matter," said Little Guy #3. "None of them would talk to us anyway."

"You're the first human who was willing to have a conversation," said Little Guy #1 mournfully.

I wasn't really paying attention to them. "Even if

you did hire a gunslinger," I said, "where would you hold the shootout?"

"In our village," said Little Guy #2.

I looked at him. "Really? Because your town is as small as you are, right?"

They nodded. In unison. Again. I was beginning to find that creepy.

"Two gunslingers would stomp your town to pieces before the first shot got fired," I said. "I mean, have you looked at the size of human feet?"

I instantly regretted that question. Fortunately, they hadn't heard it. Instead, they leaned on each other, and Little Guy #3 began to cry.

"We're going to be troll slaves," he said. "I would rather die. But I can't die. I don't want to be a troll slave."

The others patted him on the back and murmured something that I couldn't hear. But they weren't being soothing or at least, they weren't being successfully soothing, because he didn't look soothed.

"Does this meeting of the champions have to occur in your town?" I asked.

Little Guy #1 raised his tiny head and frowned at me. "Why?"

"Because," I said, "I have an idea that just might solve your problem."

And that was how I ended up in a one-horse town in a part of the Great State of California that made the butt-end of nowhere look like New York City. I'd like to say I didn't know that places like this existed, but that's not true since I'm the one who suggested it to the little men.

It was high noon. I stood in the center of the main street wearing a pair of my brother's discarded breeches, a loose cotton shirt, a vest with two bandoliers stuffed with bullets of all types crisscrossed over my chest, and my trusty six-shooters on each hip. I can shoot equally well with either hand, unlike any other prizewinning shooter I know. I wore a hat pulled down over my forehead, and I waited for my opponent to appear.

The little men and their little families sat on the wooden rails that separated the wooden sidewalks from the dirt street. There must've been a thousand little people, looking like birds on a rooftop, watching and chattering and all wearing hats with one tiny feather.

The big people were all inside the various buildings, mostly the five saloons that dotted the main drag, drinking charmed beer and unable to come outside. I didn't ask what magic made that possible, although I did ask if the charmed beer would hurt them. It seemed the charmed beer made them all very, very happy and very, very forgetful.

I wasn't sure exactly what they had to forget.

Until the trolls showed up.

You don't forget moving gray boulders. Particularly when they were ugly gray boulders with craggy features and massive arms that reached all the way to the ground. They had hands the size of horse's heads and teeth that made the little men's look like metal shavings.

As these creatures approached, the ground shook like it did in a cattle stampede. Everything bounced, everything moved. Wafting ahead of them was a great stink, like a thousand million buffalo rotting in the sun.

If the little men had trouble hiring a gunslinger, I had no idea how these massive creatures managed to hire one. As I saw them approach, I wanted to turn and run.

But I didn't. I held my ground. (All right. Technically, I was rooted there.) I watched as this lumbering gray stinky mountain of troll flesh approached, and I wondered how the hell I could get out of there.

And then I saw the human man in the center. He was tall, whip thin, and dressed in black. He walked at the head of that column of stench like it didn't bother him at all.

Next to him stood an ethereally beautiful creature seemingly made of light. The creature wasn't human—it was too bright, too lovely—but it wasn't an angel either, because it had no wings. Its hair was long and silver, and it wore some kind of gray robe. It would have blended into the gray troll army if it weren't for that brightness, which made it hard for me to take my gaze off the thing.

The trolls stopped on the outskirts of the one-horse town, just like the little men told me they would. It wasn't that they had to be invited in (apparently some creatures are like that), it was more that they didn't want to overwhelm the spectators with their stink. Or maybe they didn't want to scare me off.

Or maybe they were shy.

I didn't have a lot of time to think about it because the man in black kept walking toward me, and that was when I realized—

"Hey!" he said at that same moment. "Those are my pants."

Yep. It was my brother, Kid Vicious. Only he didn't look like his usual slovenly self. That black outfit made him look both older and thinner and almost dapper. The guns on each of his hips had mother-of-pearl inlay grips and his boots were as shiny as the ethereal creature at his side.

The creature, who had a long, bony and somewhat homely face (from this distance), moved to the sidewalk, displacing maybe five dozen little families.

"Renn!" he said as he stopped, feet spread. "What the hell—heck—hell—ah, heck—heck are you doing here?"

I swallowed. "I thought I was going to have a shootout with a bad guy."

"Oh, God, Renn," he said, and turned toward the ethereal creature. "I can't fight her. She's not just a woman, she's my sister."

The boulders behind him rippled. I guessed that meant they had some kind of reaction, but from my vantage, I couldn't quite tell what it was. The ethereal creature raised its head and glared at my brother.

"Besides," my brother said plaintively. My brother was only plaintive with authority figures. When he was being Kid Vicious, the West's Second Most Famous Kid Gunfighter, he wasn't plaintive at all. "If we go through with this, she'll win. She's the one who taught me how to shoot."

The ethereal creature raised its hand and my brother jerked forward. Then his arm went for his gun, even as his face squinched in disapproval.

It was shoot or be shot, so I grabbed my trusty six-shooter from my left holster, raised the gun in one quick motion, and shot the shit out of that ethereal creature off to the side.

As it tap-danced its way off the sidewalk, my brother tapped and jerked too. His mouth moved, he shook his head, and his gun went off.

The bullet hit me before I could move out of the way. It felt like one of those boulders had landed on my chest. I flew backwards and landed on my back, my remaining air knocked out of me.

Ralphie screamed and ran toward me. The area got lighter and I thought for a minute I was going to pass out.

"Renn, Renn, Renn," he said as he got to my side. He put some kind of filthy cloth on my vest, pushing down on the wound. "I didn't mean it. Talk to me, Little—"

"Shut up," I said. Or whispered. Or breathed. It was an effort, whatever I did to make the sound come out. I just didn't want him to say my full name.

Ralphie never was the sharpest knife in the drawer.

"They had me prisoner. I was magicked." He was pressing hard. It hurt, but I wasn't sure if that was because of the pressure or because of the damn wound. "You broke it somehow, Renn. I'm so, so sorry."

I broke it with the silver bullets I had in my left-handed trusty six-shooter. My right-handed trusty six-shooter had regular normal lead bullets. I just figured a girl had to be prepared, so I spent the previous day with Old Gus, making bullets of every single kind I could think of and every single material that was mentioned in those stories I had read in all of those books.

"Leave her," the little men said as they crowded around me. "She's ours now."

Some were climbing on my boots and I knew they would pull the damn things off. Apparently toe jam to them is as delicious—and rare—as chocolate is for us.

Some of them started climbing Ralphie and he was batting them away with one hand, loosening the pressure on my chest.

"You have to save her," he said.

"They can't," I managed. My heart's desire wasn't to live. My heart's desire was to be taken as seriously as a man, to be recognized for my strength and skill just like a man, to be—

"Of course they can," Ralphie said. "They owe you three wishes."

"Wrong kind of creature," I said.

"Heck, no," he said. "I've spent the past month with all kinds of very strange magical folk, and believe me, they owe you three wishes."

I saw Little Guy #3 gingerly avoiding the bullets crosscrossing my chest. "Is that true?" I wheezed.

He froze and I could see on his beakish little face that it was.

"You mean you were going to cheat me of two wishes?" I said, then started to cough blood. "My heart's desire is a wish, right?"

He nodded, reluctantly.

"You cheating little snake." I sprayed blood on him. I was dying. Tears were running down Ralphie's cheeks.

"We don't owe you anything," Little Guy #3 said. "We own you, Renn Visch."

He said my name like it had magic. Ralphie went white, and I realized someone had said those words to him. That was how he had gotten ensnared. (That and probably the charmed beer.)

"That's not my real name," I said or rather gurgled. The blood was getting thick inside my mouth, which now tasted of rust.

Little Guy #3 looked horrified.

"Three wishes," I managed. "First, heal this wound."

Little Guy #3 glared at me, then glared at my brother, and then waved his tiny fist.

I could breathe. Whatever had been on my chest or in my chest or near my chest was gone. The blood wasn't, though, and I spit out a whole pile of it onto the dirt around me. My shirt clung to my healthy chest.

"Ask for riches, ask for riches, ask for riches," my brother repeated.

Anyone who asked for money in all the old stories got screwed. And I wasn't thinking clearly enough to make sure I beat the system. But I tried anyway.

"Make my parents wealthy," I said.

"Noooooo," Ralphie said. "You should've done it for us too."

Little Guy #3 waved his fist again. I had no idea if the wish was granted, but I had to assume it was.

"And finally," I said, "grant me three more wishes."

All of the little creatures raised their little heads and their little feathers bobbed in the little wind created by the little movement. For an instant, time stopped, and I thought I had truly screwed up for a moment.

Then Little Guy #3 waved his fist and said, "Done."

"But," said another little man, and I had to assume that was Little Guy #1, "our power isn't limitless. You must wait a day to wish again."

I had no trouble with that. I knew the pitfalls. I had to wipe the words "I wish" from my vocabulary, and I had to think before I spoke.

My brother was cackling like he had gotten extra wishes, but he hadn't.

"Come on," I said to him. "Let's get out of here."

He helped me get up. Little people fell off me like fleas off a mangy dog. I realized as I stood that the reason it had gotten light earlier was the boulder blockade was gone. The trolls had vanished when it became clear that their champion had forfeited.

We staggered out of that one-horse town and headed home.

When we were finally free of the little people, I said to Ralphie, "What was that creature? The one I shot?"

"He said he was an elf. But I don't think so. They called him fae. I don't know what that is, but you made him explode. I don't think he'll bother me again."

As we walked (staggered) Ralphie confirmed what had happened. He met the fae/elf in a bar after too many (charmed) beers and told the fae/elf his real name, which enslaved him. I broke the enslavement when I killed (exploded?) the fae/elf.

He'd been with them at least a month, maybe more. And there I'd been cursing him for drinking, carousing, and not coming home while he'd been living among the trolls, never getting used to their stink.

"That was some shooting," he said.

"I was the one who taught you how," I snapped.

"Yeah," he said with admiration. My brother wasn't the sharpest knife in the drawer, but he was loyal. "We have to come with a nickname for you, Little—"

I put my finger on his lips. "Don't say that. Ever."

It took him a minute to understand what I meant. Renn was my name so far as outsiders thought. But inside my family, from the moment I was born, I had a different name. One given to me by my whimsical father, who thought I looked like a small brown bird.

I had three names, only one of which made it onto the rolls, and on that, it was misspelled.

"Yeah, all right, got it," Ralphie said, and I sure as hell hoped he wouldn't say it if the time ever came again.

We made it home, and I thought Ma would give me holy hell for wearing breeches, but she didn't even notice. Instead, she was sitting on the porch, staring at a pile of gold coins and crying.

Guess that second wish came true, just like the first.

Which meant that the third had come true too, so I had to be extra careful, and I had to choose my two fresh wishes per day wisely. I figured I'd mess up eventually, but until then, I had a series of wishes to get through.

And the first would be that Ralphie would forget my real name. I still don't know the second.

But I will always know the third.

SHOWDOWN AT HIGH MOON

Jennifer Brozek

"There's never enough, is there?" Mena asked with a sigh as she watched the night sky.

"Of course there will be. We'll have what we need," Will said. He stopped counting the money from their latest coach robbery and shifted around the low campfire to sit next to the love of his life. "We'll get married, go west and claim our homestead." He pointed across the plains. "Out there is our future. There's a farm just waiting for us to come get it. Just as soon as we've got the seed money, we'll go."

She smiled at him. "All right. Then the 'Star-crossed Bandits' can disappear into legend, never to be heard from again."

He gave her a peck on the cheek. "That's my girl. I'm going to make all our dreams come true."

* * *

Mena Scott. Will Brogan. Wanted for robbery. We would speak with you.

As Mena sat up with a jerk, her gun already in her hand and looking for a target, she saw that Will had woken up in the same manner. Both of them squinted at the flashes of bright light twinkling at the edge of their camp, confused as the rising sun pulled shadows from the surrounding land.

Will Brogan. Mena Scott. We would speak with you. We mean you no harm.

The voice, without inflection, reminded Will of a Chinaman learning to speak English by rote. Within the flashing lights he could see things hovering on the edge of the camp, but not the silhouette of a lawman as expected. He blinked again. The things looked like bejeweled metal teacup saucers.

"Will, it's them." Mena gestured to the flying things. "They're talking."

"I see that." He raised his voice at them. "Speak to us about what? And would you stop flashing the light in our eyes?"

Immediately, scores upon scores of the flying things stopped hovering and landed on the ground. One of them, one almost the size of a soup bowl but as flat as the rest, landed just inside the camp. Not quite sure of what to point her gun at, Mena lowered her weapon and looked at the thing next to her foot. It was silver, edged with flickering jewels on its rim, and adorned with a bronze, maybe gold, top that had an engraving on it. The engraving was something she recognized. "A scarab," she murmured to Will.

The thing within their camp began to hover again. It slowly rose to eye level.

Scarab is an acceptable classification, Mena Scott. We would speak of hiring you for a job.

Mena and Will looked at each other. She nodded to him, letting him take the lead. He lowered his revolver. "Just Will and Mena, if you please. Hire. For what?"

Mena and Will, you are wanted for multiple robberies. You are not wanted for murder. We would have something stolen. We would not have humans killed.

"What do you want us to steal?"

In the dirt between them, the Scarab projected the image of a poster advertising a traveling carnival called "The Wild West and Mystical Wonders Show." While they watched, the poster changed to another showing some of the wonders to be displayed. It featured a painted woman with black hair wearing a simple white linen dress, holding a staff. At the top of the staff was a disk that looked a lot like the Scarab before them, only bigger.

We would have you rescue our queen.

"What? The woman?"

No. Our queen. Held by the woman.

Will shook his head and wondered if he was crazy. "All right. I see her. Just the staff. Shouldn't be that hard. What's the pay?"

Gold.

Will and Mena looked at each other. "How much gold?"

Enough for your needs. We have watched you. Listened to you. You will have enough.

Will frowned. It sounded too good to be true. "What's the catch? What aren't you telling us? Why can't *you* go in and get her?"

Our queen is a captive. Our enemy watches. He keeps her from the light. She is weak without the power of the sun.

"Enemy?"

A foul creature that can morph into other biological entities.

"Pardon?"

The enemy is a shapeshifter, like the legend of were-wolves. He does it on command. He is in control. He looks human now but he is not human. We are long-standing enemies. Will you help us, Mena and Will?

Mena gave a slight nod to Will who said, "We will, but you've got to tell us more about the enemy, this shapeshifter."

Over the next couple of hours, Will and Mena prepared themselves as they heard the story of a long-standing feud between a race of small creatures made of "circuits and light" and a war-like race of beings that could take on the shape of things around it but were, by and large, "hostile biological entities." One of these creatures, dubbed Shifters by Mena, had managed to capture the Scarabs' queen and had kept her in the dark ever since. He wanted the Scarabs to cede Earth to the Shifters so they could immediately colonize it.

Despite not understanding all the Scarab told them, Mena and Will agreed that this Shifter was bad news and needed to be dealt with—starting with the rescue of the Scarab queen.

After setting the Scarabs to wait for them about a mile away from the Wild West show, they went on ahead, pretending to be some of the locals just looking for a good time. The whole thing was less of a Wild West show and more of a carnival with its emphasis on the "Mystical Wonders" part of the traveling venue. The tents with their private shows of extinct creatures, weird animals, weirder humans and other such wonders were a definite draw.

As they walked arm-in-arm through the dusty show, they saw a couple of the locals trying their hand at target practice for a prize. Easy enough for anyone who had had real practice with a rifle, but not so much for a man with his girl looking on. Just down the way was a strong man daring a slender farm boy to "ring the bell" and another hawker shouted for people to toss rings around the bottle tops—three rings got a prize. It was all good fun as the summer dust puffed around everyone's feet.

In one outdoor ring, a pretty woman, who would be mistaken for a jilly by the cut of her short dress in another time and place, was doing some fancy trick riding on a horse, while a very old, tired looking cowboy performed trick shot after trick shot in the ring next door. The man looked like he could do his routine in his sleep; Mena wasn't certain he was actually awake while she watched.

As they strolled deeper into the tent aisles of the carnival, barkers from food tents, knick-knack displays and private shows vied for their attention. Will allowed Mena to drag him over to the tent showing "Wonders from Around the World." He paid their two nickels along with several other couples and they entered the darkness of the tent with anticipation.

There were four exhibits inside, each showcasing a different part of the world: a Zulu warrior, several Mongols, an Indian serpent tamer, and, of course, the Egyptian queen. The Zulu warrior was interesting mostly because neither Mena nor Will had seen a man with such black skin before. There was little doubt that he was an actor but the man played his part well. If they had not been on a job, Mena would have spent more time looking at him. The Mongols were loud Chinamen and the serpent tamer was fascinating with his lunging snake. The exhibits were worth the nickel, much to everyone's surprise.

The beautiful Egyptian queen was stretched out on a chaise longue. She looked regal, bored and hot. There was an Egyptian warrior fanning her with a giant fan made of leaves. Mena smiled at him. Clearly not Egyptian, he was still a man. While she strolled near him, she let Will examine the queen and the object of their quest.

"Our Egyptian beauty is available for a private showing, should you have the appropriate offerings for her," the barker murmured to Will as soon as Mena was out of earshot and then glanced at her. "Assuming the gentleman is available."

"The gentleman is and his sister seems to have an eye for the warrior."

The barker leered, "The business between the warrior and your sister is theirs alone. My business is with our queen." He tilted his head back towards the woman on the chaise. Will saw that her gown was suddenly that much more revealing.

"How . . . what sort of offering does our queen take?"

"Five."

Will considered. "Five if you let this showing be in here." He allowed his eyes to greedily follow the lines of her curves.

"Your wish is our command. Come back at sunset." The barker paused, "And I'm certain your sister will find the warrior loitering nearby then." The two men grinned at each other.

Mena said nothing with words while she examined the Egyptian exhibit. But she used every bit of her feminine wits to let the Egyptian warrior know she was much more interested in him than in what she was looking at. By the time Will retrieved her and the barker was ushering them out, she knew she had her target snared.

"Come, sister-dear. We'll be back later. Sunset."

Mena glanced coquettishly between the warrior and her "brother" and smiled as she left arm in arm with Will.

They returned to the tent just as the barker was ushering the last of the customers through the exit. He grinned at them, watching Mena saunter off around the back of the tent to where her assignation loitered, and then waved Will into the entrance of the tent. While the rest of the exhibit workers had ducked out the back, Will saw that heavier curtains were drawn around the Egyptian exhibit, mostly obscuring what was inside.

He steeled himself to fight the Shifter if he had to, while pretending to be nothing more than an eager gentleman ready for a good time with the Egyptian queen.

The barker stepped in between him and the curtain. "I'll be out front. You have an hour. I'll holler when you have fifteen minutes left." He held out his hand for the money. As Will paid him, he added, "It's always polite to tip our queen for her graciousness."

"We'll see how gracious she is," Will said, and stepped around him. He waited at the curtain until the barker left the tent.

"Do I have a supplicant?" a heavy feminine voice called.

Will opened the curtain and stepped into the Egyptian exhibit. "You do, my queen."

Before him, on the chaise longue, the queen lay, posing for him—nothing revealed but everything intimated. Then she sat up. "Join me."

All around her were the false artifacts of a side-show exhibit. Stepping to her, he saw the chipped paint revealing wood instead of bronze and the hurried stitching in all of the fabric in the ground covering, the fur throws and even in the queen's costume. He took one offered hand and kissed her knuckles.

He smiled at her laughter. "I have a gift for you, if you'll allow it."

"Of course," the queen said, enjoying her role and used to such gestures.

Will went to one knee before her, reached into his bag and brought out a small bottle. "It's perfume. I hope you like it." He opened it and offered it to her.

She accepted it, delight clear on her face, and took a delicate sniff. The look of delight changed to something more neutral "I . . . it's very interesting." She put on a brave smile and inhaled again. "I . . ." She blinked several times and collapsed towards Will. He caught her and the bottle before either hit the floor. After arranging her on the chaise, he waved the bottle under her nose a few more times to make sure she was out.

Will stowed the bottle away and stood up. Looking down at the pretty woman, he smiled. "Guess ether works on Shifters, too." He turned to the thing that really mattered and approached it with caution.

The Scarab queen was still in her box standing on top of a pole that was supposed to be a staff. He saw that the box was simple to close and, as part of her capture, was probably locked in the dark at all times. The shadows within made her silver and bronze finish dull, lifeless. Even the jewels on her rim looked like paste within the box. He walked around the staff, careful not to knock over any of the set pieces, looking for security, but found none.

Coming back around, he shrugged to himself and reached into the box for her. The Scarab queen came free without resistance. In the scant light inside the tent, he could now see the scarab etching on her bronze plate. It was that much more intricate and beautiful than the etchings on any of the other Scarabs he had seen.

"Let's get you home," he said to her before sliding her into his pouch and slipping out the back of the tent.

Mena walked with her Egyptian warrior, keeping her head down in pretend shyness. He had not bothered to change out of his costume and makeup. Other workers from the Wild West and Mystical Wonders Show gave them a knowing look. Such traveling shows did a brisk trade in the flesh of locals whether or not it was paid for.

"What's your name?" she asked as they reached the back part of the show campground. This part of the campground was quiet despite the festooned wagons that made a half circle around a central firepit. She could imagine the nightly gatherings that happened here.

"They call me Olaf. It's Norse."

"Norse? A Norse name for an Egyptian man?"

"I can be many things, my lovely." He stopped at a large wooden wagon painted with the bright colors of the Wild West show. He opened the door and invited her in.

Once inside, she could see that a couple of people lived in this wagon. She turned to say something to him but he was on her, hungry and passionate, kissing her and his hands exploring where they would. After allowing him to paw her, kissing down her neck, she pulled away. "Whew . . . slow down there. I don't need to be taken like a conquest yet. Let me freshen up."

He chuckled, low in his throat. It was almost a growl of amusement. He bowed his head and moved past her to sit on a bunk, his presumably, while she shifted closer to the door. From her reticule, she pulled a damp handkerchief and dabbed at her throat. Then she turned, allowing him to see her dab at the cleft of her cleavage with it.

"I have a new perfume. Would you like to smell it?" She came close and offered it to him.

He smiled and took a deep whiff of the handkerchief. "It's pungent but I like it. It will smell good on you." He pulled her closer.

Mena laughed, dabbing it up on her cleavage again before pulling it away from her face. She could feel the ether working on her and that was not what she wanted. Playfully, she dabbed it on him—his throat, his face—and he breathed deeply of the ether again, showing no signs of being affected by it. She was wondering if she was going to have to go through with her part of this little ruse when a noise sounded from a jewel on the wall she previously thought was just decoration. That jewel sparkled and flickered with many colors, just like the jewels on the Scarabs.

She stepped back, realizing that she and Will had guessed wrong. The fake Egyptian queen wasn't the alien Shifter; the fake warrior was. And she was in deep trouble if she did not escape now. Mena turned and got two steps towards the wagon door before something hot, strong and pulsing wrapped itself around her throat and lower half of her face. She tried to scream and grab for something to fight the creature, but to no avail. He was just too strong.

Forced to face him, she saw his eyes were pure black and the thing that held her was one of his arms, elongated into a tentacle of boneless flesh. "So," he said. "This is your game. I assumed you were here to rob me like some whore with a bit of ether, but you and your *brother* are so much more, aren't you?" He shook her for emphasis. "I was going to let him rob Jane and eat you, but he's escaped with my prize, hasn't he? Well, not for long."

Mena tried to pull back in revulsion as she saw a lump rising up Olaf's throat. The Shifter opened its mouth to reveal a large, fat bug, black as his eyes and gleaming like oil. Without a word, the bug flew out one of the wagon windows. "I'll have my prize back, and then I'll eat you and the man both."

With that, he picked up the forgotten handkerchief and loosened his hold on her just enough for him to use Mena's own weapon against her.

Will reached the waiting Scarabs and horses. He was unhappy that he had not seen Mena trailing behind. The plan was to drug both of the carnies and get out as quickly as possible. That meant something was wrong. But with the Scarabs hovering around him, waiting to see their queen, he did not leave them in suspense.

As soon as the queen was out of the dark bag, her jewels began to glow with a faint gold light. The larger Scarab, the one who had hired them, hovered nearby.

She is free but she needs the sun.

"You've waited this long. Tomorrow's another day."

No. The situation is still dangerous.

Suddenly, the smaller Scarabs descended upon Will and the queen. As each one alighted upon her in Will's hands, her jewels glowed a little brighter and the small Scarab fell away and all but crashed to the ground in an ill-controlled fall.

"What are they doing?"

They are powering her.

Will looked at the ground, now littered with small Scarab bodies. "Are they dead?" He could not keep the horror out of his voice. In the dying light of setting sun, the Scarab bodies once again looked like teacup saucers abandoned in the sand.

No. Dormant. They will power up with the sun. I ask that you take them with us.

"Sure. As soon as Mena gets here."

Then the queen was hovering on her own and the other Scarabs moved back from her. She made no sound but the lead Scarab approached and the two of them hovered in tandem.

"What's happening?"

The Scarab queen answered. *I am now informed of*

all that has occurred during my captivity. I thank you for
your assistance.

"You're welcome." While the queen had the same
uninflected voice as the other Scarab, the queen's
voice did sound almost female. "I just want Mena to
get back soon."

Mena Scott. She is your queen.

"Yes. She's the queen of my heart and—"

His words were cut off at the sudden flurry of the
still-hovering Scarabs. They surrounded something
in the distance coming closer. He hoped it was Mena,
but by the time he could actually see what it was
they surrounded, he knew it was not his wife-to-be.
"What is it?"

None of the Scarabs answered him. Instead, the
fat black bug issued a series of ear-piercing sounds.
Then it turned and flew away into the night, towards
the faint lights of the now closed Wild West show.

The queen, who remained at Will's side, spoke.
The enemy has captured your queen.

"Mena!" He could not keep the anger or fear out
of his voice.

*It is demanding a prisoner exchange in the largest tent
on the campground when the moon is at its apex.*

Will looked at the Scarab queen, knowing that rescuing her had also been rescuing the planet. But at
this moment, he did not care. He would give the
queen back to make sure his Mena was safe.

If the prisoner exchange does not occur, the human fe-
male, Mena Scott, will be eaten.

He looked at the hovering Scarabs, knowing he

could not force them to give up their queen again. Scowling, he looked at the moon. Hours before it was at its highest point. "I'm not letting that thing hurt her." He turned to his horse and grabbed his holsters.

What will you do, Will Brogan?

"Fight."

We will fight with you.

He looked back at the queen and gave her a grateful nod. "Then let's plan."

Mena woke with the smells of horse shit and ether warring for attention. She turned her head and groaned. Ether left a nasty headache; one she recognized—you have to test a tool before you used it. She opened her eyes and looked around. She was lying on her side in the dirt inside a large tent at the edge of the center ring. The scent of horse shit came from the shovel lying next to her, used to remove the pungent offal after any show with animals.

"You better hope they come soon. I'm hungry and I *will* eat you alive."

She looked forward and saw Olaf standing in the center of the ring. At his feet were at least five score of those horrific black bugs. The light was coming from a couple of smokeless lanterns placed on either side of the ring. She sat up with some effort, still woozy from the effects of the ether, compounded by the fact that her hands were tied.

As she shifted towards the shovel, Olaf turned around and advanced towards her, the carpet of oily blackness moved with him. "You will lie on the ground and do nothing or I will kill you right now." His voice rose to a shout and she threw herself back to the ground, curling up there. She did not have to feign her fear. "When this is done, you'd better pray to your gods that I kill you quickly."

As she hid her face from his distorted features—elongated jaw, too-large eyes and clawed hands—the smell of the shovel told her that she had reached her goal. She waited until the Shifter and his retinue returned to his spot in the center of the ring to risk shifting her wrists onto the shovel's edge.

Will was surprised and a little unnerved at the complete silence of the showground. Whatever hold the Shifter had on these people, he made sure that they were all tucked away in their tents and wagons He took a breath and readied himself with a revolver in one hand and his saddlebag in the other. He stepped through the front flap of the main tent..

Inside it was dark except for a man and blackness in the center of the ring. All of the risers were still in place as if a ghost audience watched what was about to unfold. As he got closer to the ring and its meager light, he saw two things: there was something very wrong with the man and the blackness at his feet was moving.

Then he saw Mena's body lying at the other end of the ring behind the Shifter and cocked his gun.

"She isn't hurt. Just scared," Olaf said. "Have you come to rescue your dear *sister*?"

Will saw her faint movement and his heart was glad. *Just let me get her out alive,* he prayed.

"You demanded the exchange." He lifted up the saddlebag.

"Toss the queen here. It's fine if she bounces. She's made of stern stuff."

He did and everything seemed to happen at once. As soon as the saddlebag hit the ground in the middle of the sea of black bugs, a dozen Scarabs exploded from it and started shooting bursts of light in all directions. As random as the bursts seemed, each one hit a cluster of bugs, some still on the ground and most flying. Every bug hit stopped moving, lying where they were or falling out of the air.

In the middle was the Scarab who had hired Mena and Scott. That Scarab flew at Olaf, firing light bursts, one after another. Through the haze of black wings and light bursts, Will aimed his revolver and fired two shots. Both struck, but only one struck true, taking out one of the Shifter's eyes. The other one grazed his forehead.

"My turn," Olaf said and whipped an impossibly long tentacle at Will. It would have struck if another Scarab hadn't thrown itself in the way of the weapon. Will dodged left and then right. Every tentacle whipped out at him ended with a Scarab embedded in it that then exploded like a small stick of dynamite.

The next two shots Will took were to Olaf's chest. These shots were accompanied by much larger bursts of light from the Scarab queen who came out from hiding. Olaf roared at the sight of her and turned his attacks that way, while shrugging off the wounds the bullets made in his flesh. More Scarabs sacrificed themselves to protect their queen and Will knew he had only two shots left to hit the brain in the chest of the monster or to blind it. He decided to go for the kill and fired.

Both shots hit but did nothing to slow the Shifter down.

The Shifter's tentacles captured the Scarab queen and it roared again in triumph. By this time, it could barely be called a man. Opening its mouth to a pro-digious size, it looked as if it was about to swallow the Scarab queen whole when it suddenly stilled, with its chest area pushed forward and a surprised look of real pain on its face. As its tentacles let go of the queen, it looked down with its remaining eye and saw the slim edge of metal poking out of its chest.

"My turn," Mena said and gave another hard thrust on the shovel she had used to penetrate the Shifter. Half of the shovel head came out the front of its chest. What was left of the creature's face col-lapsed, and the body fell over as Mena released the shovel. Will and Mena watched in disgust as the Shifter disintegrated into a noxious goo.

We need to leave, the queen said. She only had eight Scarabs left. All of them hovered in a protective pat-tern around her.

Mena ran to Will, who kissed her once, hard and glad, before turning and leaving with the Scarabs.

As the sun rose over their small camp, the Scarabs that had sacrificed their energy for their queen and those who went into battle began to glow in the morning's light. Soon they were hovering about the queen while Mena and Will sat close together.

"I'm sorry to see that your lead guy didn't make it," Will said.

He will be rebuilt. His core programming has been saved.

"Will we have to deal with any more Shifters?" Mena asked.

After a pause, the queen spoke. *I do not believe so. There are no records of other Shifters on this planet. We will investigate further as a matter of caution.*

They watched as the Scarabs formed up into orderly lines. The queen spoke again. *Will Brogan, lay your coat on the ground.*

Mena and Will looked at each other. She shrugged as Will pulled his duster from his saddle and laid it out on the ground with the lining towards the sky.

Mena Scott and Will Brogan, you were offered gold as payment for rescuing me. We do not have the gold we promised but we know where it is.

The queen then flashed a bright light onto the lining of the coat. When they blinked the spots out of their eyes, they could see that some sort of map had been drawn there.

There should be a sufficient amount of gold at this location for your needs. We thank you. If our paths cross again, may they be in good times.

With that, the Scarab queen rose high in the sky

and moved faster than the eye could follow towards the rising sun. The rest of the Scarabs followed, twinkling briefly before they disappeared.

"Well, I'll be . . . it's a treasure map," Will said, as he knelt to examine his coat.

"No one's going to believe this."

"They don't have to."

Mena smiled at him, "I guess another adventure or two can't hurt before we find our homestead."

Will stood and pulled her to him. "Not as long as I'm with you. That's homestead enough for me."

THE CLOCKWORK COWBOY

J. Steven York

It was a Texas scorcher in Calliope Springs, and the main street was all but empty. The place looked dry and dead, like the whole town just might snap off at the roots and blow away. The wind whipped through town in little gusts that sent clouds of dust in the air, covering everything with a fine layer.

Every time I moved, I could feel the grit grinding at the metal in my joints, and I had to keep wiping my glass eyes clean with the corner of my bandanna. That's why I'd rode into town, to pick up a can of grease at the mercantile for my old clockwork warhorse Piston and me.

I heard my friend Rusty well before I saw him, clumping his way slowly up the boardwalk behind me, one heavy step after another. Rusty is a winderman, and he's built like a pot-belly stove, all cast-iron, legs like steam-engine push-rods, and an oversized-chest nearly as wide as a man's spread arms just to house his enormous main-spring. Like most winder-men, he isn't too bright, but he's got a good governor in him, and I'm not much of one for small-talk anyway.

"Hey Rusty, how's it going at the mill?"

Rusty stopped and turned his head slowly towards me, looking at me with big glass eyes for a while before answering. I could hear the Greek gears in his head spinning, trying to put a sentence together. He reminded me of an old tortoise when he did that. Slow, but none too concerned about it.

"Not good, Liberty. Not good at all. The river is down to a trickle, and the wheel, she's barely a-turning."

They call me Liberty Brass, because brass is what my head is made out of, and there's a crack along the right side of my face where a cannonball grazed me in the War. I nodded that sorry excuse for a head at Rusty. "Sorry to hear that. I saw some clouds out over the hills yesterday. Hoped their might be some rain up there."

Rusty tilted his head a little, and his neck made a noise like a hinge that needs oil. "Ain't just the rain, Liberty. It's the Black Oak ranch upstream. They've gone and dammed up the river!"

You might think it strange that a town of clockwork men would run on water and that getting our metal hides as far away from that rust-producing stuff as we could would be the best thing for us, but that just ain't the case. If a clockwork man doesn't like rust, there's one thing he likes even less: *winding down.*

It was that winding that made us beholden to the folks that built us and the folks that bought us. But there are other ways to wind an automaton than the hand of man: with the powers of steam, and wind, and yes, water; and for those of us who have chosen to flee the world of flesh-men and their misadventures, that is a godsend.

So it should hardly be a surprise that when a band of freematons led by the famous dance-hall steamman Calliope Jones headed west into Texas about 1855 they should set up camp in the remains of an old grist mill and simply never leave, rebuilding the mill for their own purposes. Jones broke down a few years later, as steam-men often do, but his rusting bones are propped up on a hill overlooking the town of Calliope Springs. They say at night sometimes, when the wind blows just right, you can still hear his pipes sing its praises.

But I didn't come to the place until much later, until after I walked away from Gettysburg. It was there I had learned of Lincoln's Second Emancipation Proclamation, which set free us automatons forced to serve the South, in word if not necessarily in fact. I had seen enough killing, and I was already across the Mason-Dixon long before the War finished winding down.

Me and Piston headed north for a while, ending up in Chicago where I worked in the stockyards and learned a little about cattle. Then we rode west on an empty stock train to St. Louis, then south to Texas. We worked a herd or two, but clockwork men weren't welcome most places, and we kept moving on and on.

Until we found Calliope Springs, anyway.

Here we fit in. Calliope Springs might not have been the most prosperous of towns, built as it was on the grave of an earlier town, failed and abandoned during the Indian wars. But it was a home for cast-off toys like me. Not just clockwork and steam men, but a few freemen, Chinamen, "fallen women," and other flesh-and-bone people who were shunned most everywhere else.

I didn't mind hard work, long as I could keep my spring wound, and worked odd jobs and as a round-up hand at some of the local ranches saving every penny I could. I was able to buy up a piece of land to start a small ranch of my own, if you could call it that. I had a shack just big enough to keep the rain off, a small barn, and a herd of cattle just big enough to be called a herd. It weren't much, but it gave me pleasure and provided enough to keep me and Piston's springs wound and our joints oiled.

Thinking of that, I reached into the coin purse hanging around my neck and fished out a bit of silver. "How about a wind, Rusty? I'm running a little low."

Rusty looked both ways up and down the street. "Don't know if I should, Liberty. With the mill being like it is, it's hard for us just to keep ourselves wound."

"Come on, Rusty. For a friend?"

"Well, I guess so."

He came over close to the warhorse, hoping maybe nobody would see us and demand to be wound too. I turned around. My winder is a round recess behind my right shoulder, with a lift-up key that couldn't be lost.

Rusty grabbed the key with his right hand, and there was a clunk as the gears connected his wrist directly to his mainspring. There was a whirring noise as his hand spun, doing in seconds a wind that would have taken a flesh-and-blood man twenty minutes to do.

As he did, I heard horses and a wagon come around the corner off the Hill Road. I heard them pull up behind us, and I heard a man laugh. "Well ain't that fine, boys? We come up on a couple of clock-men screwing each other right out in the street!"

My winding finished, I turned to find the man talking. He stood tall in the front of a fine black carriage, the reins still hanging from one hand. He was tall, with a pointed nose, long hair the color of a silver dollar, and a neatly trimmed beard to match. Though there is a saying among clockwork-men that all flesh-men look alike, he seemed familiar to me, and I knew I had seen him somewhere before.

Next to him sat a broad-shouldered cowboy with a carbine resting casually across his lap. Two other rough-looking cowboys rode along on horseback. But it was the final member of the party who drew all eyes to him.

He was a steam-man, tall and painted black as night, astride the biggest, blackest plow-horse I've ever seen, who still seemed weary under the big automaton's weight.

The day of steam-men was long past and most had fallen into disrepair, but this one was painted, polished and oiled so he looked brand-new. His arms made Rusty's look like tooth-picks, and his glass eyes glinted down at me, dark and evil, a dim orange glow behind them, like his firebox was connected right up to his head.

Without taking those dangerous-looking eyes off me, he reached back to a saddlebag, pulled up a hunk of coal as big as a man's head, and casually shoved it through the firebox door in his chest. A puff of black smoke rolled out of the smokestack on his right shoulder, and steam hissed from a valve on his right side.

As he slammed the firebox door closed, I saw there was an iron name-plate on it: MOGUL. I had heard there was a big locomotive by that name up north, and wondered if that was where the name had come from. If so, it fit.

Up and down the street doors and curtains were pulled open a smidge, and both people and automatons cautiously peered out to see what the ruckus was. A few of the braver souls and soulless actually stepped outside to get a better look.

A door creaked open behind me, and Ben Jackson stepped out of his metalsmith shop. Ben had been a slave in Georgia, and like me came west looking for a better life. Now he was book-studying to become a full-fledged gearsmith, something the town needed almost as bad as water.

"Get on out here!" shouted the man in the carriage. "I got something for all of you to hear!"

More folks began to wander into the street. Some leaned out of windows or stood on balconies.

"My name is Winston Hudd, and I own the Black Oak Ranch upstream. You may have noticed that I've built a dam across *my* river to secure *my* water rights."

There was murmuring from the street. Inside my head, my governor started to whine and rattle as it did when I got riled. It had never been right since that cannonball, and I could feel it heating up behind my right eye as it thrashed around, trying to find some kind of balance.

"I also know that you folks—have been used to sucking hind-tit off my water these many years, but those days are over. You want *my* water, you're going to have to pay for it—a thousand dollars for every foot I let my slip gates down. No money, no water!"

"He cain't do that!" said Ben.

"Reckon he already did," I said, trying to be calm, but just thinking about it made my head rattle.

"Well, somebody should stand up to him!"

I was grinding my gears for an answer when Ben stepped forward into the street, too fast for me to stop.

He walked right up to the wagon, the rifleman looming over him. "That river belongs to Calliope Springs just as much as it does to you!"

The man with the rifle jumped down from the carriage and slammed the butt of it against Ben's face, sending him falling backwards into the dust.

"Show some respect, you filthy niggra!" said the rifleman. He spat into the dust next to where Ben lay, then looked at the faces watching him up and down the street. "Ain't none of the lot of you worth licking Mr. Hudd's boots!"

Behind him, the other cowboys casually pulled out and cocked their irons, aiming them at the sky, but clearly ready to use them if need be.

I ran over and went down on one knee next to Ben. Blood ran from a crack along his left cheek that was near a mirror to mine, and his eyes looked off at the sky like he had forgot where he was for a minute. "Ben, you okay?"

His eyes twitched, then looked at me for a minute like I had just showed up. "Liberty? Yeah, I . . ." He tried to sit up, and just as quickly fell back down.

I took off my bandanna and gave it to him to wipe the blood. "You stay put," I said, and stood to face the man on the wagon, my governor buzzing in my head like an angry hornet.

I stood and stepped up next to the carriage. The rifleman stepped away, startled by the suddenness of my movement. The other men with the guns watched closely, but did nothing. They figured they had no reason to fear me or what I'd do to their boss.

He looked down at me, his eyes narrowed against the glare of the sun shining off my polished head. "What do you want, tin man?"

"Seems to me," I said, "you're stirring yourself up a big pot of trouble here. There's five of you, and a whole town of us."

He laughed. "'Cept for you and your *boy* here, I don't see nobody stepping up. And besides, you and most of this town is nothing but *tin-men*. That whirl-a-gig in your heads won't let you hurt me and my boys, and ain't a one of you my machine, Mogul, couldn't rip in half." He laughed again. "You ain't worth the trouble of a real man to fill you full of holes like an old can!"

And he was mostly right about that. Every clock-work man was built with a governor attached to his Greek gears so that he couldn't harm a flesh-and-bone man, no matter how much he tried or how bad he wanted to.

But it was just then, having seen him closer, that I remembered where I had seen him before: at the county auction where I had bought my spread. He had run the price up on me considerable, and had come near to beating me out. He had been a sore loser about it, too.

Later I heard tell I had been lucky in that he had lost a good deal of his cash money earlier in the day in a card game, and had been caught up short.

I wondered if Hudd recognized me. I'm right conspicuous, with my cracked face and my right arm all patched together on the battlefield with spare parts from other clockwork men. But it didn't seem that he did, clockwork men seeming to be mostly beneath his notice.

That meant I knew more about him than he did about me.

That set my gears to spinning, and gave me an idea.

"If it's gonna be me against your steam-man, then let's make it count for something. Are you a betting man, Hudd?"

He chuckled. "You want to wager on a fight between you and Mogul? Now that's a bet I'd be a fool not to take! What do you mean to bet?"

"It's me against him, one on one. I take him down, you tear down your dam and share the river like always."

"That's a big wager, tin man."

"You said yourself, how can you pass on odds like these?"

"And if my Mogul wins?"

"You get your water money."

"Seems to me like I get that already!"

"That remains to be seen. And anyhow, I'll sweeten the pot, and throw in the deed to my ranch, the Walking C, and everything on it. Livestock too. Seeing as how you lost *that* one already, you might want a chance to win it back."

His grin turned to a suspicious frown. It's hard for clockwork man to read a flesh-man's expressions, but I had learned much during and after my time in the War, and I believe I have come into a deeper understanding of many of the emotions they convey. He remembered me now, but still he studied me, looking for something else.

"I seen your like in my days with the Confederacy. You're an artilleryman, ain't ya? Got them special gears for aiming? Them gears that don't miss."

Which was true. A clockwork man's governor won't let him fire a cannon, but he can tote shells, load and aim just fine, long as a flesh-and-blood man pulls the firing cord. It wasn't what I was, but it was what I was built for.

He continued, "I reckon those might work with a pistol as well as a field-gun. That your plan? Hope to stand back and take out my steam-man's vitals 'fore he ever gets near you?"

"You're too smart for me, Boss. I was thinking that way, but you got me now. We'll do this bare-handed."

His suspicion was gone. He threw back his head and laughed. "You still want this? I swear, that crack in your head has done scrambled your gears and made you loco! But I ain't one to turn down free entertainment. When and where?"

"Here and now is as good as any."

He laughed again. "Make it tomorrow, noon, at that quarry south of town. I'm gonna give all my hands the day off so's they can come watch Mogul pull your arms and legs off!"

"Liberty has a plan!" said Rusty, faithfully.

"And I tell you, I don't," I said, looking down at my cobbled-together right arm as Ben tinkered with it.

The arm had never worked entirely right since it had been put back together just before Gettysburg, but Ben swore he knew enough to fix it now. "It just came to my mind, and I just up and said it. Figured if he was gonna kill off the town, I had nothing to lose. At least this way, we have a chance."

"Even the town ain't worth getting torn apart over," said Ben.

"For you maybe, Ben. Lots of places a freedman can go. But for us clockwork men, ain't never been a town like Calliope Springs, and there might never be its likes again."

I had seen so many things in the War. I had never understood why men volunteered to give up their lives for a place, for an idea. Just then, I thought I finally understood.

"Hold the lantern closer, Rusty. I need to see up inside here." Ben took the magnifying lens out of his good eye, the other one nearly swollen shut and partially covered by the bandages that wrapped his head, and looked up at me. "Why did you go and do it, Liberty? Why did you call them out like that?"

I looked back at him. "Why did you? I was only walking in your footsteps, friend."

He thought for a moment. "Somebody had to. Nobody else was stepping up, and I didn't see how no clockwork man could do it at all. I guess I was wrong on that."

"Maybe," I said, still wondering why I had done what I'd done, even though my gears gave me no doubt that I was doing the right thing. "In the retreat, after Gettysburg, we had lost our cannon and our horses, nothing but four run-down clockwork men and our commanding officer who was near to insane with anger at our losses. And on a road we passed some infantrymen with four Negroes as their prisoners, a man and a woman and their two children.

"The soldiers said they were escaped slaves and they were taking them back to our lines. They complained that the children were slowing them down, and my commander got a wild look in his eye that I didn't understand at the time. He just had all that anger left over from the battle and from the losing of it. All that anger just buzzing around, looking for a place to light.

"He struck them down with the butt of his rifle, like Hudd did to you, right with their ma and pa watching. But then he put his bayonet into them to finish them off, and kicked them, still twitching, into the ditch."

Everybody was quiet for a while. "No offense to you, Ben . . . Your courage goes without saying. But I don't take to see the strong prey on the weak."

He sighed and went back to the arm. "No offense taken, Liberty."

There wasn't much to say after that.

When it came time to ride out, I found that Ben and Rusty had spent the morning polishing up my old war-horse so his steel hide and his brass and copper fittings gleamed in the sun. I would have liked to set him running, to tear on out to meet my destiny, but instead we walked slowly, leading a parade consisting of most of the population of Calliope Springs.

The limestone quarry was cut into a hillside about a mile out of town. It had been abandoned early on, and was little more than a smooth notch into the hillside, still cluttered with abandoned pieces of mottled gray stone.

Despite what I'd told Rusty, truth be told, I had a bit of a plan. Or at least, a hope.

I was faster than the steam-man, and without being modest, smarter. Ben was no steam-smith, but he had done some reading on steam-men, and put me on to some of their weak spots: coils, tubes, valves and such where I might do him harm with something short of a cannon-shot.

But to make it work, I'd have to get close, and that would be near to suicide.

Hudd and about twenty of his men were already waiting there on horseback, spread out in a loose half-circle with the quarry walls to their back. I couldn't help but notice that they were all packing, and most carried rifles. They didn't look like they were out just for a day of friendly sport.

Mogul stood near the center of the quarry next to that big plowhorse of his. He was busy stoking his firebox 'til his chest looked nearly red hot, clouds of black smoke coming off his stack, steam and scalding water escaping from every valve and joint.

I stopped about ten yards away and climbed down off Piston.

Mogul turned towards me, and removed a huge holster from where it hung from a bolt on his hip. In it was basically a small field gun with a steel stock attached. He hung it on his saddle, and turned to face me. I had never heard him speak, and his voice was like a chord of the low notes on a pipe organ. "Let's do this," he said.

"Last tin-man standing and in one piece!" shouted Hudd from behind him. "Fight!"

The clockwork folk mostly looked on silently, while some of the flesh-townsfolk shouted and cheered encouragement. Only Hudd's men seemed truly excited by the event, whooping and whistling and eager to watch hot-oil spurt.

Mogul moved towards me like somebody had flipped a lever, and I waited till he was almost at me to dash to one side and run behind him. There was a grate on his back with a coil underneath that. Ben called it a condenser, and said it could be holed with a sharp blow or a good poke. I tried to go for it, but Mogul was already spinning around.

I just managed to duck under his arm. As I did, I tried to strike at an exposed valve there, but I was too far to reach and had to back away.

Hudd's men booed and jeered.

"You can take him, Liberty!" I heard Ben shout.

I rushed him again, going for some exposed tubing under his firebox, but his massive head of steam made him faster than I expected.

An arm like a derrick slammed across my chest, denting in my chest-plate and sending me flying.

I landed ten feet away, my body ringing against the hard stone like the bell I was named for. Another blow like that, and it would be as cracked as my head.

I tried to get up, and found the problem with our makeshift coliseum. The stone gave my metal hands and feet little purchase, and I was having trouble getting up.

Mogul pivoted and began moving towards me like a train leaving the station, slowly building up speed.

I tried to get up again, and fell back.

Mogul could have run right over me, but he stopped just short, and turned to look at a slab of limestone there that must have weighed half a ton.

He picked it up like it was nothing, raised it over his head, and stood over me, blotting out the sun.

His arms started to swing down with his mighty load.

My left foot caught in a crack in the rock, and I was able to get enough leverage to stagger up into a wobbly run. I just got out of the way before the slab hit the ground and split right down the middle.

I realized something was in my left hand.

I had come up with a hand-full of small rocks, little more than pebbles. We had said bare-handed, but if Mogul could throw rocks, then I reckoned it opened the way for me to do the same.

I am not strong, not in the way that Mogul was strong, but springs are fast, and I have an artillery-man's gears in my head. On a good day, I can throw a small rock like a musket-ball, and *I never miss*.

Mogul turned towards me, and I let off a throw that cracked against the tubing I'd aimed for earlier, letting out a little jet of steam.

Mogul didn't seem to notice, so I put the next one right into his left eye, shattering the lens full of spider-cracks.

Ben had done a right fine job of fixing my arm.

He whistled in anger, a sound that was part train, part devil. But I was already taking off at a right angle again, forcing him to turn.

He was slow at turning. I couldn't give him a chance to get going in a straight line, where he could built up speed.

Snap!

Another rock hit that valve under his arm.

Mogul turned to protect himself, and I put another two more straight through the grate on his back. Steam and water started to spew out.

Hudd's men's cheers and calls fell silent, unable to believe what they were seeing.

Mogul backed away, and I scooped up a rock the size of my hand off the ground.

Snap!

His other eye shattered completely, smoke curling up from the empty socket.

The big steam-man staggered blindly, turning in circles for a while until the valve I'd jammed with my rock built up too much pressure. Something in him just burst, and with a screaming whistle, he vanished in a cloud of his own steam.

He was gone for a moment before the steam lifted just enough for me to see him falling to the quarry floor, a sputtering wreck.

It was a while before Hudd found his voice. "You cheated, you tin-traitor!"

"Not near as much as Mogul did, " I said. "And I'll just bet you were the one what told him to do it!"

Hudd looked at what was left of Mogul and laughed bitterly. "Damned thing was more trouble than he was worth anyways! Anyhow, don't matter none," he raised his voice to a shout. "I never intended to give you any water anyway. I figured I'll just wait 'til enough of you are wound down, and then my boys will ride in and burn the whole place! By next spring, I'll be grazing my cows over your ashes!"

Inside my head, my governor whined and growled until I could feel it heating up from the friction.

Hudd pointed at me. *"Take him down, boys!"*

Suddenly all his men were going for their iron, but I was already moving.

The bullets flew around me, and one grazed off my shoulder, but I was moving towards Hudd fast and they had to hold their fire. He pulled his Colt Paterson and got off a wild shot that came nowhere near me.

Before he could get off another one, my hands were on him. In one move I had yanked him out of his saddle, had my left arm around his neck, and his pistol in my hand.

I pushed the nose of the Colt hard against his right temple. He flinched as I cocked the hammer.

"Tell your men to drop their arms and ride out!"

Hudd coughed and managed a laugh. "You won't hurt me, tin man! You *can't!*"

I tightened my grip on his neck, moved the barrel of the gun just a little and squeezed the trigger.

Half of Hudd's ear vanished in a spray of red.

He started to scream.

I recocked the gun and put it back to his temple. "You said this crack in my head made me loco, and you was right, Hudd! Cocked up my governor but good. I've already killed one man that deserved it, a heartless southern bastard not much different than you! Second time should be easier . . ."

He moaned in terror. "Drop your guns!" he screamed. "Get out of here! He means to kill me!"

They were slow about it, unable to believe that an automaton could hurt a flesh-man. But one by one the cowboys lay down their guns, turned, and rode away.

The townsfolk just looked on in quiet horror at me, my face splattered with blood, and my terrified prisoner.

Hudd looked up at me, his eyes wild. "You won't get away with it, you tin monster! You can't stay here now that your secret is out. They'll hunt you down! Every right-thinking man in Texas will ride out and hunt you down! I can wait! Even if you kill me, I got a son, and he and my boys will be back when you're gone, to finish off this town!"

"You're right, I can't stay. But you'll leave this town be, and you'll tear that dam of yours down, and I'll tell you why.

"If I hear of any harm coming to Calliope Springs or its people, if I hear you mess with the water supply in any way, I'll be back for you, and you'll never see me coming.

"You do it, and you'll spend the rest of your short, sorry life looking at every tree, every rock, every hill, every building, wondering if you're going to die. 'Cause I got a Kentucky long rifle that will take the wings off a fly at 500 yards—and I *never* miss!" I kicked him loose, so he landed in a heap at my feet.

He looked at me, eyes wide and crazy, but he said nothing as he climbed on his horse and rode off, looking back over his shoulder the whole way, till he was lost in the trees beyond the quarry.

I left my spread to Rusty, who promised to pay market value for my stock when he had the money. He said I should send him a telegram from wherever I ended up. I packed up the few things I had left in my saddle bags, mounted up old Piston and headed west.

I thought of the way Rusty and Ben and the rest had looked at me after the fight, not as their rescuer and benefactor, but as something to be feared, or at best, pitied.

I knew that there was no way I could have stayed, even if I hadn't made myself a hunted automaton. As I thought this over, my governor moaned slightly, and I looked down at my hands.

I thought of my commanding officer laying dead, his neck snapped, along that blood-spattered battlefield road. I remembered his body lying in a ditch next to two small graves I had dug with my own hands.

I thought of him and I wondered if he had always been a monster, or if, like me, he had ended up scarred and broken by the madness of war.

I rode west, thinking about the fight, and wondering who had won, and who had truly lost.

BLACK TRAIN

Jeff Mariotte

On the third day out, the cat had turned away from the high country.

The men had been expecting him—for they believed it to be a male cat, a mountain lion with tracks bigger than any Evan had ever seen—to head for the rocky upper reaches of the Chiricahuas. Instead, he had skirted the edge of the range and then struck westward.

There were two men on the cat's trail. There had been three, but the third, a hand from the Sierra Bonita, had been summoned home because of a family illness, one of his sons riding out with the news.

"You'd think Hooker would have sent another hand to help out," Charlie said when they were gone. "Bonita's the biggest spread in the territory."

"Might be why." Evan was watching the men ride south, the late afternoon sun rimming them with golden light. "You and me, we can't spare the beeves. Hooker loses ten or fifteen to this damn cat, he barely feels it."

"Reckon it's just us, then."

Evan hadn't answered. There was nothing to be said to something so obvious, and Evan was a man who had never been much for talking except when it was necessary. Lucinda complained about that sometimes. Since they had wed, she seemed not to lack for things to complain about. She was a fine wife otherwise, fair of skin, helpful around the ranch, and not much afraid of Indians since Geronimo's surrender two years ago.

The men stopped for the night in a canyon, which provided shelter from the chill late-winter wind and plenty of downed mesquite branches for the fire. They cooked up three rabbits they had taken that afternoon, and as Evan sat eating his, burned skin flaking under his fingers, meat falling off the bone, fat sizzling fragrantly on the flames, he watched glowing sparks drifting skyward. He didn't believe it to be true, but at that moment it wouldn't have taken much to convince him that all the stars above were nothing more than sparks from every fire ever lit on Earth, trapped in the sky.

"We'll get him tomorrow," Charlie said.

"Could be."

"We're closer."

"He's probably not stopping for the night."

"We have to."

"I know. Just saying he's not."

"He has to sleep sometime."

Charlie unscrewed the lid of a flask and took a couple of swallows. Lucinda had said that he drank. Everybody drank sometimes, just about, but Charlie did it too much, and when he did he got mean.

Charlie and Lucinda had never been church-wed, the way Evan and Lucinda were, but they had been together just the same, common law, for a few years. Lucinda's father had died suddenly. She had needed a man, she said, or else would have had to go to St. Joe and live with a maiden aunt whom she despised. Or take up whoring. She had settled for Charlie, who was tall and handsome and had a good-sized ranch that bordered on Evan's. Then she and Evan had fallen in love, and she had moved from one ranch to the next.

Charlie had lost four head to the cat over the past two weeks, Evan six.

There was something wrong with the animal, Evan thought. He didn't eat much of the cattle he killed. He didn't act like a lion should. Maybe he was sick. Either way, he had to be killed, and he was leading Evan and Charlie a merry hell of a chase.

While Charlie stared at his flask, Evan looked at Charlie, at the curve of the back of his head, and wondered what it would look like with a bullet in it.

He would have to do it tonight or tomorrow. He could take the cat himself, he wasn't worried about that. But if they did catch it tomorrow then he would lose his last, best chance to get it done out here, where no one would witness it. A hunting accident, that's what he had decided.

He thought: probably Charlie is thinking the same thing about me.

That night, he hardly slept.

The next morning, they saw the train.

The winter had been a dry one, and the grasslands they crossed were a dull gray color. The wind had subsided during the night, but the morning air was cold and brittle. Evan rode with his barn coat buttoned all the way up, his hat tugged down as far as it would go on his head.

The cat had turned north, as if making for the Sierra Bonita again. Evan and Charlie followed, and when they started down off a swell toward the valley through which the tracks rain, the train was sitting there. They expected it to start up again, but it didn't. No smoke issued from it, or sound.

As they got nearer, Charlie said, "It looks burned."

He was right.

The train couldn't have been there for more than a day or two. Others would have come along, stacked up behind it or pushed it out of the way. There were no side tracks here to park it on. Its sides were coated with black, like scorch marks. There were some passenger cars, and the black licked up from the windows; the freight cars behind those were covered in it. At the front of the locomotive a couple of American flags were mounted; the black even coated most of those, just a few stars and a couple of stripes visible at the top.

But if flags had burned, they would not still be flag-shaped, Evan thought. They would be in tatters.

"Something's not right," he said. "I don't think there was a fire."

"Well, it's black. Something happened."

"Something," Evan said.

They rode closer. The black still looked like the streaks made by fire, and yet it didn't. The edges of things were softer, blurred somehow. Fire hadn't done that.

Evan counted nine cars plus the engine and the coal tender. Four were passenger cars, lined up behind the locomotive, boxcars behind those. The train just ended with the last boxcar. It looked unfinished, like a sentence begun but then forgotten halfway through.

The men rode even closer, right up to the train, and around it. The cat had come this way, too; they saw his tracks approach it, then he had gone underneath. For the moment, they didn't look for the trail to continue on the other side. Instead, they looked at the black coating the train. It was some kind of black fuzz, as if the train had skipped shaving for days on end.

Trains, however, did not shave.

"What do you think?" Charlie asked.

"It looks like mold."

"What I thought too. But I've never seen so much."

"No." Evan dismounted, tied Goldie to a yucca far enough from the train that Goldie wouldn't be drawn to it. She put her head down and munched on grass, content. One of the tall yucca stalks had fallen, and Evan picked it up. It was about seven feet long, thick as a man's wrist at the end that grew from the plant, thin and branching out into twigs that held seed pods at the other end. He raked his hand across the thin end, breaking off the twigs and pods. Holding it by the thick end, he scraped the other against the train.

It left a red mark, the color of the boxcar's paint, where it touched. He scraped away more of the black fuzz. Some of it clung to the end of the stalk, but the rest just fell to the gravel patch beside the tracks.

"I don't like the way it smells," Charlie said. He had tied his mount by Evan's. "It's sour. Tart. Like mildew."

Evan hadn't known how to describe it, but Charlie's words were true enough. He dropped the yucca stalk and went to one of the passenger cars. Black mold carpeted the stairs, but he figured it wouldn't hurt the soles of his boots. He stepped up, careful not to touch anything with his hands.

A moment later, he stepped down again. "Charlie . . ."

"Yeah?"

"You ought to take a look."

"At what?"

Evan had to spit. Bile had risen up inside his throat. "There're soldiers inside."

"Soldiers?"

Evan jumped down to the ground and got three

steps from the train before he lurched forward, bent over double, retching until his gut was empty.

When he looked back, Charlie was stepping down from the car. His face had a greenish tint to it. "What in the hell happened here?" he asked.

Evan knew he had to look again. Someone had to. If any of those soldiers were still alive, they needed help. He forced himself up the steps again, back into the car.

They were in seats. One soldier had his head thrown back, mouth open. Black fuzz came from inside his mouth, or had traveled down into it. It linked mouth and nose in bushy trails of black. It climbed his cheeks, grew thick in his eye sockets. The man's hair, reddish brown and cut short, was hardly touched. But the stuff went into his ears, and down his neck and under his shirt.

And they were on the floor. A soldier had one arm thrown out in front of him, the other at his side, as if he were swimming. The spaces between his fingers were covered in it, and the floor on which he lay. It coated his arms and disappeared into his sleeves and came out again at the collar, and like the other one, had entered and become thicker, more lush, in his eyes and ears and mouth and nose. The soldier's shirttail had pulled out from his trousers, and it was there too, in the gap, extending up his spine and down toward his buttocks.

Evan counted the men in the train and got nineteen. One, in the seat closest to the back, to the boxcars, he had to simply assume had been human, because he had been entirely covered in the stuff, the way a stone sitting near a creek can become encased in moss.

Outside, Charlie gave a squeaky whimper. Then: "Evan!"

Evan turned and started for the stairs, accidentally forgetting himself for an instant and touching the corner of a seat. His bare hand felt the soft, furry growth, and he swore and spat again and wiped it on his trousers. Charlie called him again. "I'm coming!" Evan shouted.

He clattered down the stairs, hearing something else, muffled cries from somewhere down the line, back in the boxcars. Outside, he found Charlie dragging his Henry rifle from a saddle scabbard. Charlie stared at a soldier who had evidently come down from one of the other passenger cars. He, too, was covered in the mold: face, neck, hands. It came down from his pants legs and covered his boots, outside and likely in as well. A shock of blond hair was visible above the black, but there was no flesh showing anywhere.

But he was walking. His mouth moved, and his hands were held out in front of him, reaching.

Reaching for Charlie, who raised the rifle.

"Charlie, don't!" Evan cried.

Charlie settled the stock against his shoulder and fired. The bullet slammed into the soldier, staggering him, but not knocking him down. Charlie fired again, with a similar result. The smell of gunpowder wafted through the air, a light gray cloud that Evan sucked in

greedily, since for the moment it blocked the stink of
mold.

"Evan, hell—" Charlie said.

The soldier was still reaching for him, closer now.
Evan wore an old Remington .44 Army when he was
hunting, mostly for rattlers and the like, and he drew
it. For an instant, he hesitated and remembered.

When Charlie had come to collect him for this
trip, Evan had been out in the barn, saddling Goldie
and stowing his gear. Leading her back to the house,
he had come upon Charlie and Lucinda, standing
close. She dropped her hand to her side, and Evan
couldn't tell, but it might have been touching Charlie. When she bade him farewell, there was a distant
coolness to her kiss, and she couldn't meet his eyes
for long.

She had been with Charlie before, and swore it
was over when she took up with Evan. But was it?
Did such a flame ever die out, or did it remain a
spark that could be kindled, under the right circum-
stance, to blossom as fire once again?

"Evan, for God's sake!" Charlie had turned the
Henry around in his hands, ready to use it as a club.
Motion from another car caught Evan's attention,
and another soldier, almost invisible inside his cas-
ing of black fuzz, climbed down the stairs.

Evan took aim at the first soldier's right knee,
thumbed back the Remington's hammer, and fired.
Black fuzz and flesh and blood and bone flew and
the soldier went down, not making a sound but continuing to writhe and reach on the ground. Then

Evan trained the revolver on the new soldier and fired again, hitting this one in the upper thigh. Another shot, also to the knee, dropped that one. Both soldiers writhed on the ground, clutching at the earth with blackened hands, but with their knees blown out they could not rise.

"What the hell is it, Evan?" Charlie asked. His eyes were huge and liquid, and ribbons of spit joined his teeth. "What is it?"

"The hell should I know," Evan said. "Listen."

He heard it again, the cries coming from a boxcar. The soldiers hadn't made a sound. "Back there. Someone's alive." Saying it, he realized what he meant—that the soldiers weren't alive, despite the fact that they were up and moving around.

Another came from the first passenger car he had looked in. He recognized this one, the auburn-haired soldier who had been sitting up in a seat with his head tilted back. He didn't even wait for the soldier to get to the stairs, but shot him in the knee. When the soldier lurched forward and tumbled out, he went as close as he dared and shot the blackened figure in the head. The soldier pawed at the earth a few times, then was still.

"The brain," Evan said. "We got to get their brains."

Charlie had rushed back to his horse and was grabbing ammunition from a saddlebag, fumbling it into the rifle with shaking hands. "Evan, let's get out of here," he said. "Let's just ride for all we're worth."

"There's someone alive in there," Evan reminded him. "We got to help him."

"Oh, Jesus God," Charlie said. He was near panic. Bits of white foam flecked the corners of his mouth and glistened on his chin. Another soldier stepped awkwardly down from a passenger car, and Evan fired a single shot into his head. He flopped backward and was still.

"Hello!" Evan called. He went to the boxcars. "Where are you?"

"In here!" a voice returned.

"Keep calling!" Evan said.

The man in the boxcar did as he was told. Evan listened, and determined that the man was in the second of the five boxcars. He picked up a rock to hit the latch with, so he didn't have to touch it with his hands. When it was released, he used the rock to push open the door.

Inside the car, there was little of the black mold, just a faint coating on the walls. Toward the front of the car was cargo of some kind, wooden cases stacked and tied in place. Rifles, Evan guessed. Then there was an open space, and at the back of the car, by himself, was a man.

He was short and wiry and he had long dark hair. He wore black trousers, a white shirt with a black vest, and a black topcoat over it all, but there didn't appear to be any mold on him. He had a high forehead and bushy eyebrows and a mouth that seemed somehow too big for his face. His neck was scrawny and his Adam's apple pronounced. He was a singularly unattractive man, Evan thought. But he was alive, and he was not covered in black fuzz.

Behind Evan, Charlie's rifle boomed. "Christ, Evan, there's more!" he cried. "Let's go!"

"Come on," Evan said to the man.

"Believe me, I would love to oblige, sir," the man said. He shook his right leg. That was when Evan noticed the manacle around the man's ankle, the short length of chain looped around a ring set into the boxcar wall and locked with a brass padlock.

"What are you, some kind of prisoner?"

"It's not how it looks," the man said. Evan didn't see how it could fail to be how it looked. "I'll happily explain, but for the moment, we've got to get out of here, sir."

"Reckon so," Evan said. "Don't suppose you know where the key is."

"Last I saw it, Lieutenant Montgomery was putting it into his shirt pocket. I don't imagine you'd like to go find him."

"Do you know what—"

"I said I can explain!" The man's voice conveyed urgency. "First get me loose of this!"

Evan didn't see much choice. He stepped into the boxcar and stood close to the man, trying to shield him with his body in case shrapnel flew. He aimed the Remington at the padlock and fired. In the enclosed car it sounded loud, but the lock broke and the man was able to free himself from the train car. The manacle and length of chain remained connected to his ankle. "We'll have to take care of that later," Evan said. "After we get away from this train."

"My thoughts exactly," the man said. "And thank you, sir. You're a true gentleman."

"Not hardly," Evan said. An image of Charlie on the ground, his brains leaking from his head, flashed in his mind. "Nothing like it."

The man hopped down from the boxcar, and Evan followed. "You can double up with me," Evan said.

"Yes, yes," the dark little man said. "In a moment. First, though . . ." he started toward the last boxcar in the line.

"Mister, we got to get out of here!"

Charlie's Henry boomed again. "Ev," he said. "Now!"

"Mister," Evan said.

The little man whirled on him, fury animated his homely countenance. "In a minute, I said. Do you want to put a stop to this, or don't you?"

"You know how to—"

"I know everything about it," the man replied. "Open that car."

Evan had dropped his stone in the other boxcar. He found a suitable substitute and opened this car the same way. This boxcar held even less than the first one, and what it did hold, Evan didn't understand.

There were crates of something, but amid the crates was a device like none he had ever seen. Parts of it were black, but not with fuzz. It was cast iron, he thought, or something like it. Other parts were brass, and there was copper tubing and a wooden box attached to the front. "What in blazes?" Evan asked.

"It runs on steam, and we haven't time to get it going," the man said. "But for the moment we don't need it." He climbed up into the car, the chain dangling and scraping behind him. He tugged open one crate and then the next, and then he brought out a smaller device, hand-held, made of polished wood and brass and copper. It looked like some sort of wand, except it had a handle shaped to fit a man's grasp on one end and was wider on the other, where it split into a Y shape. Between the two outer ends of the Y was a thin coil of copper.

Evan had never seen anything like it. He had heard that there had been all sorts of marvelous devices shown at the International Exhibition of Inventions in London back in '85, but he had not been there and didn't know anybody who had. "What does that do?"

"It's my demoldificator. It'll do what we need it to," the man said.

He hopped down from the boxcar, holding it in his hands. Charlie had three soldiers around him now, moving stiffly, arms out to grasp him, and he was trying to reload the Henry. Evan raised his Remington, but he should have reloaded already and hadn't. There were two more soldiers coming off of passenger cars.

Almost calmly, the little man turned a small dial on his device, pushed a couple of buttons, and the copper coil between the two tines of the Y began to glow and spark. He held it out toward the nearest soldier, aiming it like some sort of weapon, and when he pushed yet another button, a bright flash, earthbound lightning, streaked out toward the soldier. The soldier fell instantly, and the black fuzz coating him began to smolder and dissipate, showing patches of flesh beneath it.

"I *told* them I could control it," the man said. "But they wouldn't let me have my instruments. I told them I needed it, needed it all, but they said no." As he groused, he repeated the process twice more, and the three soldiers who had penned Charlie in went down, the mold drying out and fading away with a thin blackish smoke.

"Can that thing bring them back?" Evan asked.

The little man shook his head. "Oh, they're quite dead. Quite dead. Nothing to be done about that."

"But—they're up and moving around."

"Quite dead, just the same."

"What—?"

"Oh, your hand!" the man said. Evan looked at his right hand, the one that had brushed the train seat. Black mold grew over his palm, between the fingers, and was threading back toward his wrist and arm.

"God!"

"This'll burn," the man said. He pointed his device at Evan and pushed the button. The brilliant light flared and Evan felt a pain as if he had plunged his hand into a roaring fire. But it lasted only a moment, and when it was gone, the mold had turned to dry dust. He shook it off.

"Thanks," he said.

"The big machine you saw?" the man said. "That's

a full-size demoldificator. It'll clean up this whole train, and more, if I can get enough water to it. As long as we have time. You're the first people I've heard since we stopped, sometime during the night. Do you know if anyone else has been here?"

"I don't know," Evan said. Charlie was barely listening, watching the train cars for more soldiers.

"Because if they have, then we might not have time to spend on the train."

Evan remembered something, from what seemed like days ago. "Does it have to be a person?"

"Not necessarily."

"That damn cat."

"What cat?"

"Charlie, find his tracks!" Evan shouted. "The cat!" He ran around the train. Charlie and the little man joined him, the chain clanking in the man's grip.

Sure enough, on the far side of the train, the cat's big tracks continued.

Only this time, each track had a trace of black mold in it, growing thicker and heavier the farther the cat got from the train. "What's over that way?" the man asked. The cat was moving west again.

"Willcox. A few miles out."

"That's a town?"

"Yes, a town."

"Then," the man said, "we had better hurry, hadn't we?"

The man, who gave his name as Franklin, rode behind Evan. They had bashed the manacle off his leg with a shovel from the coal tender, after the man had cleared the mold from it. He swore that he could wipe the mold out from the whole train, but not just now. The mountain lion, he said, was the bigger danger. If it reached the town . . .

Evan got the picture. He wondered about the traces of mold left in the cat's trail. If a snake slithered across one, or a coyote, a bird. Anything. Franklin shrugged. He could not, he said, guarantee the safety of the whole world. Not since the Army had interfered.

"I went to Washington, to show the generals there," he said. "I knew how formidable a weapon it could be, given the right circumstances. I offered to teach them how to control it."

"What'd they do?" Evan asked.

Franklin's grip around his middle tightened. Evan wished he would relax. "Treated me as if I were insane," he said. "Separated me from my devices, put me on this train. They were taking me to the territorial prison, in Yuma, because I had told them that it grew more slowly in an arid climate."

"What is it?"

"In layman's terms, it's a mold," the man said. "A sort of fungus. Spores form in a moist environment and spread. Mine just spreads more quickly than most. It likes warm, wet things."

"Like people."

"Yes."

"Who die, and then get back up—"

"It goes in through every opening it can find.

When it reaches the brain, the filaments encircle it and compress. They essentially squeeze the brain to death. But then they meld with it, and they can make the body move again. They aren't truly bringing a person back to life—it doesn't think, doesn't feel. But it can move."

"But . . . why does it do that?"

"Because it wants to spread itself."

"So you made some kind of smart mold, that's what you're saying?"

"Yes!" Franklin said. He sounded proud. "That's it exactly."

They rode hard, and soon Willcox lay before them, a flat valley town with a rail line cutting right through it. All the way, they followed the cat's tracks. Closer to town, the mold was thicker in the cat's pawprints, spreading out slowly beyond them, to the grasses and weeds the animal walked on. "That going to be a problem?" Evan asked.

"We'll take care of it on the way back," Franklin said. He sounded sure of himself.

Evan started to ask him why, or how, this had all come about, but then he caught himself. He didn't want to know how Franklin had come to experiment with mold, to turn it into a weapon that could be controlled with bizarre instruments. He wished he had never encountered the man or his inventions.

When they reached the town, the first person they saw was a butcher wearing a bloodstained apron and carrying a cleaver. But he was blackened from the hairline down, and walking with the jerking, awkward steps Evan had come to recognize, down the middle of the main street.

Evan stopped Goldie so Franklin could dismount and use his machine on the man. "No, not yet," Franklin said. "Keep riding."

"But what about that guy?"

"He's already dead. Don't stop until we're at the bank."

"The bank?"

"Do what I say!" Franklin snapped.

For the first time, Evan wondered if they had done the right thing in unchaining him.

From his horse, Charlie drew his Henry and shot the butcher in the head. He hadn't said much since the train, but Evan noticed his hands weren't nearly as shaky as they had been. The butcher collapsed in the street.

On the way to the bank, a brick building with white wooden trim standing in the middle of a block, they passed several more dead people. Franklin refused to use his machine, so Evan and Charlie took turns, trying to hit each one in the head with the first shot. Evan didn't figure a dead man could feel pain, but just in case he wanted to spare them that agony.

When they drew up outside the bank, Franklin slid off the horse before she even came to a full stop. There was more to this than he had said—he rushed for the front door with real enthusiasm, threw it open, and dashed inside. Evan dismounted, looped Goldie's reins around a hitching rail, and followed. "Keep an eye out," he told Charlie.

Charlie just nodded, holding that Henry rifle in his hands with something like religious devotion.

Inside, Franklin had gone around behind the counter and was pounding on the vault door. "I know you're in there! Come on out! I told you I'd be back! I told you!"

"Franklin?" Evan said. "What is—?"

Before Franklin could answer, the vault door started to open. Two men stood inside it with rifles, and there were three women behind them. The man in front was wearing an expensive suit. He had gray hair, and he was a little taller, but his resemblance to Franklin was unmistakable. "Son? What are you . . . you can't be responsible for . . ."

"What do you care?" Franklin asked. "I gave you a chance to be part of it all. You just threw me into the street and slammed the door, didn't you? Your own kin. Laughed in my face!"

"It wasn't like that, Franklin . . ."

"You remember it your way, but I remember the truth. The humiliation, the sorrow. All I ever did was love you, and all you ever did was hurt me and torment me and then throw me out like a dying dog!"

"Franklin," Evan said. "This is a touching reunion and all, but that cat—"

"Hang the cat!" Franklin shouted over his shoulder. "*This* is why we're here!"

"You, maybe," Evan said. He was not the world's smartest man, but it was dawning on him that Franklin had used him—used them all, even the Army. He didn't know where Franklin had gone after his father had tossed him out of the house, but wherever that had been, he had used the time to creat his weapon—his mold, which he somehow controlled with his machines. It was no coincidence that the train had been overtaken and stopped just a couple of miles from Willcox.

"You think you're safe in that vault?" Franklin asked. "Maybe you are, for now. But you can't stay in there forever. How much food you got in there? How much water? Whenever you come out, it'll get you. It's already in town, and spreading fast."

"Franklin, you said that thing you have can kill it," Evan said.

"Kill it? Sure. But it does more than that, doesn't it?"

"I don't know what it does."

"Trust me. It does a lot more."

"I don't know who you are, sir," Franklin's father said. "But I'm afraid my son is quite mad. Brilliant, but completely beyond my control. Anyone's control."

"Hope you don't think that comes as a surprise to me, mister," Evan said. "Tell you the truth, I'm sorry you threw him out instead of chucking him down a well or something."

Franklin shot a vicious glare at Evan. "Now you're turning on me, too?"

"I was never with you, amigo. I thought you could do something to help, that's all. You did all this just to get back at your pa?"

From outside, Evan heard the crack of Charlie's Henry, twice. Then the bank's front door opened and

Charlie put his head in. "You'd best come quick, Evan," he said.

Any excuse to get away from Franklin and his father was a good one. Evan joined Charlie at the door.

"This stuff is bad," Charlie said. He moved aside, letting Evan out.

The street was full of the dead.

Evan saw men and women and children and dogs and even the mountain lion. There must have been a hundred of them, more, coming from every direction. They were all moving with seeming purpose toward the bank, toward the only living things in sight. The black mold had taken hold, not just of them, but of the town. It scaled buildings, coated walkways, dripped from hanging signs.

Evan shoved the door open. "Franklin! Get that machine of yours working!"

Franklin threw back his head and laughed. He held the device up in both hands, and then he brought it down, fast and hard, over his lifted knee. It snapped in two pieces, the ends splintered and jagged.

"Damn you to hell!" Evan said.

"I told you," Franklin's father said. He slammed the vault door again. Evan could hear a whirring sound as he spun a wheel on the inside. Franklin pounded on it a couple of times, then turned back to Evan, the sides of his fists red.

"Now what?" Evan asked. "You got a plan for this, Franklin?"

"I suppose I do," Franklin said. "It won't take

long. The mold. It's over fast. A couple of minutes, maybe, as you feel it snaking into your nose and your ears, fingering its way into your mouth, coating your tongue. The worst part might be the eyes, because it has to burst those to get past. But then all the feeling goes away, the shame, the betrayals, they're all left in the past, and then—" He stopped, staring at Evan.

Evan thumbed the hammer and pulled the Remington's trigger twice. He had taken care of the old gun, and it took care of him. When he put it away, Franklin was sliding down the vault door, leaving a wide streak of red behind him.

Charlie barged through the front door with his rifle at the ready. "What happened?"

"I did him a favor."

Charlie looked at Franklin. His left foot was still moving, tapping out an unheard beat, but it went still a moment later. "Might be the best way out of this."

"Are the horses all right?" Evan asked.

"I think so."

"Let's get back to the train. He said that machine there, the big one, could take care of a whole lot of this stuff."

"You know how to work it?"

"Don't reckon I do, but I'd rather die trying than not."

"Well, hell, let's ride, then."

They burst from the bank and ran toward the horses. There was a little mold on Goldie's left leg,

just surrounding her hoof. She only had to go a few
miles, though, and Evan figured it would take a
while to get to her brain.

The dead tried to stop them. They lurched in front
of the horses. The cat tried to pounce, but Charlie got
off a shot—from the saddle, at a trot, Evan was
impressed—that took off the back of the cat's head
and dropped it in its tracks. Evan had never been so
glad to see a damn dead lion in his whole life. He
emptied the Remington and reloaded, kicking the
horse on to greater speeds, and hoped Charlie was
impressed by that.

Then they were out of town, riding hard.

The mold left in the cat's pawprints had spread.
The mold on Goldie's leg was spreading fast, too, up
past her hock and still climbing. She gave what she
could, though, and Evan had never known a horse
like Goldie for pushing herself when it counted. His
hat blew off and he let it go, feeling the wind in his
hair and his face, clean and alive, and looking out at
the countryside, the grasslands he loved, the mountains standing brown and firm and solid to the east,
his country, and he knew then that everything would
be all right.

The train was a solid black mass.

The mold had grown to twice the train's original
dimensions. It still had an essentially train-like
shape, long and rectangular and close to the earth.
But it was massive, impenetrable.

"Now what?" Charlie said.

Evan stared at it for a long while, unwilling to admit defeat.

Goldie nickered, stamped the ground.

"You got any of that stuff on your horse?" Evan asked.

"I don't think so."

Evan got off Goldie's back, petted her muzzle. "You got to shoot her," he said. "I can't do it. But I don't want her to go that way, neither."

"Step away from her, then," Charlie said.

Evan did.

"Now what?" Charlie asked when it was done.

Evan wiped his left eye. A cinder, he told himself, that's all. Damned horse. "We need to get to that de-moldi . . . whatever. That machine."

"But—" Charlie gestured toward the shape that contained an unseen train.

"We know it's in the last car," Evan said. It occurred to him at that moment that only he and Franklin had seen it there. And he had shot Franklin.

If someone had to go in after it, it would be him.

"Let's start a fire," he said. "We'll need steam to run the thing."

"A fire with what?" Charlie asked. "Grass?"

"Start it with grass, I reckon, but then we'll need coal, from the tender," Evan said. "Got to fetch water from there as well."

Charlie spat into the grass. "Damn waste of time," he said. But he squatted and started pulling hand-fuls of grass.

When they had the fire going with grass and the few branches and dried yucca stalks they could find, Evan got one of the larger stalks burning. Putting things off would serve no purpose.

He held the torch up, trying to prepare himself. "I'm going in there, there's one thing I got to know first."

"What's that?"

"Do you love her?"

"Who?"

"You know what I'm talking about, Charlie. Don't play dumb now."

Charlie was quiet for a while. Then: "I'll allow as how I just might."

"You think she loves you?"

"I know she loves you."

"That ain't what I asked."

"Might be."

"Good enough," Evan said. If he lived through the next few minutes, they could talk again. If they needed to.

He tried to guess about where the open boxcar door was, and with the torch in his hand, he plunged into the black.

It was cloying, gagging. He was as blind as a man with no eyes out on a moonless night. Filaments clung to his whiskered cheeks, his hair, his hands, writhing atop his flesh like the tiny feet of a million ants. When he sucked for air he felt some climbing down his throat, imagined it slithering into his lungs. Nausea roiled his gut. Wherever the flame from his torch touched, the mold retreated, sizzling and melting, and dropped around him in moist, heavy clumps.

He slammed into the boxcar wall, but an outflung hand found air. He shoved the torch through, illuminating space inside that the mold had not filled. He hoisted himself up, found the machine. It was remarkably free of mold, as if the horrible growth recognized an enemy it could not defeat. The thing was big, but he could skid it across the floor. Laying the torch on the boxcar floor, he muscled it to the doorway. There would be no gentle lifting the machine down, and it would crush Charlie if he tried to catch it. If it didn't survive the drop, then they were dead anyway.

Evan pushed. The machine balanced on the boxcar's lip for a moment, then tumbled out, ripping through shreds of mold as it went. Seeing daylight, Evan grabbed the torch and jumped.

Evan cleared out the tender and the locomotive as best he could, figuring he was already exposed to the stuff, and no matter what, someone had to survive to take care of Lucinda. They had hauled the machine up next to the death train's locomotive. Tubes uncoiled from inside the thing's belly, and they found a way to connect those to the boiler. Once they had the fire raging, steam ran through its pipes and issued from a slender iron chimney with a whistling sound. There was a big wheel at the machine's center with a brass knob for turning it with, and that wheel turned a smaller wheel, which turned one that was still smaller. When all three were going, a shade slid open, and light glimmered through. The beam could be directed by turning it with a brass handle.

"You reckon that's all there is to it?" Charlie asked. "Spin that thing?"

"Worth a try."

Evan cranked the big wheel a few times. As he did, the steam engine took over, and he had to let go quick, lest it tear his arm off. The wheel spun faster and faster, but the light remained dim, showing the barest flicker.

"Evan?" Charlie said.

"Yeah?" Evan couldn't tear his gaze from the spinning wheels.

"It ain't working."

"What?"

"Look."

Charlie was right. Not only was the mold not diminishing, it was growing thicker, quickly marching across the grassland toward Willcox and spreading out in every direction from the patches left in the cat's tracks.

"That rummy lied?"

"Or we're doin' it wrong."

The wheel! Evan tried to catch the brass knob when it came around. It slapped his fingers away, then punched hard against the palm of his hand. Finally, he got a grip on it, slowed it down. "Other way, mebbe," he said. With a great heave, he got the wheel moving in the opposite direction. Again, after a few turns, the steam took over, propelling it faster and faster.

This time, the light glowed brilliantly, beaming through the little window like a captive sun.

And where light fell, mold smoked and crisped and evaporated in wisps of grayish smoke.

Evan ran around front and bathed in the light. Mold had reached his ears. He tasted it on his lips. It caked his limbs and trunk. He had been trying to ready himself for death, working out when he should ask Charlie to shoot him as he had Goldie. But now he let the light burn it off. For the first time in hours, he thought he would survive. He laughed, and Charlie joined him, and their laughter wafted into the sky along with the smoke.

As the wheel spun ever faster, the beam widened and reached out farther. They cleared the train, the grass, the high desert plants. Then, carefully mounting the machine on the train itself, making sure they didn't divert too much steam from the device, they got the engine going and chugged slowly toward Willcox.

They had almost reached the station when the machine began to vibrate. Its whistle had gone from loud to piercing and most of the way to deafening. "Thing's spinnin' too fast," Charlie said. By this time, the beam had spread even more, blocking evening's dusk from reaching the landscape. Above, the sky was dark, but daylight washed the earth. "Think we can slow 'er down?"

Evan had been afraid to touch it for some time. "Might cut off the steam."

"But the town. That stuff's . . ."

Charlie was right. They had to clear Willcox or all their efforts would have been wasted. "Speed up the train," Evan said. "Let's hurry."

The machine wouldn't wait. It coughed and shuddered and barked and then it flew apart in a blast of steam that seared the skin of Evan's face. Pieces flew this way and that, and the light—before it extinguished itself for good—flooded the plain and the town and the desert beyond in a blinding flash, as if that captive sun had broken free and for just an instant, unleashed its full fury on the landscape.

The men sat on hard wooden benches inside the train station, speaking little, sipping from a flask once in a while. They waited until morning before they entered the empty town. In the sun's first glow, they saw no traces of the mold. Bodies were scattered everywhere, human and animal alike. The only living people they found were those who had holed up inside the blood-streaked vault, and it took some convincing before they would emerge.

"You men did this?" Franklin's father asked when they led him, blinking against the light, into the street.

"If you mean stopping what your boy started," Evan said, "then yes."

Tears slid from the man's narrowed eyes. "But . . . this town . . ."

"You can start over," Evan said. "Sometimes a man's got to reconsider things."

He had been doing some reconsidering of his own.

When the hunt began, he had been planning to kill Charlie. But things changed. Sometimes they changed faster and more dramatically than a man could account for. He and Charlie had been thrown together in a new and different world than they had started in. After what they had gone through, he couldn't just put a gun to the man's head.

As for Lucinda, she was a fine wife, and he would miss her something fierce. But things being what they were, he thought the choice should be left up to her.

He started to say something else, to try to soothe the sobbing man and the other people who slowly stepped into the light, but his attention was caught by a dove, descending from the sky and coming to an awkward, fluttering landing on a balcony rail across the street.

He couldn't have said for sure, not from this distance, but it appeared there might have been a black patch on the bird's breast, where the shadow should not have been so dark. Maybe a little something around its eyes, as well. He felt a chill on his neck, as if someone had draped a wet string over it and then yanked it away.

He watched the dove for a minute, but he didn't say anything. Pointing it out would only upset the survivors. And Evan wasn't a man who put much stock in words anyway, in talking just for the sake of it.

Not when there was nothing left to say.

LONE WOLF

Jody Lynn Nye

"Ayoooooooo!"

The cry chilled Duncan Hopkin's blood, but he kept on walking behind Carson McCreary and cranking the dynamo hanging around his neck on a strap. The pair of them was heading right for the sound, instead of going back home to their warm beds in their nice, safe houses on the edge of Kansas City. Couldn't blame Carson, really. Josephine had been the girl he wanted to marry. And she was Duncan's kid sister, which is why he was out under the moon in the middle of the night on the prairie. The grass hissed beneath his heavy work boots. He wished he had on a suit of armor instead of work pants and his heavy canvas coat.

"I will kill that damned wolf if it takes the rest of my life," Carson had vowed. Duncan, his true friend from childhood, knew he meant what he said. It had been nearly a month since Josie had gotten dragged out of the farmhouse in the dead of night. At least that was the tale the marks on the ground had told—that and the inexplicable behavior of their hound dog. Nelson had been found in the morning hiding underneath the chicken coop, shaking like he had been dipped in an icy river. He had been no use as a guard dog ever since. Little noises made him jump to the sky, and a howl set him running in the opposite direction. Duncan might have shot Nelson for failing to do his job, but he felt so sorry for him he just couldn't do that. The dog had a bite mark on the back of his neck from a much bigger animal with long, sharp teeth. A wolf. He'd be all right, but his ma's poodle had taken over protecting the family.

Duncan stumbled on a stone and heard the scrabbling of claws as small animals fled the noise. At least they had a full moon to see by. That set them and this wolf on an even basis—sightwise, that was. The world was all silver and black, with the moist, rich scent of the earth rising around him. It would have been a pretty nice night for a walk, if it wasn't for the reason.

For a thriving city, Kansas City was still troubled by wild things roaming around. Shawnee Indians came and went as they damned well pleased as if it was all still their territory. Duncan had a friend who was a famous hunter and tracker who also worked for his family's mineral springs business. Owl Feather sometimes turned up at five in the morning sitting next to the fire in the Hopkin family kitchen, scaring Duncan's ma half to death when she came in to get breakfast going. Deer ate the hen feed. The biggest problem was varmints. They had to lock up the hens and lambs at night so they had any in the morning.

Owl Feather ought to have been out there with them hunting this wolf. Carson and Duncan had asked him, but he gave them a flat no.

"Ain't no wolf," he said. "You're looking for two critters with one soul. And they don't want to be found."

Carson scorned Owl's advice. No one had ever been able to tell him what to do. On the other hand, he was plenty good at convincing other people. So, every night for three weeks, Duncan had accompanied him, and every day after he finished his job in Argentine for the railway, he had been in his workshop laboring away at his wolf-detector. It took him two solid weeks and almost seven dollars worth of new parts, but he did it. If tracks weren't going to lead them to the wolf, this would.

Duncan had what his granddaddy called a mechanical bent. Pieces of wire and horsehair and old bits of glass turned into useful devices in his hands. He made a pin-collector for his ma so she didn't lose no more straight pins down between the floor boards. You wound up the little clockwork gizmo that looked like a cross between a spider and a pillbox and let it go. Saved her a lot of money when she made clothes. His best invention had been inspired from when he saw lightning strike a tree and split it in half. He was currently waiting for word from the United States Patent Office on the Duncan Hopkin Log Chopper. It could turn out a cord of wood in twenty minutes. Some people laughed at his inventions, but his ma and pa were proud of him. They hoped he would find Jo's body, but they didn't hold out much hope for it. They had already mourned her.

The wolf detector worked by sniffing out the scent of the tufts of long gray fur that had been left in Jo's bedroom and on the window-sash. It drew air in with a miniature bellows and weighed it for similarities with the samples. At least that was how it was supposed to work. They hadn't had much luck with it the first few nights. Tonight, though, it was going like wildfire. The gauge, made out of an old part from the engine of a locomotive, whistled softly and more insistently than usual.

"We're on the trail now!" Carson said hoarsely. He carried the detector. The dynamo that powered it was kind of fragile and touchy. Duncan didn't trust him with it. Carson broke almost everything. Jo had sent him home a dozen times because he was too rough in his courting. She had several other beaus, including Tim Pettigrew, whose family lived in a huge mansion in the fashionable neighborhood near the river and who had been to Harvard University in Cambridge, Massachusetts. Duncan wished he could afford to go to college. He felt wasted in Kansas City. Maybe once he became a famous inventor, like Mr. Thomas Edison, he could move to a big city on the east coast.

"*Ayoooooo!*"

The howl came so close that Duncan jumped halfway to the moon. He stopped cranking. The detector's whistle died away. Carson rounded on him angrily, his face a pale blob in the moonlight.

"Start 'er up! Do you want us to lose him?"

Duncan seized the handle and wound it up. The whistle rose from a murmur to a shriek. They must be almost on top of the wolf. He leaned his head toward the comforting length of his rifle barrel. The gun hung over his shoulder on top of the dynamo strap.

The detector shrilled like a frantic train. A dark figure not ten yards ahead of them shot across the silverlit landscape. It made for a thicket of jumbled shade. Neither of them could miss the long, shaggy brush wagging behind the fourlegged shape.

"There it goes!" Carson bellowed. He dropped the detector. Whipping his rifle off his shoulder, he pounded after the figure. Duncan slung the dynamo out of his way. He fumbled for his own gun and followed. They crashed into the brush, thrusting branches and twigs out of their way.

In the daylight, the thicket was an ordinary blackberry patch. At night, with moonlight lancing through the tangles, it was a nightmare of clawed hands tearing at his face and clothes. Thorns clutched at his trouser legs.

"Carson, I can't see nothing," Duncan whispered. His friend was a hunched black silhouette ahead of him.

"It's here," Carson said. "Right there!" He leveled the gun. Duncan blinked his eyes and squinted. A long-tailed shadow flitted across a pool of light.

Then the smell hit them. His eyes watered at the sour muskiness.

"Ayooooooo!"

The cry was right under their noses. Carson swung the barrel toward the noise. A pair of glowing orange eyes were inches from the two men. Duncan got a glimpse of shaggy gray fur and two tall ears. How could it move that fast?

BLAM!

Duncan almost jumped out of his skin at the sound of the shot. The eyes faded for a second then lit up again, stronger than before. A growl erupted, low and menacing. Duncan froze. Carson cocked the gun and pulled the trigger again. The smoke went right between the golden lights. The eyes didn't even close.

"That ain't natural!" Duncan gasped.

The beast bared long white teeth in a growl. It sprang at Carson. The young man swung the rifle like a bat. It hit the creature right in the jaw. It reached up a paw and grasped the gun around the barrel. It had hands like a man!

He had no more time to analyze the problem. He threw himself on the beast's back and put an arm around its throat, trying to pull it off Carson. Its muscles rippled under the coarse fur, hard as iron. Carson kicked and punched at the beast. Its teeth snapped at his neck.

"Get it off me! Get it off me!"

Duncan hung on its back, flopping around like an opera cloak. He kicked at it with both feet, hoping to hit a kidney or some other sensitive spot. The beast howled. It gave a mighty heave, and Duncan went flying off. He landed hard in the grass and lay stunned for a moment. His hip hurt, but he rolled over and felt for his gun. He managed to cock it, closed his eyes and fired.

KER-POW!

"Yaller-bellied sows, Duncan, you almost hit me!" Carson shouted.

Duncan opened his eyes. Carson stood alone in the moonlight. His right sleeve was torn off, and he was holding his pants up with one hand.

"Where's the wolf?" Duncan asked.

"Gone," Carson said. "Shoved me off and ran away. Damn it to hell."

Duncan got up and brushed himself off. "I think it might've been from hell, Carson. That wasn't a natural creature. You hit it square with two bullets, and it didn't even stop."

"I thought you didn't believe in hell," Carson said, sourly.

"I believe in science," Duncan said. "And physics says when you hit a solid object with another solid object you're going to get a reaction. Nothing happened. And it had a man's hands. That's not a normal wolf."

"That's against God and nature," Carson agreed. He was too mad to be scared, like a sensible man.

"Got to be some kind of enchantment. Let's go find Owl Feather."

"It's got to be three in the morning!"

"Then he'll be easy to find."

Duncan sat blearily next to the fireplace in Owl Feather's small two-room house, listening to the same set of questions and answers over and over again. He knew he'd hear them in his sleep. Carson jabbed his forefinger into his other palm.

"I shot it twice, point blank range! Why didn't it fall down and die?"

"You can't kill one body without killing the other," Owl Feather said. He sat on his bed wrapped up in a blanket. With his long black braids framing his hawk-nosed face he looked a lot more like one of his ancestors than the respectable businessman who wore a suit to work at the mineral springs. "They can only walk under the full moon's light because they're two bodies with one soul. Divide one from the other, and both may die."

"That don't mean anything, Owl," Carson complained. "I need an answer that will help me kill that goddamned wolf!"

"That is the only answer," Owl said, imperturbably. "Now why don't you go home and let me sleep? Some of us got jobs to go to." He glanced at the window. The moon had set, and the sky was lightening to denim blue. "In about an hour." He cocked his head at Duncan. "Your ma's making buttermilk biscuits. She bakes better than anyone else in town."

"I know," Duncan said, summoning up his manners from somewhere. "Come on over and have some. I know she makes enough for the entire United States Army."

"Thank you, my brother. I will."

"You act like my betrothed wasn't important enough to care about," Carson said, lowering brows that were as black as Owl's.

"I have sung songs to ensure her spirit is at peace," Owl said. "Now I must deal with the living. So must you."

"That wolf's living! It ought to be dead!"

"Okay," Duncan said, rousing himself in hopes of getting an hour of sleep before he had to go back to the train yard. Owl never lied or even stretched the truth. No matter how much like a story by Mr. H.G. Wells the whole thing sounded, if Owl said it was true, then it was true. Duncan never argued with facts. "What do we need to do to divide that wolf in two?"

Owl studied him for a moment. His dark eyes seemed to have no pupils at all. Then he reached over to the table next to his bed and picked up the collection of necklaces he wore every day. He selected one and handed it to Duncan.

"This has virtues to bring things back to the way they started. And don't forget, silver puts them under your power. It's the only thing that will." Owl looked out the window at the paling sky and sighed. "No time to sleep. Better eat and welcome the day."

*   *   *

Ma was baking, as Owl had said. Though he lived over two miles away, he always knew what she was making. Her round, plump face was red as usual, but it was from crying instead of exertion. She dabbed tears away with her flour-dusted sleeve and forced a smile for the guests.

"Hey, there, Owl, Carson. Sit down. I'll pour you some coffee."

"Thanks, Mrs. Hopkin," Owl said, sliding into a chair at the kitchen table. "Blessings on this house."

Ma turned away toward the stove. Duncan came up and whispered in her ear.

"Ma, why are you crying? What's wrong?"

She turned fierce blue eyes on him.

"You are never to mention Nancy Bellamy to me again for the rest of my life. She is as dead to me as . . . as my poor Josephine!"

"Why? Aunt Nan was your best childhood friend."

She took a folded paper out of the pocket of her big white apron and shook it at Duncan. He opened it and read it.

Saw your Jo at Mr. Meyer's jewelry store looking at engagement rings with that handsome Pettigrew boy. Couldn't miss him with that head of gray hair. She looked so happy! So glad to know I heard wrong. Let me know when I can congratulate you.

The letter was dated only two days before. He was a little shaken by it, but handed it back.

"Well, come on, Ma, Aunt Nan is mistaken. She must have seen Tim Pettigrew. All the Pettigrews turn gray as soon as they reach their majority. He was with some other girl that he is going to marry, that's all."

Ma was adamant. "No. She's tormenting me with lies! I never want to hear that woman's name again!"

The three men ate their breakfast in silence. Owl took a few biscuits wrapped up in a napkin for later. Carson growled over his food. When he left, he glared at Duncan.

"Just find me a way to kill that wolf," he said, and stalked out.

Duncan sat for a while, thinking hard. What Owl said stuck in his mind. Separate the souls, and the bodies were vulnerable.

He kissed Ma on the cheek and went out to his workshop.

It took a wheelbarrow to manage the heavy, cylindrical black case with its curved silver arms, but he managed to carry the Log Splitter to work with him to the train yard. Over his lunch hour, he adapted it to take in Owl's beads. His fellow mechanics were glad to help, though they didn't properly understand what he was doing. The beads looked pretty mystical. Some were made of a strange gray stone that was shiny as metal. A few were garnets as big as grapes. The rest were carved buffalo horn that gave him a little shock as he handled each one. They had to go in between the emitter and the lenses in the arms that focused the power. Since none of them were shaped the same, it was tricky. He wasn't sure but that it might blow up when he used it.

When he was done, he had a gadget designed to split natures by lightning. It ran on a self-actuating dynamo with a drum wound with silver wire finer than hair. When he flipped the switch, the drum started to rotate, generating sparks that crackled between the two arms. The electrical force built up it lanced outward to a point. He experimented on a water bucket and a drop-forged ball peen hammer. They both melted into puddles of iron. The Log Splitter vibrated mightily, but it held together. There was no telling if it would work on a wolf with two bodies, but it was worth a try. He'd scorch its tail anyhow. Satisfied, he finished his shift and waited for Carson to arrive.

"I suppose you want to bring a mule team out with us?" Carson asked sourly, surveying the insulated black case and its makeshift carriage. "That thing is the size of a safe!"

Duncan put up with a lot of his guff because Carson was his oldest friend, but he wasn't taking any abuse of his inventions. He put his hands on his hips and glared.

"I suppose you want to go shake Owl's necklace at them by itself?" he asked.

Carson backed down, but only a little. "Of course not! But this had better work. I want that wolf's pelt on my floor."

"Nothing's sure," Duncan admitted. "But it's an experiment. We can only fail until we succeed."

"There it goes!" Carson bellowed, stumbling over the uneven ground under a full moon the size of a barn. He put one leg in a gopher hole and measured his length on the ground. Duncan saw his arm go up, pointing desperately. "Shoot it!"

"Can't! Too far away!" Duncan panted. He shoved the Log Splitter along in the wheelbarrow yards behind his friend. It was heavy, kicking dirt up from under the wheel. It sprayed him in the face. He spat out grass and dust.

The gray shadow flitted out of reach as if playing with them. It seemed to enjoy frolicking in the eldritch light. It disappeared from plain sight and popped up in another place entirely as if distance meant nothing to it. Carson clambered up and followed, swearing loudly.

They followed it downhill into Edward Posner's orchard. The shadow ducked back and forth between the apple trees. Showers of sweet-scented blossoms fell on Duncan as he maneuvered the wheelbarrow over the gnarled roots. Mr. Posner would be mighty angry if they damaged any of the trees. He could smell his own sweat.

No, that wasn't him. The bitter stench welled up, giving Duncan his only warning.

"Carson!" he shouted. The wolf loomed up out of nowhere, grinning at him. It heeled over and galloped down the row, out of reach. It looked like it was laughing over its shoulder. Carson pursued it, winging off shot after shot with his rifle. The two of them went around and around the orchard, while Duncan tried to spot the wolf and level his Splitter on it.

He figured he had a maximum of four tries with the Splitter before the insides slagged. Each successive try would be weaker than the one before. It'd be best if he could take the wolf down with the first one. Carson, if he had any ammunition left, could finish it after that.

The wolf, with Carson shouting and puffing in pursuit, came roaring around four rows up. They were heading straight for him.

"Shoot it!" Carson yelled at him.

"I might hit you! Get down!"

Carson threw himself face first on the ground. "Shoot it!"

Duncan flipped up the switch. The dynamo wowed as it came on. He urged it to hurry up and gather up power. Tiny sparks were playing between the ends of the curved metal arms, but they wouldn't stop a hummingbird.

Come on! he begged it.

But the wolf moved faster than a man could think. The wolf gathered itself and sprang. Duncan's eyes went wide. It crashed into him, bearing him over backwards. He hit his head against an apple tree and saw stars. The wolf grabbed his throat in its teeth and started to squeeze.

"Duncan!" Carson shouted. Duncan heard the sound of his friend's rifle. The wolf jerked several times as each bullet hit it, but it didn't fall. Duncan thought he was done for.

Suddenly, it let out a yelp and loosened its grip. Duncan wriggled away under the boughs of the apple tree, clutching his throat. Carson must have gotten it at last.

But it wasn't Carson that had the wolf at bay. It was another wolf. There were *two* wolves!

The newcomer was smaller and had a browner coat than the first one. It snarled fiercely at the bigger wolf. They circled one another, then leaped for each other's throat. Growling, they separated and ped again.

"It's his mate," Carson croaked, hurrying over to help him up. "They're fighting."

"We'll get him while he's busy," Duncan said. He staggered to the Splitter. Blue sparks were now arcing between the arms. Plenty of charge. "This is our best shot, Carson. You be ready."

Carson cocked his rifle again. "I'm ready."

"Okay, then."

Duncan threw the switch.

The whole orchard turned to stark black and white as lightning leaped out of the Splitter. It hit the big wolf square in the side. It let out a whine of pain and staggered sideways.

Duncan thought it was a trick of the light, but the creature *blurred*. Suddenly, it stood up tall, and split into two pieces, one dark and one light. It was two bodies with one soul!

It took him a moment to realize that the light one was the shape of a man, all but hairless and naked as a jaybird. The dark one, still a wolf but much diminished in size, opened terrified red eyes at all the people and fled down the rows, yelping. The man tottered and fell down.

Carson strode to him, with Duncan tagging along behind.

"I know him," Duncan said, peering down. The man on the ground looked young, but his hair was pale silver gray. "It's that Tim Pettigrew."

"That's impossible! How could he be a wolf?"

"He's gotta be like one of those loops in the stories the French traders tell," Duncan said. "A loop garoo. A wolf-man."

"Well, then, he's a monster." Carson put his foot on Tim Pettigrew's chest and aimed the rifle right up his nose. "Did you kill my Jo?"

"She's not your Jo," Tim said. He looked more meek than he ever did on the street, but it was hard to look dignified when you're stark naked and lying on your back in the dirt. Duncan had to admit that he was a pretty good-looking man. He had a long, square jaw and a straight nose not unlike a muzzle. His eyes, though, were plain blue. Tim stared up at the moon in shock, then examined his arms, pale in the moonlight. "What have you done to me?"

"What did you do with her?" Carson demanded. "It had to be you who snagged her out of her room and killed her! You're a dead man, Pettigrew!" He cocked the rifle.

"No!" Tim protested, holding his hands up. "She's not dead!"

The smaller wolf let out a fierce growl. Its haunches twitched like a cat's, and it bounded at Carson's chest. The rifle got knocked upward, and the shot pinged into the trees. The wolf grabbed the rifle out of Carson's fingers with her teeth and tossed it to one side. Then it went for his throat with her teeth.

Duncan stared in disbelief. He realized suddenly what he must be looking at. All logic was against it, but intuition was for it. Aunt Nan wasn't wrong!

"Josephine Hopkin, leave him be, or I will tell Ma what kind of hijinks you have been up to!"

The small wolf stopped chewing on Carson's throat and looked up at him with wide, bewildered eyes. Carson fought his way free.

"What's the matter with you, Duncan? Wolves can't understand human speech!"

"This isn't a wolf either," Duncan said. "That's my sister Josephine. Like *he* was, until we split him up. She's a loop garoo, too." He kicked Tim in the leg. "That means you bit her, you scoundrel! My pa is going to take you to court, but not until I finish kicking you around this whole orchard!"

"I can explain," Tim began.

"You're talking nonsense," Carson said, bewildered. "He must have been next to the wolf in the bushes."

"He was the wolf, and she's one, too," Duncan said stoutly. "I can prove it." He looked at the sky. A line of blue glimmered at the eastern horizon. "In about an hour."

He broke his dynamo down and took out the silver wire. The wolf backed away from him, but he jumped on her back and looped it around her neck. It fell on the ground, crying as if it was in pain.

"You oughta cry, after what you put Ma and Pa through," he said severely, shaking her. The female wolf lay on the ground, whimpering.

"She didn't mean to," Tim said. He had gathered a couple leafy branches off the nearest apple tree and had covered his privates with them. "It was my idea. We were going to surprise everyone."

"You took her in with your wild, university-man ways," Duncan said. "She was a respectable girl, and now what will people say?"

"I'll make it right for her. I swear to you!"

"You're as crazy as bedbugs, both of you," Carson said hoarsely. Duncan could tell this was all getting to be too much for him. He didn't have a scientist's dispassionate interest. He was just in love with Jo. "What do we do now?"

"We wait," Duncan said.

It seemed to take forever, but the sun eventually came up over the orchard. The wolf, who had given up complaining about the silver tether, began to show terrible signs of distress. She curled up on herself, writhing and moaning. Duncan watched with a scientist's eyes. As light washed over the wolf, the fur started to fall off in handfuls. Carson crossed himself. Duncan took off his coat and threw it over her body for decency's sake. Her muzzle shortened and smoothed out. Her feet lost their claws and shrank to dainty proportions. All the hair seemed to gather itself up on her head then fell in a neat brown braid down her back. She sat up, pulling the coat close around her. She looked as healthy as she had the day she went missing. Carson gazed at her in open-mouthed disbelief.

"It's good to see you, Jo," Duncan said, swallowing his pleasure and favoring her with a stern look, "but Ma is gonna have a heart attack. What were you thinking?"

"Tim and I ran away together," Jo said, apologetically. "We were gonna get married, but I want a proper church wedding. His family's afraid to set foot in a church because of the curse. Each of them gets it when they grow to adulthood."

"The parson might be able to cure them," Duncan said.

"You don't understand," Jo said. "They *like* it. I like it. It's fun. Tim . . . well, he bit me that very same night we ran away, and I changed for the first time. I have never felt so free in my life. Whenever the moon's full, we can run together. I felt like he was my other half." She glared at him accusingly. "Then you spoiled everything! His wolf half is gone!"

"Two bodies with one soul," Duncan said, nodding. "Owl Feather was right."

Jo smiled up at Tim. "That's the way I feel. We're meant to be together."

Tim touched her chin with a gentle forefinger.

"That's my sentiment exactly, my wild rose."

"Maybe we can restore the curse and get your wolf back. It might just take a little nip. A love bite," she said, then ducked her eyes shyly. Duncan felt embarrassed. He wished he wasn't watching them.

"If not, I'll live with it," Tim said manfully. "As long as I have you, nothing else is important."

Carson let out a sorrowful cry.

"But you were gonna marry me, Jo!"

Jo regarded him with weary impatience.

"I was never going to marry you, Carson McCreary. The only person who ever thought so was you!"

"You can't marry a loop garoo," Duncan said, reasonably. He never argued with facts. Jo didn't want Carson and that was that. "You wouldn't want a wife who went running around naked in the moonlight."

"I could," Carson said stubbornly. "She could bite me and I'd be one, too. Won't you, Jo?"

"Never in a thousand years," Jo said. She flung a hand at Duncan's Log Splitter. "I'd let Duncan use that thing on me first."

Carson stood up. His eyes blazed as much as the wolves' had. "Well, if that's the kind of gratitude you give a man who almost lost his life for you, then I wash my hands of you."

Gathering as much dignity as he could muster, he stalked off into the glare of the sunrise.

"There goes a man who is going to be lonely all his life," Jo said sympathetically.

"Well, you're going to have a hard time ahead of you, too," Duncan reminded her.

Jo reached out and put her hand into Tim's. "I'm prepared. I thought it through pretty thoroughly before I let him do it. You're not the only scientist in the family. I'll cope with being a wolf."

"I don't mean that," Duncan said, standing up to load what was left of his greatest invention into the wheelbarrow. He grinned down at Jo. "How are you going to tell Ma and Pa where you've been for a month?"

ABOUT THE AUTHORS

Jennifer Brozek is an award-winning editor and author. Winner of the 2009 Australian Shadows Award for edited publication, Jennifer has edited five anthologies with more on the way. Author of *In a Gilded Light* and *The Little Finance Book That Could*, she has written more than thirty-five published short stories and is an assistant editor for the Apex Book Company. Jennifer also is a freelance author for many RPG companies including Margaret Weis Productions, Savage Mojo, Rogue Games, and Catalyst Game Labs. Winner of the 2010 Origins Award for Best Roleplaying Game Supplement, her contributions to RPG sourcebooks include *Dragonlance*, *Colonial Gothic*, *Shadowrun*, *Serenity*, *Savage Worlds*, and *White Wolf SAS*. She also writes the monthly gaming column *Dice & Deadlines*. When she is not writing her heart out, she is gallivanting around the Pacific Northwest in its wonderfully mercurial weather. Jennifer is a member of Broad Universe, SFWA and HWA.

Brenda Cooper is a Seattle-area futurist and writer, and also the CIO for the City of Kirkland. Brenda writes a monthly column for Futurismic called Today's Tomorrows, and is the author of the Endeavor award winner for 2008: *The Silver Ship and the Sea* and of the sequels, *Reading The Wind* and *Wings of Creation*. She co-authored *Building Harlequin's Moon* with Larry Niven. Her next book is *Mayan December*, coming in August 2012. See her website at www. brenda-cooper.com.

Jay Lake lives in Portland, Oregon, where he works on numerous writing and editing projects. His 2012 books are *Kalimpura* and *Love in the Time of Metal and Flesh*, along with paperback releases of two of his other titles. His short fiction appears regularly in literary and genre markets worldwide. Jay is a past winner of the John W. Campbell Award for Best New Writer and a multiple nominee for the Hugo and World Fantasy Awards.

Jeff Mariotte is the award-winning author of more than forty-five novels, including the border horror trilogy *Missing White Girl*, *River Runs Red*, and *Cold Black Hearts*; *The Slab*; and the *Dark Vengeance* teen horror quartet. He also writes comic books, including the long-running horror/Western comic book series *Desperadoes*. He's a co-owner of specialty bookstore Mysterious Galaxy in San Diego and lives on the Flying M Ranch in Arizona's historic Sulphur Springs Valley. Find out more by visiting www.jeff-mariotte.com..

Seanan McGuire was born and raised in Northern California, where she grew up with tarantulas, rat-

tlesnakes, and her own mountain: all the necessary
components for the weird Wild West. Naturally, she
now writes urban fantasy, and is the author of the
October Daye series (published by DAW Books). She
also writes science fiction under the name Mira
Grant—the pseudonym lets her preserve the illusion
that she sleeps (she doesn't sleep). Seanan shares a
crumbling farmhouse with three enormous blue
cats, several thousand books, several hundred horror movies, a lot of little plastic horses, and the occasional trespassing tarantula. She is very proud of
her complete set of Monster High dolls, and feels
this is worthy of inclusion in a professional
bio. "Flower of Arizona" is set in the same universe
as her InCryptid urban fantasy series, several decades earlier. You can keep up with the madness at
www.seananmcguire.com.

Christopher McKitterick's short work has appeared
in *Analog, Artemis, Captain Proton, Extrapolation,
Mythic Circle, Ruins: Extraterrestrial, Sentinels: In
Honor of Arthur C. Clarke, Synergy SF, Tomorrow SF,
Visual Journeys*, and elsewhere, and he was honored
to edit the special science fiction issue of *World Lit-
erature Today*. Chris recently finished a far-future
novel, *Empire Ship*, and his debut novel *Transcendence*
has just been published. He is Associate Director of
the Center for the Study of Science Fiction (ku.
edu/~sfcenter) and lives in Lawrence, Kansas,
where he teaches writing and SF, restores old vehi-

cles, and watches the sky. Visit Chris at his website (sff.net/people/mckitterick), blog (mckitterick.live journal.com), or on Facebook.

Jody Lynn Nye lists her main career activity as "spoiling cats." She lives northwest of Chicago with one of the above and her husband, author and packager Bill Fawcett. She has published more than forty books, including seven contemporary fantasies, five SF novels, four novels in collaboration with Anne McCaffrey, including *Crisis on Doona* and *Treaty at Doona*; edited a humorous anthology about mothers, *Don't Forget Your Spacesuit, Dear!*; and over a hundred short stories. Her latest books are *Dragon's Deal*, the third in Robert Asprin's *Dragons* series, and *View from the Imperium*.

Kristine Kathryn Rusch is an award-winning writer who writes too much weird fantasy, but usually under the name Kristine Grayson. In fact, her latest Grayson novel *Wickedly Charming* has hit a number of bestseller lists, as has the reissue of *Utterly Charming*. *Thoroughly Kissed* (also a reissue) will appear in June 2012, and *Charming Blue* will appear in fall of 2012. Her other Grayson novels, *Completely Smitten* and *Simply Irresistible* are out, along with some Western short fiction. You can find her more serious fiction under the names Kristine Kathryn Rusch (latest novel: *City of Ruins*) or Kris Nelscott. Find out more about all of her fiction at www.kristinekathrynrusch.com.

Steven Saus injects people with radioactivity as his day job, but only to serve the forces of good. His work has appeared in print in the anthologies *Mages & Magic*, *Timeshares*, and *Hungry for Your Love*, and has fiction and nonfiction articles in magazines both online and off. He professionally converts books to eBooks, and has started his own foray into digital publishing with the release of *The Crimson Pact*, an anthology edited by Paul Genesse. You can find him at stevensaus.com and his digital publishing ventures at alliterationink.com.

USA Today bestselling author **Dean Wesley Smith** has written more than ninety popular novels and well over 200 published short stories. His novels include the science fiction novel *Laying the Music to Rest* and the thriller *The Hunted* as D.W. Smith. With Kristine Kathryn Rusch, he is the coauthor of *The Tenth Planet* trilogy and *The 10th Kingdom*. He writes under many pen names and has also ghosted for a number of top best-selling writers. Dean has also written books and comics for all three major comic book companies, Marvel, DC, and Dark Horse, and has done scripts for Hollywood. One movie was actually made. Over his career he has also been an editor and publisher. Currently, he is writing thrillers and mystery novels under another name.

Anton Strout is the author of the Simon Canderous urban fantasy series and of *Alchemystic*, book one of the Spellmason Chronicles. He is also the author of over half a dozen tales in anthologies published by

DAW Books. Anton was born in the Berkshire Hills mere miles from writing heavyweights Nathaniel Hawthorne and Herman Melville and currently lives in the haunted corn maze that is New Jersey (where nothing paranormal ever really happens, he assures you). He's been a featured speaker and workshopper at San Diego Comic-Con, Gencon, New York Comic-Con, and the Brooklyn Book Festival. In his scant spare time, his is a writer, a sometimes actor, sometimes musician, occasional RPGer, and the worlds most casual and controller smashing video gamer. He can often be found lurking the darkened halls of antonstrout.com.

Larry Sweazy won the WWA Spur award for Best Short Fiction in 2005 and was nominated for a Derringer award in 2007. He has published over forty non-fiction articles and short stories, which have appeared in *Ellery Queen's Mystery Magazine; Boys' Life; Hardboiled;* Amazon Shorts, and other publications and anthologies. Larry is also the author of the Josiah Wolfe, Texas Ranger series, and a standalone mystery novel, *The Devil's Bones.* He is member of MWA (Mystery Writers of America), WWA (Western Writers of America), and WF (Western Fictioneers). He lives in the Midwest, with his wife Rose, two dogs, Rhodesian ridgebacks, Brodi and Sunny, and a black cat, Nigel. www.larrydsweazy.com

J. Steven York collects hobbies the way some people collect stamps, dabbling in robots, electronics, rock-

ets, action figures, radio-controlled vehicles, gad-
gets, and a dozen other things to keep his hands
busy. Meanwhile, his brain (with help from fingers)
has turned out over fifteen books and a bunch of
shorter fiction. Meanwhile, brain and hands collabo-
rate on his weekly photo-illustrated web-comic
"Minions at Work," starring a cast of action figures
performing on tiny sets. He lives on the Oregon
coast with his wife, fellow writer Christina F. York,
who writes mystery, romance, fantasy, and other
stuff under a variety of names. He invites readers to
their shared site at www.YorkWriters.com.

About the Editors

Martin H. Greenberg (1941-2011) was the CEP of Tekno Books and its predecessor companies, now the largest book developer of commercial fiction and nonfiction in the world, with over 2,100 published books that have been translated into thirty-three languages. He was the recipient of an unprecedented four Lifetime Achievement Awards in the science fiction, mystery, and supernatural horror genres—the Milford Award in science fiction, the Bram Stoker Award in horror, the Ellery Queen Award in mystery, and most recently the Solstice Award for his work in science fiction—the only person in publishing history to have received all four awards.

Kerrie Hughes has edited ten anthologies: *Maiden Matron Crone, Children of Magic, Fellowship Fantastic, Dimension Next Door, Gamer Fantastic, Zombie Raccoons and Killer Bunnies, Girl's Guide to Guns and Monsters, Love And Rockets, Chicks Kick Butt,* and now *Westward Weird.* She has also been a contributing editor on two concordances: *The Vorkosigan Companion* and *The Valdemar Companion.* She has published nine short stories: "Judgment," in *Haunted Holidays;* "Geiko," in *Women of War;* "Doorways," in *Furry Fantastic;* "Travelers Guide," in *The Valdemar Companion;* "Bog Bodies," in *Haunting Museums;* "Pennyroyal," in *The Courts of the Fey;* "Corvidae" in *The Beast Within;* with her husband John Helfers in "Between a Bank and a Hard Place," in *Texas Rangers;* "The Last Ride of the Colton Gang," in *Boot Hill;* and "The Tombstone Run," in *Lost Trails.* Kerrie is currently working on three novels and attempting to sell more anthologies.